Moving On

ANNA JACOBS

Allison & Busby Limited
12 Fitzroy Mews
London W1T 6DW
allisonandbusby.com

First published in 2011.
This paperback edition published by Allison & Busby in 2018.

A CIP catalogue record for this book is available from
the British Library.

10 9 8 7 6 5 4 3 2 1

ISBN 978-0-7490-2312-6

Typeset in 10.5/15.5 pt Sabon by
Allison & Busby Ltd

The paper used for this Allison & Busby publication
has been produced from trees that have been legally sourced
from well-managed and credibly certified forests.

Printed and bound by
CPI Group (UK) Ltd, Croydon, CR0 4YY

Moving On

By Anna Jacobs

THE PEPPERCORN SERIES

Peppercorn Street
Cinnamon Gardens
Saffron Lane
Bay Tree Cottage

THE HONEYFIELD SERIES

The Honeyfield Bequest
A Stranger in Honeyfield
Peace Comes to Honeyfield

THE HOPE TRILOGY

A Place of Hope
In Search of Hope
A Time for Hope

THE GREYLADIES SERIES

Heir to Greyladies
Mistress of Greyladies
Legacy of Greyladies

THE WILTSHIRE GIRLS SERIES

Cherry Tree Lane
Elm Tree Road
Yew Tree Gardens

—◆—

Winds of Change
Moving On

Chapter One

'Why don't you bring a friend with you to the wedding, Mum? Then you won't have to sit alone.' Avoiding her mother's eyes, Rachel twisted and turned in front of the mirror, holding her hair up and checking her profile.

'I don't need to bring a friend to my own daughter's wedding, surely?' Molly picked up a tissue that had fallen to the ground, suddenly feeling apprehensive. What did Rachel want to change now? You'd have thought they were organising the premiere of a Hollywood blockbuster movie, not a wedding.

'We-ell, Dad's a bit worried that with him and Tasha sitting together, and Brian sitting with Geneva, you'll be on your own at the family table.'

Craig worried about her? No way. The last time he'd worried about her was when he'd asked for a divorce two years ago and been desperate to take as much money he could out of the marriage with him. And the house. He'd badly wanted to stay in the family home, but she'd dug her heels in there, at least.

When Rachel said nothing, Molly added, 'Anyway, I won't be on my own. My son and daughter will be on the top table with me.'

'Yes, but . . .'

Here it comes, thought Molly, more bad news. It felt as if she'd been standing alone against the rest of the family ever since Craig left. She braced herself, determined not to weep or make a scene. She'd done that all too often over the first few bewildering months of sorting out a new life for herself.

'Well, Mum, Tasha thinks she and Dad should sit on either side of us, and Jamie's parents don't mind.'

'Tasha isn't the mother of the bride. I am.'

'I know, and no one can take that away from you, but you see, it's her money that's paying for such a swish venue. Dad's not been exactly flush since you took the family home and he had to buy the flat.'

'You don't want me to sit next to you.' She got no answer to that. Thank goodness she'd come to her senses before it was too late. And thank goodness her friends had found her a good lawyer. 'It was *my* family home, actually, which *I* inherited. Why should your father take it from me?'

'You have to keep harping on about that, don't you? It was Daddy's home as well for ten years, and he misses it terribly. He looks so sad when he talks about it.'

Molly breathed in deeply. She'd promised herself not to do anything to spoil Rachel's special day, because bad feelings about important occasions could linger for years, but it was hard sometimes to bite her tongue. 'I thought we were having traditional seating.'

Rachel shrugged. 'It's a bit old-fashioned to stick to a formula. And does it matter that much where you sit, as long as you're on the top table?'

'It matters to me. Very much.' Molly looked at her daughter, but Rachel had brushed her hair over her eyes and was pretending to try out a new style. When the fiddling with the hairbrush went on for longer than it needed to, Molly realised the seating change was a done deal. If she made a big fuss she'd be the one in the wrong, as far as her daughter was concerned.

She moved to stand by the window, colours blurring as she blinked her eyes and looked out at the garden. She suddenly remembered her own wedding day and had to stuff her hand into her mouth not to sob. So much hope, so much joy.

She had to start fighting back more skilfully. They were steamrollering her. Only . . . was it worth creating a fuss about this? It was Rachel's wedding, after all, not hers. The trouble was, these days she couldn't be bothered to fight back most of the time. It was all just – too much. Her friend Di said she was depressed. Well, she had reason to be.

A bright yellow delivery van turned in to the drive and pulled up at the house. A minute later the doorbell rang and Brian yelled up the stairs, 'It's a parcel for you, Rach, from that shoe place.'

Rachel squeaked and dived out of the bedroom.

Molly wiped her eyes hastily, but couldn't wipe away the sick feeling. Thanks to her husband's rich and extremely slim second wife, she now felt totally excluded from her only daughter's wedding – and was dreading the event.

She went to her own bedroom and opened the wardrobe door to stare at the blue dress and jacket she'd bought. 'Perfect for the mother of the bride,' the sales assistant had assured her.

'It's a pretty shade of blue,' Rachel had said. 'One of your favourite colours.'

But her daughter hadn't seen it on, and the dress didn't look half as flattering once Molly got it home. Dresses never did. She wasn't good at choosing clothes. And anyway, she'd put on two kilos since then, what with all the hassles, all of it round her waist. She'd let herself go since the divorce and she wasn't naturally slim.

No. 2 wife was not only slender but ferociously elegant, never seemed to have a hair out of place, and was the perfect partner for an ambitious man who'd climbed almost to the top of the executive ladder and was still going.

There was a joyous squeal from the hall. When Rachel squealed like that she wanted an audience, and if she didn't get one here she'd go round to her father's, where Tasha would take an intense and clever interest in anything to do with clothes.

In the hall, Molly found her daughter balancing on shoes with impossibly high heels, moving to and fro, beaming at her reflection in the full-length mirror. 'They look beautiful, darling,' Molly lied. In reality, she thought heels that high not only looked ridiculous but were dangerous to walk in. But what was one minor lie in the confusion her life was in now?

Rachel wobbled across to the dining room to find the swatch of ivory satin and hold it against the shoes. 'Oh, yes. The dyers got the shade exactly right.'

'They certainly did.'

Beaming, Rachel walked up and down the hall again. 'I'd better practice.'

'I'll go and start tea. Chicken breasts with salad all right? I've found a new low-fat sauce recipe.' She turned towards the kitchen.

'Oh. I'm not going to be here for tea, Mum. Didn't Brian tell you? We're both going over to Dad's tonight.'

'But we agreed we'd have a family meal here tonight! I bought some champagne and . . .' Molly had been looking forward to an evening with just her two children, something which wouldn't be likely after the wedding. She'd wanted them to reminisce about old times and get closer again, as they used to be. She'd hunted out some old photo albums for them to go through, something Rachel usually loved doing.

Of course, Brian would still be living at home after the wedding, but apart from piling his dirty clothes in the laundry and regularly eating the last of the bread, he wasn't around very often, especially since he'd started dating his stepmother's daughter, Geneva.

Molly turned away, hearing her daughter go in the other direction. Once this wedding was over, she'd have to find something more interesting to do with her life, something for her. What did they call it? Moving on.

But what could she do? She'd never had a career, just a series of jobs when they were first married and short of money, then years of being the perfect hostess for Craig. She was a good cook, at least; prided herself on that. She looked down at herself and grimaced. Too good a cook, maybe.

Only she wasn't professionally trained, and anyway, the joy of cooking was giving pleasure to others . . . and soon she wouldn't have any close family to cook for. She felt as if the world had tossed her on the scrap heap.

On the afternoon of the wedding Molly dressed carefully, sucking in her stomach and tugging the dress down over it. When she let her breath out, she moaned aloud because the dress was stretched too tightly. She should have tried it on a couple of days ago, while there was still time to buy another. But there was nothing she could do about that now. She slipped the jacket on and it looked marginally better – but it'd look frumpy and wrong against Tasha's outfit, she knew.

When she put the hat on, she realised she'd made an even bigger mistake. The hat was huge, fussy and more suited to an English lady in Edwardian times than a modern woman. It was pretty in itself, but it did nothing for her. She tried it several different ways, but couldn't get it to flatter her. Should she leave it at home? No, her hair had been messed up by it now. She wished she had nice bouncy hair, instead of straight fine hair with built-in flop.

Last week Rachel had decided she would be getting ready at her father's house, so that Tasha could help her with her make-up. It seemed you had to be specially made-up for weddings these days, though with a complexion as good as her daughter's, Molly wondered why she needed so much make-up.

Molly and her son were going to the church in a taxi. She tried not to mind too much about being left out of the preparations, and tried not to mind having a taxi instead of a limo, like the rest of the family. But she did mind. She should have ordered a limo for herself and Brian, only she had to be careful about money these days.

Oh, stop it! she told herself crossly. *Stop moaning. You've done nothing but moan for days, Molly Peel. Just get the wedding over, then get a life.*

'Right,' she told her reflection and squared her shoulders. 'I will.'

Brian yelled along the corridor. 'Geneva just rang. She wants me to ride to the wedding with her in the limo. Do you mind, Mum? After all, the taxi is booked. You'll just have to sit in it like a queen and be swooshed away to the church.'

He didn't wait for an answer – he never did these days – but rushed out of the house.

Molly looked away from the mirror with a sigh and picked up the tiny bag that matched her outfit. Rachel had begged her not to take her roomy shoulder bag today and had helped her choose this silly thing.

Standing by the front door, she waited for the taxi. It was late. Five times she glanced at her watch, which equated to four minutes.

Ten minutes passed. She was getting seriously worried now.

Just as she was about to ring the taxi firm, a vehicle with a sign on top turned into the drive. With a sigh of relief, she locked the house door and got into the back seat.

'Meesis Taylor? St Jude church?' the driver asked in strongly accented English.

'Yes. Can you hurry, please? I don't want to be late.'

He set off as if he was fleeing from justice, screeching round corners and exceeding the speed limit whenever he could. But inevitably the traffic got heavier as they reached the town centre. People were starting to go home from work. Five o'clock was a stupid time to hold a wedding.

As the minutes ticked relentlessly past, Molly kept glancing at her watch.

It happened so quickly, she didn't even see the other car approaching, but she felt the impact as it slammed into the side of her taxi. In spite of the seat belt, she bumped her head hard against the side of the car, and she really did see stars for a moment or two.

The taxi driver began to swear and tried to get out to check the damage, but his door wouldn't open.

A crowd gathered and someone yelled that they'd called the police.

With the aid of a passer-by, Molly managed to unfasten

her seat belt and get her door open. As she climbed out, she had to clutch the stranger because she felt dizzy, couldn't seem to focus properly.

The driver of the other car was holding a handkerchief to his bleeding forehead. The taxi driver was yelling at him in a language Molly didn't recognise and gesticulating wildly.

As the argument continued, all she could think of was her daughter waiting at the church. She suddenly lost patience and yelled, 'Never mind that, I have to get to a wedding!'

They both turned towards her looking surprised.

'My daughter's getting married in five minutes' time. *Five minutes!* I'm going to be late.'

Just then a police car drew up and two officers got out.

Molly went across to the female officer. 'I'm the passenger and—'

'We need to speak to the driver first.'

'I'm going to be late for my only daughter's wedding.'

That got the woman officer's attention. 'Tough luck. Hey, John, can we take down this lady's details first and let her go? Her daughter's getting married today. At what time?'

Molly glanced at her watch and sobbed. 'In three minutes' time.'

'You'll never make it.'

They took her name and address, while the driver summoned another taxi by radio, but more precious minutes were ticking past. The new taxi wove in and out of traffic jams and Molly tried in vain to ring her ex-husband, then her son, to let them know what had happened. But of course their mobiles were switched off. She could only hope they'd delay the wedding till she arrived.

She crept into the back of the church in time to hear the words, 'I now pronounce you man and wife.'

She could only stand at the rear, tears streaming down her cheeks and watch as her daughter and son-in-law went off to sign the register.

Craig turned round, saw her and slipped out of the pew. 'Where the hell have you been? Brian said you were ready ages ago.'

'The taxi was involved in an accident.'

'Only you could manage to miss your daughter's wedding. Rachel was extremely upset.'

'We were in an *accident*, and no, I'm not badly injured, thank you for asking, just a few bruises.'

'It certainly didn't affect your mouth.'

'You could have waited for me.'

'We did. We waited ten minutes. Rachel was nearly in hysterics. In the end, it was either cancel the wedding ceremony or get on with it. There are other weddings planned for today, you know. Those people waiting outside aren't *our* guests. Anyway, never mind that. You'd better move to the front, so that Rachel can see you're here.'

He grasped her arm and tugged her forward. 'And straighten your hat. The brim's bent. You look a mess. As usual.'

She jerked away from his hand. 'I told you not to touch me – ever again.'

'Don't be such a bloody drama queen.'

Head held high, she walked to the front of the church and slid into the second pew next to her son.

Brian scowled at her. 'What the hell happened to you? Rachel's really upset.'

Molly was too busy fighting back sobs to answer him.

When the newly-weds came out of the door at the side of the church and began to walk down the aisle, they stopped for a moment next to her.

'I will never, ever forgive you for this!' Rachel hissed, not letting her smile slip. Then she moved on without allowing her mother to explain.

At the reception, pride alone kept a smile on Molly's face. Well, she hoped it was a smile. She explained several times about the taxi accident, and only a cousin of her ex showed any real sympathy.

'Why didn't they take you with them in the limo?' Sally asked, then gave her a quick hug. 'Stupid question. Because Madam didn't want you.' She cast a sour look at Tasha, who was queening it as if she were the mother of the bride.

Molly didn't trust her voice and could only hug Sally back.

'Craig always was a selfish bastard, even when we were children. I think you're well rid of him, actually. Not a man to grow old with, my dear cousin. Oh look, we have to sit down now. Look, if you get fed up of talking to *them*, come and chat to me once the meal's over. Pete's working off shore, so I'm here on my own.'

That kindness nearly destroyed Molly's self-control, and it took her a minute of deep breathing before she could carry on round the room to the top table, where she'd been ousted from her rightful place by Tasha. She hesitated for a moment or two, feeling slightly nauseous and seriously considering going home. When she found her place, not the place the mother of the bride should be in, she shot a reproachful glance at Rachel, but her daughter gave a slight shrug and turned away.

There were all sorts of stray relatives scattered around the room to remember for ever if she fell apart at the wedding, so Molly kept it together. Just.

After an hour of sitting in stiff silence at the end of the table, ignored by her son who was in the next seat and had eyes only for Geneva, she excused herself and went to the restroom. Her head was thumping and she felt dreadful. If she'd had her proper handbag she'd have had aspirins, but she only had this ridiculous little blue thing, which barely fitted tissues, money, her house key and a comb.

She stayed in the cubicle for ten minutes, feeling sick and dizzy. But she couldn't stay there for ever so stood up. Just as she was about to open the door, two women came in.

'Did you see the mother of the bride roll in late?' one asked. 'She looked as if she'd been drinking to me.'

'Tasha told me Craig's ex was putting on weight. The

woman must be at least a size sixteen. Talk about porky.'

As they tittered, Molly let her hand fall from the latch and stood absolutely motionless.

'No wonder he left her. The wonder is a man like him stayed with her for so long.'

'He's still good-looking, isn't he, though he must be going on for fifty . . . ?'

They left and Molly crept out of the cubicle, staring at herself in the mirror. Her face was chalk-white, not rosy as usual. She felt so unsteady she had to lean against the wall after she'd washed her hands. As she opened the outer door, the room spun round her and if Sally hadn't come in and caught her, she'd have fallen.

'Are you all right, Molly love? I was worried about you. You've been gone a quarter of an hour and you looked so pale.'

'I do feel . . . a bit dizzy.'

'Look at me.' Sally, who was a nurse, stared into her eyes. 'You might have concussion. Ouch, look at this bruise. Good thing it was hidden under your hair for the photos. You must have hit your head in the accident.'

'I suppose. Can't remember.'

'I think I'd better take you to hospital.'

'No.' Molly clung to Sally's arm. 'Just call me a taxi. I'll go home and lie down, take it easy.' She wasn't wanted here, anyway.

'You shouldn't be on your own. I'll come with you.'

'No. I'll be all right, I promise you.'

'Are you sure? Is there someone else you can call? You really shouldn't be alone tonight.'

'Oh, yes. I've got plenty of friends.'

'I'd stay with you, but it's a five-hour drive back to our part of Yorkshire. I'd not have come here at all today, but Mum made such a fuss about the family showing up to support Craig. Ha! As if *he* needs our support. Look, I'll see you into a taxi, then go and tell your family what's happened.'

'No. Don't say anything. I don't want . . . to spoil things for Rachel.'

'But what will she think if you're not there for the speeches?'

'The worst. She always does lately.'

Sally gave her a sudden hug. 'She'll grow up now she's married.'

Molly shook her head, wincing as it thumped with pain. The headache was getting worse by the minute and everything seemed a bit blurry. Suddenly she couldn't move, and everything went into slow motion as she started falling. She could do nothing about it but close her eyes and let the blackness swallow her up.

She woke in a strange bed and in spite of the curtains drawn around it, the light hurt her eyes so much she shut them again.

'What's your name?' someone asked.

She didn't want to speak but they asked her again, so she said, 'Molly.'

'Surname?'

'Taylor – no, Peel.'

'Aren't you sure?'

'Divorced. Keep forgetting.'

'What date is it today?'

'Look at the newspaper. I can never remember.' She opened her eyes again, squinting in the harsh flow of light, and found a young nurse staring at her anxiously. 'Where am I?'

'In hospital. You were brought in last night with concussion.'

Molly stared at her in shock. '*Last night?*'

'Yes. Just look at me, please. Oh good, you're focusing properly now.'

She realised she was wearing a short hospital gown, the sort that fastened down the back and made you feel horribly vulnerable. 'My glasses.'

'They're here.' The nurse opened the drawer next to the bed and passed her the spectacles.

With a sigh of relief, Molly put them on and the world became clearer. 'I want to go home.'

'You can't leave till the doctor's checked you out. Is there someone who can fetch you and keep an eye on you for the rest of the day? A woman called Sally brought you in, but she said she didn't live near here. She promised to tell your son and your ex, but I'm afraid no one's phoned.'

As that information sank in, tears welled in Molly's eyes. They couldn't even be bothered to look after her, could they, her precious children? Well, Rachel had some excuse. She and Jamie would be away on their honeymoon now, but what about Brian? And Craig. Her ex could have called one of her friends. He could at least have done that.

But he hadn't.

She'd never have gone away and left one of her family alone in hospital, without even a change of clothes to go home in. Well, she wasn't going to beg for their help now. She sat up and pushed the covers back. 'I need to use the bathroom.'

'Perhaps a bedpan until—?'

With only curtains round the bed and other people nearby to hear her. 'No way!'

'OK. Let me help you. You're in the end bed, so it's quite close.'

'Why am I in a public ward? I have private medical insurance.'

'You didn't have anything on you to show that.'

She remembered the stupid little handbag. She'd throw it away as soon as she got home. 'Just . . . stand outside the bathroom and let me see how I manage.'

'Well, OK. You're not sounding slurred.'

Molly closed the bathroom door, used the facilities, then stared at herself in the mirror, trying to smooth her hair a bit. Bruised forehead, huge bruise on her arm, but her head felt clear. Very clear. Clearer than it had been for over a year.

She opened the door, holding the open-backed hospital gown together with one hand. 'I feel fine now, better by the minute, so I'm getting dressed and going home.'

'The doctor hasn't discharged you yet.'

Nearby someone moaned and asked for a bedpan.

Molly shuddered. 'If the doctor doesn't come quickly, I'm discharging myself.'

By the time she was dressed, they'd found a junior doctor, who looked dead on his feet. He shone a light in her eyes, watched her walk up and down the room and signed the release papers.

Her clothes were wrinkled and she looked a mess. She threw the hat in a rubbish bin near the hospital entrance. Then she called a taxi from the free phone near the entrance. At least she had some money in her handbag to pay for it.

When she got home, she saw that Brian's car was missing. That was unusual. Tasha didn't encourage him to stay overnight with Geneva.

The empty house seemed to echo around her, every sound she made magnified, in her head at least. She made a piece of toast, but couldn't force more than a few bites down. Shoving the plate aside, she went up to Brian's room. It was a mess, as usual, but she wasn't going to clear it up this time.

If Rachel had still been at home, she would have refused to clear up after her any longer, too. Jamie was welcome to the perpetual mess.

She rang Brian's mobile, but got no answer. Where was he?

'What's the point?' she asked the empty house. 'Why did I have children at all? Rachel believes the worst and won't listen to me, and Brian doesn't give a stuff about me, except when he needs an unpaid servant.'

Anger welled up so strongly she had to do something, anything rather than sit around talking to herself and waiting for her son to return. Why should she wait for him anyway? He'd not waited for her, or come to visit her in hospital.

Suddenly she knew exactly what she was going to do.

In Wiltshire, Euan Santiago picked up the phone because his secretary hadn't arrived yet. 'Yes? Ah, Becky. How are things in the IT world?'

'Your new website's finished. It's ready to go live as soon as you've checked it all out.'

'Great. I'll get on to that straight away. The sooner it's out there the better. I've got a few sales brewing by word of mouth, but I want to start selling in earnest now that we've got six finished houses ready to show people. I'll get back to you by noon at the latest, after which, if there are no glitches, you can put the site up online.'

As he put the phone down, there was the sound of an outer door opening. He strode out into the reception area, having trouble keeping his voice calm. 'You're late again, Penny.'

She looked at him resentfully. 'The traffic was bad.'

'That's what you always say.'

'Well, Swindon's famous for it.'

'Then set off earlier or come here by another route.' He bit back more sharp words. After years of Miss Buttermere being in charge of his office, and having a larger staff at his disposal, he was finding it hard to put up with such inefficient help. But he'd set himself this business challenge and he was going to make it work, whatever it took. Unfortunately, Avril Buttermere couldn't be coaxed out of retirement at any price and he didn't want to be without a secretary, even an inefficient one, not at this crucial time.

Avril still lived nearby and always waved cheerfully if he passed her in the car. When they met in the village, she stopped to chat, sounding to be involved in a dozen community activities already. Lucky them to have her help! She was the most capable organiser he'd ever met.

'I'll be checking out the new website this morning,' he told Penny. 'Cancel my first appointment and fit it in another time. I don't want interrupting unless it's important.'

He got the new website up on the screen. It looked very attractive. 'Marlbury Golf Club and Leisure Village', it announced at the top in gold lettering on a teal blue background. Below that, it showed the architect's concept sketch for the whole development, with the golf course in the background.

The golf course had been there for years, of course, but the leisure village was his own idea. He'd bought the golf course and adjoining land, and set out to make his long-time dream come true without impinging on his other business interests. That had left him a little tight for money, but he was determined to cope. He didn't want any backers who might interfere with his plans. Fortunately, he'd leased the hotel and golf course to someone else, so that left him free to do what he wanted with the development.

This time he wasn't building cramped little flats someone else had commissioned and trying to cram too many into the space, or office buildings that looked like a stack of crates. He was attempting to create a community, somewhere people would enjoy living – somewhere *he* would enjoy living.

He'd spotted a niche market – he was pretty certain about that – and was offering people second homes, suitable for expats or people who wanted to spend part of their time in England, or homes for the over-fifties. Most retirement housing offered only small places, as if you needed less space when you spent more of your time at home. He was offering small, medium and large places.

Lodges was the official term for these wooden houses, but he always thought of them as homes. He was going to move here himself shortly and just keep a small flat in London. He was over fifty, after all.

His present house was far too big for one person. Once he'd got over his wife's death, as much as you ever did when you'd loved someone, he'd bought a new house, thinking – hoping even! – that he might end up marrying again one day. Karen would have wanted that. Now that his sons had completely left home, he didn't like living alone.

He'd spent several months in one relationship, but it hadn't lasted, not because of quarrels or infidelity, but simply because he didn't want any more children and it turned out she was aching for a late-in-life child. He wished her well, but the thought of raising more young children didn't appeal to him at all.

Euan didn't see much of his sons at the moment. Jason was working in Newcastle upon Tyne and Grant had set off to see the world as soon as he'd obtained his degree.

Jason had done the same thing, and you couldn't help worrying about their safety while they were overseas. But you couldn't hold them back.

Forcing himself to concentrate, Euan clicked on every link he could find on the new website, moving from the artist's concept sketches of the finished development to computer images of larger detached dwellings to a photograph of the first group of six finished lodges, painted in a dark blue-grey with white window frames and doors.

The house plans came up clearly, but he didn't linger on them because he knew them by heart. He wasn't an architect, but the houses were basically his design and he'd put a lot of thought into them. The architect who'd checked them out for him had congratulated him on their workability.

Two hours later he smiled at the screen. Perfect. Not a single link that didn't work. Becky was a talented woman, young as she was. She'd worked hard on this, knowing it would be a feather in her cap and could bring other major business her way. He had her on retainer for regular tech support and maintenance, which would give her a steady part-time wage.

When he went out into the reception area, he found it unoccupied. Frowning, he went to the corner and saw Penny standing further down the corridor next to the automatic food dispenser, which sold rubbish snacks for people staying at the hotel. He made a mental note to do something about that tendency of hers to wander off, but couldn't just sack her without a better excuse.

She was making eyes at one of the waiters, her whole face animated as it never was in the office. He frowned. She was in a steady relationship, talked a lot about her partner, so shouldn't be flirting like that. Not in his book, anyway.

Euan didn't draw attention to himself, but watched for a few moments then went back inside the office, keeping an eye on the time.

Ten minutes later she came back just as he was answering a call at her desk. He looked at his watch and finished the call, then stared at her until she wriggled uncomfortably.

He'd hired Penny because she had all the necessary qualifications on paper and seemed enthusiastic, but it was clear now that she was a better actress than secretary. He needed to find someone else who really could do the job – and quickly.

He rang Becky and congratulated her on the website. 'Every link that I could find works. We can go live now.'

'Do you have sales staff ready to go.'

'I'll handle that myself for the moment. Thank you, Becky. You did a great job. Send me your bill, then we'll go on to the monthly maintenance budget we discussed. And if you want to use me as a reference, don't hesitate.'

She couldn't hold back a few squeaks of joy and he smiled. He loved the enthusiasm of young people setting out to make a life.

Putting the phone down, he wondered what to do next. He fiddled with some papers. He really ought to get into these accounts. But he couldn't settle, which wasn't like him.

Since there was half an hour before his next appointment, he went out to stroll round the leisure village – well, what would be the village one day. The roads for the first stage were there, and the lamp posts, plus a great deal of cleared land where grass and wild plants were already growing back. He'd miss the wild flowers once the development was finished; hoped he could keep some growing in the nature patches; hoped the people who bought his houses would like that and not want billiard green lawns everywhere.

Wooden-framed houses went up quickly once you started building, but the group of six looked lonely at the moment. It was all happening so much more slowly than he'd expected. Maybe he should hire more admin staff. No, he'd set himself to managing this project himself, so that he didn't lose touch with the grass roots. There was no deadline to meet, except in his own head.

If he did it right, this project would come in at a good profit – as well as giving him a sense of pride in his creation, which the more lucrative office blocks never could.

On the way back to the admin suite, he stopped to watch two men playing the sixth hole, his hands twitching to pick up a golf club. He could play better than they were doing and he *would* once he'd got the village on its feet. He sometimes managed nine holes, but couldn't remember the last time he'd had a whole afternoon free to play for pleasure.

The office closed around him like a stifling blanket. He gave a wry smile. He infinitely preferred being outdoors. Was he stupid to take this on single-handed? No.

He'd been growing stale, had needed to move on, make changes, find a challenge.

Chapter Two

Even though she had a dull headache and the doctor at the hospital had told her to rest, anger drove Molly to start packing her son's things at once. She put his better clothes in his old suitcase because she couldn't find the fancy new one he'd bought last month. Some of his clothes were missing, too, surely? She stuffed his remaining clean underwear into his backpack.

There were about thirty T-shirts in various stages of wear; from ragged to near new. Some had mottos on them, one or two distinctly rude. She grimaced. As usual, Brian's dirty clothes were scattered all over the place. He was nearly as bad as his sister for that.

She went to fetch a roll of dustbin liner bags and filled two with his washing. She found some sticky labels and wrote DIRTY CLOTHES – NEED WASHING, before slapping them on to the black plastic bags. Then she dumped them on the landing, ready to take downstairs next trip.

When she'd emptied every cupboard and drawer in his bedroom, stacking dirty plates and mugs on his desk, she carried the bags and bundles downstairs. Reversing her car out on to the drive, she began piling his things in the garage. Although it was a double garage, she'd need the whole of it for what she intended.

She glared at the empty cardboard boxes, which her new son-in-law was supposed to have cleared out. They were leftover from the presents Rachel had taken with her to the flat. 'Leaving me to get rid of the boxes!' she exclaimed, then began to smile. Actually, these were just what she needed.

Back in the house, she began filling the boxes methodically with Brian's books and CDs. His old boxes of toys were already in the garage and if he wanted them, he could lift them down from the shelving unit. Otherwise they were going to a charity shop.

She hesitated about his laptop, knowing he'd spent a lot of money on it, but then anger took over again and she disconnected everything. She cushioned the laptop and printer in boxes with some of his sweaters, and shoved the leads in any old how, then labelled them.

It took nearly two hours to clear everything out of her son's room, by which time she was more than a little light-headed. When had she last eaten? She couldn't remember. She made a cup of tea, sipped it without much interest, then forced down some biscuits and cheese, with some of her favourite sunblush tomatoes and olives. She still didn't feel hungry, but knew she had to take care of herself.

Nor was she going to rest. Couldn't. She had vowed to change her life and this was the first step. If she didn't do it, she'd have no respect for herself. What was there to respect at the moment? Nothing. She'd let her family trample all over her, had loved them unwisely and too well. Where was that quote from? It sounded like Shakespeare, but she couldn't be bothered to go and look it up.

After her snack she began work on Rachel's room. There were very few personal possessions left, but there was a huge pile of wedding presents – and the usual pile of dirty clothes.

She could remember Rachel saying, 'You don't mind if I leave the presents here, do you, Mum? It's such a small flat and they'll make the place look a mess till we get a proper house.'

Why did I put up with being a dumping ground? Because I've been a stupid doormat, that's why.

I should have told Rachel to clear the mess out of my house before she got married.

At three o'clock Molly went for another cup of tea and forced down a piece of stale cake, feeling her energy sagging drastically now. She swallowed two paracetamols then rang Brian's mobile again. But there was still no answer, so she dialled her ex-husband's office.

'Who's speaking please?'

'His ex-wife.' As if his long-time secretary didn't know who it was!

'Mr Taylor's busy, I'm afraid, Mrs – um, Ms Peel.'

'If Craig won't speak to me, then will you please give him a message, Judy? It's very important. Tell him his son's and daughter's possessions are piled up inside my garage, wedding presents included. I can't contact either of them, so if no one collects them by three o'clock tomorrow, I'll have everything picked up and dumped on his drive.' She heard a gasp at the other end, looked out of the window at the dark clouds building up and added with relish, 'Whether it's raining or not.'

Not waiting for an answer, she put the phone down.

Two minutes later it rang. She let it ring five times before picking it up. And if that was petty, well, she wasn't feeling at all kind today.

'Molly?'

'Who else would it be?'

'You're out of hospital, then?'

'No thanks to my family, yes. I got out this morning.'

'Your message didn't make sense to me.'

'Oh? I thought it was very clear. I've moved all Rachel's and Brian's things out of this house. As of today, Brian doesn't live here any more and I'm not going to act as a storage facility for Rachel. I don't know where Brian is or I'd have told him to find a new place myself, and I don't know which hotel Rachel's in for her honeymoon. I'm sure you or Tasha will have a key to her new flat, though.' She should have known which hotel, dammit.

'Why the rush? Brian will be back next week. He's only gone away for a few days. Surely he told you about it?'

'No.'

'Ah. Well, it was rather a last-minute thing. Friend of Tasha's has a holiday cottage and she had a cancellation, so it was going dirt cheap. He and Geneva both felt in need of a break.'

Molly breathed deeply. Brian hadn't even bothered to tell her, nor had he paid her any housekeeping money for the last two weeks. He'd have spent it by the time he got back, knowing him. He owed her a lot of money for his keep, but she didn't suppose she'd ever see any of it.

'What on earth made you move his things out today?'

'The fact that neither of my children came with me to hospital after I collapsed, or even called to ask how I was.'

'Rather childish, isn't it? A bride can't leave her own wedding and you only had mild concussion, after all.'

'Not childish. And my concussion was bad enough for me to collapse.'

'Well, you're clearly better now . . . or maybe you're not. Maybe that's why you're acting so stupidly.'

'Not stupidly, I'm being practical. I can't sell this house with the mess Brian leaves everywhere and with piles of Rachel's bits and pieces all over the spare bedroom and dining room. You have to declutter to make a place look bigger, if you want to get the best price.'

'You're selling? This is a bit sudden, isn't it?'

'Yes. Very sudden.'

He let out an aggrieved sigh. 'It's another of your wild ideas, Molly. When will you grow out of them? And where's Brian going to live once you sell the house? It'll take him time to save up for a deposit on a flat, so he might as well stay there till you move out yourself.'

'I don't care where he lives, but he's not staying here.

He's old enough to leave home. More than. You're welcome to house him, though, if you're worried about him. I'm sure Tasha will enjoy picking up his dirty washing and ironing his shirts. Or you could lend him the money for his deposit. He owes me too much for me to lend him another penny.'

'You're definitely being petty.'

'Maybe I'm just seeing things more clearly. Our son is twenty-four and in full-time employment, so he'll probably survive. Of course he'll have to cut down on his boozing and clubbing to pay for a flat and the various services like electricity – and he'll have to do his own cooking and washing too, poor thing.'

Dead silence, then, 'But you said you wanted to go on living there. You wept all over the arbitrator about that.'

'The main thing the arbitrator took into account was the fact that it was me who'd inherited the house and the mortgage was only for the extensions *you* had insisted on. All of which you'd left out of your financial settlement statements.'

'I did offer to buy the house off you.'

She laughed. 'At a knock-down price, way below the market value. I did have enough sense to check that. But if you still want to make an offer – a *realistic* offer – I'll let you have the name of my estate agent.'

Silence, then, 'Do that. Or . . . we could cut out the estate agent and save both of us some money.'

'And then you could find some other way to cheat me? What do they say? *Cheat me once, shame on you. Cheat me twice, shame on me.* No, Craig, I'm selling through an estate agent, and if you're interested, you'll have to compete with everyone else.'

'*If* anyone wants to buy it.'

'It's in a really good area with top schools nearby. The house down the road sold in the first week it was on the market. Lavengro Road is a quiet, leafy street. People love living here and don't often move away. Anyway, I've a lot to do, so please ask Tasha to contact Geneva and give Brian my message. He'll have to get someone to fetch his things. I meant what I said about having them dumped at your place tomorrow.' She put the phone down.

It upset her that she and Craig couldn't even hold a short conversation without bickering. 'Now, stop that!' she told herself fiercely as tears welled in her eyes. She'd wept and dithered enough. More than enough.

Two hours later, Brian rang. 'Mum? What's happening?'

'You've moved out.'

'No, I haven't.'

'Let me put it another way. You – have been moved – out of my house – by me.'

'But it's my *home*. I've not got anywhere else to live.'

'I'm sure your father will put you up till you find a flat.'

Silence, then, 'He won't. And anyway, I can't afford a flat.'

'Too bad. Not my problem.'

'Why are you doing this?'

'Remember the wedding, how I collapsed? I was bad enough for them to keep me in hospital overnight. No one in my family came to the hospital with me, or even rang up to find out how I was. Not one of you.'

Silence, then, 'Oh. I'm sorry. Really. I didn't think it was serious. Someone told me you were drunk.'

'No. I wasn't. I'd been in a car accident.'

'Look, Mum, can't you at least wait till I get back from my holiday and we'll sort something out? Surely I can stay there till the house is sold?'

'No, you can't. I'm too angry. And you owe me some rent and housekeeping money, too. I'll make up an account.'

She heard a yelp, silence, then, 'No wonder Dad left you. I didn't believe him when he said that underneath that sweetness and light you're a mercenary bitch. He really wanted to buy that house, you know.'

She sucked in a sharp breath. Was that what Craig was saying about her? Somehow she kept her voice steady. 'Nice to know you believed him, Brian. You don't know me very well, do you? He offered me half the market price for the house.'

Silence, and she couldn't bear it any longer. 'Anyway, I'll definitely arrange to have your things dumped at your father's house tomorrow if no one picks them up before three o'clock. They're in the garage at the moment and I need to clear it out.'

She put the phone down on her son. Her hand was shaking, but Brian couldn't see that. She no longer wanted to weep, though. She wanted to throw something. So she did. She picked up a glass vase Craig's mother had once given them, such a cheap, ugly thing that he'd not wanted to take it with him. Opening the back door, she hurled it at the patio wall. It smashed into myriad pieces, and even though she knew she'd have to sweep them up later, it still felt wonderful to do it!

As she went back into the house, she had a sudden thought. She went online and found a local locksmith, noting down the phone number. She was pretty sure Brian and Rachel didn't have back door keys, but they both had front door keys. Craig might still have one, too. The back door keys were big, old-fashioned things and there had only ever been two of them. She went to check. Yes, one was hanging on the key rack in the pantry and the other was in the back door.

She rang the locksmith, arranging to have the front door lock changed within the hour, pretending she'd had an intruder.

She must have done something very wrong as a mother, to have raised children who turned out so uncaring. Yet she'd loved them so much. Had she been too soft with them, as Craig always claimed? Yes, she decided, wiping away more tears – she had. He'd been far stricter and look how they respected him.

She couldn't help caring about them, even now, but love was a two-way street, or it should be. And she wasn't going to hang around any longer, begging for crumbs of affection, letting them walk all over her.

It was time to toughen up. No one was going to get the better of her from now on. She couldn't live through such an agonising humiliation again.

Half an hour later, the doorbell rang and when she peeped out of the window, Molly saw her friend Nikki outside.

She wasn't sure she was ready to face anyone yet, even such a close friend, but she went to answer it.

Nikki burst into the house with her usual exuberance. 'So . . . how did the wedding go?'

Molly fought for control and lost the struggle within less than a minute. With tears rolling down her cheeks, she let Nikki guide her into the kitchen and poured out her tale of woe, ending, 'And they didn't even let me invite you to the wedding, even though you've known the children since they were small. I'm sorry about that.'

Nikki listened without commenting, other than to make soothing noises, then hugged her and went to fish in the fridge. 'What you need is a glass of wine.'

'Why not.'

She poured them both some. 'Here's to your new life.'

Molly dutifully clinked glasses, but she might have been drinking vinegar for all she could taste.

'What are you going to do now?'

'I'm not sure, but I've made a start, at least.'

'You have?'

Her friend sounded doubtful, so Molly said defiantly, 'Yes. I've got as far as chucking Brian out and deciding to put this house up for sale.'

Nikki cheered loudly and did a war dance round the room. 'About time. Haven't I been telling you to give him the elbow? Haven't I?'

'Yes.'

'Did he ever pay you any rent? Or contribute towards the electricity and food?'

'Now and then.'

'How often is that?'

'About once a month.'

'He's in for a shock, then. Reality has sharp teeth.'

Molly nodded, took another sip of wine and said what she'd been thinking. 'I've been an absolute doormat, haven't I?'

'Yes. But a lovely one.' Nikki leant forward to give her a hug. 'My very favourite doormat, in fact.' She picked up her glass, swirling what was left round and round, then asked, 'Have you seen Brian yet?'

'No. He's not due back till Friday.'

'He'll try to persuade you to change your mind. Don't give in. Please.'

'I won't.'

'You might. You've always been a soft touch. Promise me you won't.'

It was Molly's turn to stare into her wine. 'I won't give in this time. I do mean that. The worm has turned.'

'Way to go.' Nikki leant forward to clink glasses. 'We should get Di round and have a girls' night in.'

'Let's do it. But not yet. Not till I'm feeling better. Besides, I want to make a start on the house.' She put her hand across the top of the glass. 'No more. I have too much to do.'

Nikki looked at her own glass regretfully and put the bottle back in the fridge. 'And I'm driving, so I'd better be sensible. Will you be all right?'

'Yes, of course I will.'

But the house felt very empty after Nikki left.

'Get used to it!' Molly told herself.

When Craig's secretary rang to say he'd be sending a removal firm round the following morning to remove all the things she'd put into the garage, all she said was 'Fine.'

'And would you please tell them which are Brian's and which are Rachel's. Mr Taylor's sending your daughter's things straight to her flat.'

'Yes.'

Once the house was cleared and tissied up to look its best, she'd contact some estate agents and made appointments to show them round the house.

She went to bed at eight o'clock, feeling exhausted. She was coping – wasn't she? Doing the right thing – wasn't she?

Why did it have to hurt so much?

Euan opened the sales office for the first time on a sunny Saturday. It was a second-hand transportable unit, but had been smartened up and painted the same colour as the houses. He hadn't forgotten how to cut corners and save money here and there.

He had a feeling of mild anxiety about today, unusual for him, but a lot depended on how the houses sold. Would people like his lodges? Want to live in his village?

He usually felt confident of what he was doing because he didn't go into any business deal without careful research and number crunching, but this was more important to him than other deals. This had been his dream for years.

He sat behind the desk, trying to look relaxed. An hour passed slowly and no one came to look at the houses. He got angry with himself for wasting time and got out some paperwork, of which there was always a pile needing doing. Penny didn't help him with the details as Avril had done.

Just as he was starting on some calculations, a car drew up outside. He didn't go out to greet them, didn't want to seem pushy. An older couple got out and studied the row of houses, then the big signboard outside which displayed the artist's impression of the finished development, the one he'd used on his website. They looked round, pointing things out to one another, taking their time.

He watched them closely, glad the sun was shining. It was a beautiful setting, not just because the land the village was being built on was attached to a golf course, but because he'd left patches of woodland here and there, with as many large trees as he could, and had created several small lakes – well, they were closer to big ponds, but he preferred to call them lakes. He'd put a lot of effort into keeping Marlbury beautiful, as well as eco-friendly.

The couple seemed pleased with what they saw, and turned to come inside the sales office.

He took them over to the model, then sat them down and explained the set-up and prices.

'We won't be here all the time,' the man said, 'because we live mainly in Spain. But we've decided we want a foothold here for the English summers. One of your smaller houses, perhaps.'

'Far too hot in Spain in midsummer,' the woman said

with a grimace. 'But before we even start doing our sums, what we really want to do is to look round and see if we like the style of your houses.'

'The first three lodges are open for inspection, the ones with the bunting across the front. I'm sure you'll do better going round them on your own than with me hovering over you.' He saw from their expressions that he'd guessed right. 'Just come back if you've any questions or want to take matters further.'

They took the brochures and left. He followed their progress on the CCTV system, watching the expressions on their faces with great attention. Positive, he thought. Definitely positive.

But when they left the houses, they didn't come back into the sales office, just drove off. He shrugged and wrote them off mentally. There would be quite a few who popped in out of sheer nosiness, he was sure. The majority, in fact. People had even driven into the building site to have a look, though it was signposted as not being a through road. But he would put it on his list of to-dos to make sure there was a chain across the road at night. And the building equipment was carefully locked up in a huge temporary shed he'd had erected behind a clump of trees.

At four o'clock the Hamiltons arrived, a couple he knew slightly socially. They had a home in the US and another in Australia, and seemed to spend their life moving from one place to another. They were charming, educated people, exactly the sort he wanted to attract as residents, but they enjoyed being fussed over, so he took them round the houses in person.

Someone else arrived as they were coming out of the first house, and he excused himself for a few moments to run up and offer them a brochure.

'This is quite a nice little cottage,' Mrs Hamilton said, after going round the final and largest of the houses.

Her husband was looking longingly at the golf course and had peered at it out of each window on that side of the houses. 'It's far enough away that we won't get hit by balls, but close enough to walk.' He nodded in approval.

'Do you want to go round the houses again on your own?' Euan asked.

'Yes, please,' Mrs Hamilton said.

'I like them all.' Mr Hamilton sighed and followed her inside again.

The other people came out of the first house and Euan went across to them. 'Sorry I couldn't speak to you when you first arrived. Do you know the rules about developments like this?' When they shook their heads, he explained. 'So, you have to be over fifty to live here and no children are allowed to be in permanent residence.'

The woman's face fell. 'Oh. Surely there's some way round that?'

'I'm afraid not.'

'It's such a lovely house,' she said wistfully.

'Thank you.'

'Come on, love. It's not for us.' Her husband took her and the toddler back to the car.

Anger carried Molly through the next few days, though she woke in the night sometimes, worrying about what she was doing, fretting for an end to this uncertainty. Once you had a house up for sale, it no longer felt to be yours.

She still hadn't got a real goal in life, apart from selling the house and moving as far away as she could from her family. A bitter laugh escaped her at that thought. Where in England would she go? Her parents were dead and she had no brothers or sisters.

Her mother's parents had lived in Whitley Bay, but even though it was a nice little town, it was much colder up there in Northumberland. She remembered the icy winds off the sea in winter when she and her granddad went for walks. No, she didn't want to live there.

Her father's parents had lived in Wiltshire, which was a beautiful part of the world. Perhaps that would be the place to go. She'd taken Craig to see her grandparents once, but it hadn't been a successful visit. They'd lived in a tiny village on an acre of land and he was an urban animal. They were dead now, but she still had some cousins living round there and kept in touch with one of them, Helen, by email.

She paused, coffee cup in mid-air. Well, why not? Why not go and live there? She had very happy memories of Wiltshire. If she sold this house for what the estate agents had predicted, and didn't go mad when she bought a new place, she'd have a nice lump of money behind her. She could look for a job, make friends, build a new life for herself.

And she'd be right out of the way of her family, wouldn't have to pass them in the street, or endure duty visits from her children. She'd even change her mobile phone just before she left, so that they could only get in touch with her by email. That way, no one could harass her and spoil her day.

She took a slurp of coffee, then picked up a chocolate biscuit. But before she could take a bite, she remembered suddenly how terrible she'd looked in the wedding outfit, like a sausage about to burst its skin. And she hadn't been able to fasten the top button on her comfiest jeans this morning. Quickly, before she could change her mind, she shoved the biscuit back into the packet and threw the whole thing into the rubbish bin.

Then she cleaned her spectacles and got online, looking at house prices in Wiltshire. Definitely cheaper than this part of Surrey. Good.

After she'd finished her research, she went back to work on the house. She'd already decluttered ruthlessly, setting aside in the garage stuff to throw away or give to a charity shop. Was it really only four days since she'd dumped Brian's and Rachel's possessions here? It felt longer, much longer.

Don't dwell on that, she told herself firmly and carried on working.

She studied the front garden. Not bad. Just needed tidying up. So much physical activity helped tire her out and she started sleeping better.

She had several chats with her neighbour while she worked. They'd always got on well. Jane Benton was about eighty, but full of life and interested in everything. Her husband was pleasant but tended to keep himself to himself. Denis hadn't looked well lately, but as Jane had said nothing about that, Molly didn't comment.

'You look tired,' Jane said to her one day.

'I am but I need to clear the house out if I'm to sell it.'

'Can't your son help?'

'Brian isn't living here any more.'

Jane looked at her sadly. 'As bad as that?'

Molly nodded.

'If you need to talk . . .'

'Thanks, but I'll be all right.' She hated the way her voice wobbled and could see that Jane had noticed it.

'I'll be sorry to lose you as a neighbour. I don't think we've ever exchanged a cross word, have we?'

'Not even when Brian put that cricket ball through your side window.'

Jane chuckled and Molly was smiling too as she went back inside. People. That was what life was about.

The next day Molly decided it was time to call in the estate agents. To her surprise, they all felt she should sell the house by auction.

The man she chose to handle this was particularly insistent. 'The market's quite buoyant again and you'll get far more for it that way.'

She let him persuade her. It had been so long since she'd sold a house. What did she know?

In the middle of the night she woke with a start, feeling suddenly anxious about going to auction, she couldn't work out why. She tried to reason herself out of this. Auctions were very common these days. What could possibly go wrong? Apart from no one wanting to buy, of course, and she doubted that would happen in this area.

Anyway she'd signed the papers now. And her agent was probably right. This was a very desirable residence. Even Craig said so.

Graysons were a reputable real estate company and all the other agents had told her the same thing.

She dozed off then woke again, after a nightmare in which no one offered for the house, or they made only low offers.

'Oh, you are a fool, Molly Peel!' she muttered.

But she didn't get back to sleep properly and as soon as it was light, she got up. She'd go and buy some punnets of flowers today to make the front garden look more appealing when people were looking round.

There was another reason why she wasn't sleeping well, one she kept trying in vain to push to the back of her mind. Brian was coming back from his holiday tomorrow. She wasn't looking forward to seeing him, but had vowed to stand firm and not let him live here again. Tough love, didn't they call it?

He had to grow up and stop using people, or what sort of a man had she raised?

And *she* had to stop letting people use her.

They were all on a learning curve – or ought to be.

She wondered how Rachel would cope with her new status. Her daughter was one of the laziest people she'd ever met, refusing to lift a finger in the house, not even picking up her dirty underwear, eating takeaway rather than make so much as a piece of toast.

Would marriage change her? She hoped so, for Jamie's sake.

What would Rachel do when she saw the pile of stuff Molly had cleared out?

No use worrying. Done was done.

Chapter Three

Euan picked up the sales phone, since Penny hadn't turned up at all this morning – or even rung to let him know she wasn't coming in.

'Gus Hamilton here.'

'Oh, hi, Gus.'

'Diana likes the end house, but she wants it by the end of the month. And she wants you to stop showing people round it.'

Euan thought rapidly. He'd intended to keep that house as a show home, but a sale was a sale. 'Fine. I'll close it as a show home as soon as you sign the contract and pay a deposit.' And he'd get people working on the similar house at the other end of the row, move the furniture into that one and open it up for show.

They discussed the practicalities of the sale, which would be easier than usual since Gus was paying cash.

'Looking forward to playing golf here?' Euan asked.

Membership was part of the residents' annual fees.

'Am I ever! Just to walk out of the door and stroll on to the course. Never had that before.' Gus grew enthusiastic, describing several recent games and the call lasted another half-hour.

Euan didn't mind listening because he'd made his first sale. It was small change compared to what he'd spent on the development, but it was the result of his own creation of a residential community, and that meant a lot to him.

He'd have to think of some way to celebrate tonight, but it wasn't as much fun celebrating on your own.

Then he'd have to think where he was going to live, because he'd just had an offer to buy his own house as well.

The phone rang again, the normal line, not the sales line.

He sighed as he picked it up. If Penny was going to be away for long, he'd have to get a temp in.

Molly's son came round to see her the following afternoon. She was in the sitting room, waiting for him, because she'd guessed he'd be coming back today, since he had to start back at work tomorrow.

She heard him try to use his key on the front door and swear when he found it didn't work.

Not until Brian had rung the doorbell for a second time did she answer it.

He tried to give her a hug and she stepped back out of reach.

'What's with the new locks? Have you had burglars?'

'No. I'm just protecting my privacy and keeping other people out.'

He looked shocked. 'Are you that mad at me for not telling you I was going away?'

'Disgusted would be a better word, or perhaps sickened by your selfishness.'

He blinked. 'I don't know why you're so upset. It was just a little holiday. Look, can't I come in to talk about it?'

'I suppose so.' She led the way into the sitting room and gestured to a chair. Now that she'd seen him, she was wondering if she was overreacting. He was her son, after all.

'Can't we sit in the kitchen? I'd love a cup of tea and I'm really hungry.'

'I want to talk to you, not feed you.'

He looked at her in puzzlement. 'I don't understand all this, Mum.'

'I was in hospital and you never even checked that I was all right. Never even made one lousy phone call. None of you did.'

'Dad said it was just a knock on the head and you were making a f—'

'Making a fuss about nothing?' She had the satisfaction of seeing her son wriggle uncomfortably. 'I wonder how he knew that? He wasn't there when it happened and he certainly didn't ring the hospital to ask how I was, either.'

Brian's face got that sulky look, as if he was still a child. Molly knew then that she wasn't going to forgive him – well, not for a good long time – not until he showed some sign of understanding that he'd let her down badly. And she definitely wasn't going to let him come back to live here.

'Look, I haven't got anywhere to stay tonight, Mum. Could you let me come back here for a few days till I sort something out? Please?'

She realised that he still hadn't asked if she was OK. 'I'm afraid I can't. I'm getting the house ready for auction and I'll be having people going round it from tomorrow onwards. You're far too untidy. Anyway, your things have all been moved out now, so it'd be silly to bring them back again, wouldn't it?'

'But what am I going to do tonight?'

She almost weakened, then remembered the amazing amount of rubbish she'd had to remove from his bedroom, which had included old crisp packets and sweet wrappers stuffed down the back of the bed, not to mention something she rather thought was a spliff, though she'd never smoked marijuana so she wasn't sure. She'd thrown that in the rubbish bin straight away. 'Go and throw yourself on your father's mercy. I'm sure Geneva will persuade her mother to let you stay there.'

'Ah. Well. Geneva and I aren't together now. We . . . um, fell out. She's, like, the Queen of Tidy, even worse than you, and well, we argued a lot about it while we were at the cottage.'

Worse than her! And he didn't even realise how condescendingly he said that. As if there was something wrong with being tidy. 'Why am I not surprised?' Molly asked, which drew her a scowl from him.

She knew he'd try to wear her down and was suddenly fed up of it, so looked at her watch. 'I've got the estate agent coming in a few minutes, so I have to get on. There's just one thing before you go. Do you want those boxes of toys from the garage? If you don't, I'll take them to the charity shop.'

'Yes, I do want them. I'll take them once I've got somewhere to stay.' He added with heavy sarcasm, 'Unless you have to have the garage perfect immediately as well.'

'Oh, I think I can find space for two cardboard boxes now that I've got rid of all Rachel's wedding presents and all the rubbish from your room.' She hadn't heard a word from her daughter, who was still on honeymoon, and that upset her a lot. Surely Craig had told her what her mother had done?

'She'll throw a fit when she gets back. It's not a big flat.'

'That's her problem, not mine. She's married and independent now. And you're old enough to be independent, too.'

She watched as Brian opened his mouth, thought better of it, then snapped it shut and walked out of the house without a word of farewell.

She was shaken by the encounter, but she'd stayed firm. Nikki would be proud of her.

Only . . . she'd now alienated both her children. Not intentionally, not at Rachel's wedding, at least. But with Brian – well, what choice did she have? She wasn't going to let anyone ride roughshod over her from now on.

How scornfully he'd spoken to her!

He really didn't understand how badly he'd hurt her. Would he ever?

Molly picked up the phone two days later. 'Oh, Rachel. How was the honeymoon?'

'Fine. Why are all these boxes here in the flat, Mum?'

'Because I'm selling the house and needed to clear them out.'

'You couldn't wait till we got back, or put them in the garage?'

Oh, the sarcasm in her daughter's voice. She sounded just like Craig. 'No,' Molly said. 'The whole house has to be immaculate, including the garage. Look, about the wedding, I—'

'I do not wish to discuss that, Mum – ever. If you can't make it on time to your only daughter's wedding, then you've got your priorities wrong. People told me you were *drunk*!'

'But—'

Rachel put the phone down on her.

Molly stared at it in shock. Didn't her daughter know she'd been in an accident, injured and taken to hospital? Surely someone had told her?

Craig obviously hadn't, the rat.

She put the receiver down gently and went back to making the house look as beautiful as she could. She held the pain of her daughter's rejection at a distance. She wasn't going there yet; had done enough weeping.

So . . . she was on her own now and that was how it'd stay.

A minute later she decided she was getting maudlin. Of course she wasn't on her own. She had good friends, a wonderful neighbour, and one or two cousins with whom she kept in touch and even caught up with occasionally.

Her cousin Helen had been talking about holding a big family reunion for the Wiltshire Peels. Molly decided to find out if that was still on and if so, she'd attend it. She'd email Helen today.

The day of the auction was blustery, with heavy clouds covering the sky and a grey light that seemed to dull down the colours of the garden. Molly sighed as she got the house ready for its final viewing, keeping anything she valued in the smallest bedroom, from which she'd be watching the auction that followed the viewing. This would be taking place in the garage.

She couldn't help looking at the sky anxiously, praying for the rain to hold off!

During the hour before the auction several couples went through the house and Molly kept out of sight in the smallest bedroom. She'd put a sign saying THIS ROOM NOT OPEN FOR VIEWING on the door, giving the room's measurements.

The auctioneer had wanted to wait a few weeks and put the house into an auction of several properties which was to be held at a luxury hotel, but she wanted to sell quickly and had insisted on holding the auction as soon as possible.

In the end he decided the garage was large enough to accommodate seating for twenty or more people, and others could stand along the sides, if necessary.

As the hour approached, she grew more and more nervous. She heard a noise outside and looked out of the window. To her surprise she saw a group of rough-looking youths gathering on the other side of the street, yelling, shouting and shoving one another.

The first car pulled up just then and a couple got out. The youths began to jeer and shout at them, making threatening gestures.

Molly was horrified. She'd never seen any groups of hooligans like this in the area before. What was going on?

The couple hesitated, then the woman tugged at the man's arm, shaking her head. They got back into the car and drove away.

Five other couples were treated in similar manner and four of them drove away again without waiting for the auction. Molly stayed by the window, frozen, shocked.

When she heard a voice behind her, she turned round to see the auctioneer scowling at her.

'I asked if this often happens, Ms Peel?'

'It's never happened before. Not once.'

'Well, I've rung the police and they're sending a car.'

There was a shrill whistle outside and when they looked, they saw the group of youths running away.

'That's got rid of them,' he said. 'But unfortunately they've already driven away several potential buyers. We should definitely have waited for the mass auction at the hotel.'

The police stayed for a while, then drove away again. Within minutes the group of youths had re-formed and the jeering and taunting had begun again.

As she watched, Craig got out of a new vehicle and stopped to watch the group drive another car away. He smiled. *Smiled!* It was the satisfied smile of a cat which had just caught a bird. She'd seen it before when he got the better of someone.

He continued to smirk as he went across to the garage, and stopped at the entrance, turning round to watch and smile even more broadly as another car stopped, then drove away.

That's when she realised *he* had set this up. He'd boasted of other dirty tricks against rivals during the last two years of their marriage, and it'd been something they argued fiercely about, because he felt any tool was permissible as long as you won 'the game'.

After the arbitrator awarded the house to her, Craig had told her he'd get it at his own price before they were through, but of course, he hadn't said that in front of witnesses.

She went down to the auction, something she'd not intended to do, but she felt she had to face up to Craig, even though her stomach was churning and she felt literally sick with anxiety.

There were only six people sitting there, including him. She went to stand at the far side, arms folded across her chest, feeling numb, unable to believe this was happening.

Outside the jeering and shouts grew suddenly louder

and there was the sound of another car driving away. Craig smiled at her and drew an imaginary tick in the air, confirming her suspicions.

The auctioneer fiddled with his papers.

The sale began and the first bid was made by Craig, a very low bid indeed, even less than the amount he'd offered her after their divorce.

There followed a series of increasing bids, but the buyers sounded half-hearted and nothing came even close to her reserve price. In the end, the house was turned in unsold at well below her reserve price.

As the auctioneer was clearing up his papers, speaking in a low voice to the estate agent, Molly walked to the front and told them baldly, 'I'm not going below the reserve, so don't waste your time trying to persuade me differently.'

'We'll . . . um, see what happens,' the estate agent said.

As she walked outside, Craig stepped forward to bar the way. 'Since when have those louts been hanging around?'

'Since someone paid them to disrupt the auction, I suppose.'

'You'll never sell the house at this rate. Look, as a special favour, I'll up my bid to what I offered you before.'

'Do you think I don't realise the game you're playing?' Suddenly her anger boiled over. 'I'll burn the house down myself before I accept an offer like that from you. I swear that!' She had the satisfaction of seeing his mouth fall open in surprise.

But his scornful expression soon returned. 'Don't be

so bloody melodramatic. You know very well you'd never do any such thing.'

It was her turn to smile. 'Actually, I meant that quite literally. About burning it before selling to you. You have gone a step too far, Craig.'

Uncertain how long this frozen feeling would allow her to control her emotions, she moved past him and went back into the house.

When she turned to close the door, she saw him striding along the path towards her and slammed the door in his face, then ran through the house to lock the back door as well. She didn't want to speak to him again, was shaking now with reaction.

Craig rang the doorbell a couple of times, but she didn't answer. Eventually he strolled back to the garage, whistling cheerfully.

She waited for the estate agent to come and see her, but he seemed to be taking a long time to wind up. It was a while before the auctioneer's car drove away.

There was no sign of the youths now. How Craig must hate her to do this to her. What had she ever done to deserve it? *He* was the one who'd been unfaithful, then walked out on their marriage, not her. And the house had belonged to her family, so he had no moral right to it, whatever he might want.

Eventually Craig drove away and the estate agent came across to the house. She let him in and led the way to the kitchen. 'I want to say again that there have never been groups of youths like that in this street before. And if you like, I'll get you some signed statements from my neighbours to that effect.'

'Why should the youths suddenly be here today, then?'

'Because someone wanted to disrupt the auction and get the house for a low price, I suppose.'

'I think you should be very careful before you make such accusations.'

'Should I?'

'Your husband was extremely upset on your behalf and is worried that you're not thinking rationally.'

'He's not my husband. He's my ex and he's married to someone else. What's more, he doesn't give two hoots about me. Did he make you another bid?'

'Yes.'

'Was it anywhere near the reserve price?'

'Well, no.'

She named the sum Craig had offered her before.

'Yes, that's it exactly,' William said. 'How did you know?'

'It's what he offered me when we split up – at the same time as he told me he'd get the house at that price one way or another, so I might as well give in. But he won't get it. No one can force me sell it to him. I'll stay here for ever, if I have to.'

'We might be able to persuade him to go higher.'

'I don't think you will, but you're welcome to try. If he'll meet the reserve price, I'll sell, even to him.'

'And as we agreed, we can list the house for sale now.'

Which was what she should have done in the first place.

She didn't weep after he left. What good would it do?

She watched as a van turned up to remove the seats and auctioneer's table. There was no further sign of the youths.

The following week the estate agent rang to say he was bringing a couple to view the house. Before they'd even arrived, the gang of youths was there again. She couldn't believe what she was seeing. How could anyone have got to know about this private viewing?

It only took a moment's thought for her to realise there must be someone in the office of Grayson's passing the information on. It was the only possible explanation.

The couple looked round the house and the woman sighed. 'It's what we want, Ms Peel, but I don't like the look of those yobs.'

'I believe they've been sent deliberately to prevent me selling,' Molly said grimly. 'The only times I've ever seen them round here were during the auction and now.'

All three of them looked at her as if she was mad.

As William was showing the couple out, she touched his sleeve. 'Do you have a moment?'

He nodded. 'I'll just let the Doonans into my car.'

When he came back, she said, 'I think you may have someone in your office leaking information. Those youths haven't been back here since the auction – until the very hour you came here to show someone round.'

His disbelief showed in his face.

She looked out and saw her neighbour out in the front garden, staring open-mouthed at the youths. 'Wait.' She ran outside. 'Jane, could you spare me a minute?'

'Of course, dear.'

'Come and tell the estate agent that those youths don't normally hang around here.'

But Jane's assurances did no good. William listened impassively, then said he'd be in touch.

'You're having trouble selling,' Jane said when they were alone. 'I saw what happened on the day of the auction. I was watching out of the window. Nosey neighbour syndrome.'

'A neighbour like you can be as nosey as she wants. I think someone wants to get the house very cheaply and I can guess who.'

'Craig?'

'Yes.'

'I'm so sorry, dear. I don't know what the world is coming to when people act like that.'

'I'm sorry too. But thank you for your help today, even if the estate agent didn't believe us.'

William rang up that evening. 'I've been thinking about what you said, talking to my colleagues about the situation and I believe, given the circumstances, that it'd be better if you took the house off the market for a while. Or found yourself another estate agent. You clearly don't trust us.'

'How did he get to you so quickly?'

'I don't know what you mean. Or who you mean.'

She wasn't stupid enough to accuse Craig by name, so waited for William to speak. When he didn't, she decided he wasn't on her side anyway in this, so said quietly, 'Please take my house off your books, then.'

That evening Craig rang up again, increasing his offer slightly.

She put the phone down on him and got herself a glass of wine, but left most of it, because she couldn't settle to anything, let alone enjoy a drink.

In the middle of the night someone threw a stone through her bedroom window.

She came awake with a start as glass shattered and showered across her bed. The old-fashioned window, with its single pane of glass had broken easily. She shivered, wishing she'd not resisted having double glazing fitted.

Why would anyone do that to her?

It took her a moment or two to realise what this must be about: the house. Craig again. Trying different tactics. She'd never be able to prove it was him, but she was quite certain of it.

Breathing quietly, straining her ears to hear footsteps, she waited for another attack, but there was no sound outside and no more missiles smashed into the house.

She cried then, couldn't help it, sitting upright in the bed, surrounded by shards of glass, not daring to move, sobbing and letting the tears run down her cheeks. On the floor, a large chunk of rock sat triumphant amid the ruins.

Eventually she managed to stop weeping and shook the glass off the duvet. Leaning down for her slippers, she gave them a good shake as well, though fortunately they'd been on the other side of the bed. She risked putting them on then crunched her way to the window. Of course there was nothing to be seen, no lurking figures, no strange vehicles parked in the street, only the moonlight dappling the garden and the flowering cherry tree near the gate swaying in the breeze.

She moved to another bedroom for the rest of the night, taking care not to put the light on to give away where she was. She didn't sleep much, though, and the remaining hours of darkness seemed to pass very slowly.

In the morning she got up and went to survey the damage to her bedroom: glass everywhere and a deep gouge mark on her dressing table. 'Bad call, Craig,' she said aloud. 'I'm *not* giving in.' She felt furiously angry and the incident made her feel more determined not to let him have the house, not less.

She reported it to the police, knowing it wasn't likely they'd be able to do anything, but wanting to register the offence, at least. Then she sat down and wrote out a diary of the various events. Her father had taught her to document serious problems. He'd been a wise man and she still missed him.

He'd suggested early on in her marriage that she should stand up to Craig more, and she'd laughed, feeling secure and loved, knowing how her husband valued her help and support . . . and also, not wanting to rock the boat. She could see now that even then she'd been a bit chary of angering Craig.

She didn't know what she was going to do with her life now, but the one thing she could ensure was that Craig didn't get hold of the house, whatever he offered her, whatever he did. She held on to that thought tightly.

She wasn't giving in to him.

Euan stared at the email in amazement. Penny had resigned, in a brief email and without giving a reason. He couldn't believe she'd be so unprofessional as to do it this way, without giving him any notice. His eyes narrowed as he read the second paragraph. She felt so nervous of coming in again, she'd be sending her fiancé to pick up her things the following afternoon. Could someone please pack them?

He reread the email and the idea slowly crept into his mind that something was brewing here. He had a nose for trickery. Was she going to claim that he or his staff had done something to upset her, something against the laws of harassment, or whatever they called it these days? He'd dealt with cases of false claims from time to time in the building industry, as well as genuine claims for injuries, which of course, he'd facilitated.

No, surely Penny wouldn't dare file a claim for compensation? The working conditions here were not only fair, but he stuck to both the letter and the spirit of the law.

He read the email again and unease crawled along his spine. Something just didn't read right.

There was only one person to whom he could turn for help, only one person who knew Penny's job and was beyond reproach. He picked up the phone. 'Avril? I'm in serious trouble and I need your advice and help. No, it's not just that I'm missing you, though I am. It's Trouble with a capital T. Yes, I'd love to stop at your house for coffee on my way home and tell you about it. Thanks.'

He then sent an email to say Penny's fiancé shouldn't call for her things until two days later, since he had to find someone who knew the office well enough to separate Penny's possessions from company items. If she would provide a list, even a rough list, they could check it off and that might save everyone further trouble. He thanked her for her services and said the staff clerk from the hotel would be in touch about her pay and entitlements.

He didn't call in a temp that day, but soon wished he had, because he had to keep stopping work to answer the phone instead of doing his own job. He'd have to come back here this evening and put in a few more hours.

He didn't get away till six o'clock and when he stopped his car in Avril's drive, he sat for a moment or two, eyes closed, gathering his thoughts together.

She opened the door before he knocked, studied his face and patted his arm gently. 'It must be bad for you to look so weary. Come and sit down, Euan. I've made an apple pie.'

He tried to smile but was too tired, too worried. He accepted a cup of her delicious coffee and suddenly realised he'd missed lunch. The apple pie was delicious and he ate a second piece.

'Missed lunch again, did you?' she said, her eyes twinkling at him from behind her thick multifocal glasses.

'Yes. I didn't even notice until now.'

'Doesn't your secretary nip out for a sandwich? Or is that below a modern young woman's dignity?'

He sighed and explained the problem.

She sat frowning, then shook her head regretfully. 'I promised myself I'd never go back, but I think you're right and you do need help. That young woman may indeed be about to try something on. I'll be in tomorrow at my usual time and I'll stay until we've found decent help to replace me.' She fixed him with a firm gaze. 'I'm not coming back permanently, but if it's necessary, I'll also be able to help you investigate this Penny person, since she lives locally. I have a lot of contacts in the community.'

He took her hand and raised it to his lips. 'Thank you. You're a wonderful woman.'

She shook her head slightly, smiling. 'And you're a flatterer.'

He stared back at her, still holding her hand. 'No, I'm not. I've employed secretaries for nearly twenty years and not one of them has even come close to you in effectiveness or been such a pleasure to work with. I told you that when you left and I meant it.'

She flushed and pulled her hand away. 'I'll see you tomorrow, then.'

When he got back to work that evening, Euan felt a deep sense of relief that help was coming. There was no one around and he got a lot done. Only when he stood up to fetch some papers from the filing cabinet did he realise how stiff he was. Stretching and groaning, he glanced at the clock, amazed to see it was past midnight. He debated getting a room in the hotel attached to the complex, a hotel he didn't run, thank goodness, but had leased out to someone else.

In the end he decided to go home. He didn't intend to face Avril in the morning wearing a crumpled shirt and yesterday's underwear.

He knew she couldn't walk on water or see through walls, but sometimes it almost felt as if she could.

Chapter Four

When Molly went to tidy the front garden, just to get out into the sunshine for a while, her neighbour looked over the fence.

'What happened last night?'

'Someone threw a rock through my bedroom window.'

'How terrible! Do you fancy a cup of coffee and a chat?'

'I'd love one.'

As she sat on Jane's patio, she found herself confiding in her neighbour, fighting against tears. 'Sorry. I keep telling myself I won't cry any more, then I get upset and before you know it I'm weeping again. I'm so annoyed with myself.'

'Don't be,' Jane said gently. 'You've held things inside yourself for too long.' She hesitated, then added, 'You changed so much after Craig left, I did wonder whether you were clinically depressed. I told you if you wanted to talk, I was here, but you didn't come. I repeated my offer recently. It does help to talk, you know, dear, and one of the good things about being eighty, like me, is that you have a lot of experience under your belt and sometimes that can help others.'

Molly stared down at her tightly clasped hands, frowning. Depressed? You read about depression, but you never related it to yourself. But when she looked back, she realised she had been pretty miserable. And reclusive. 'I think you could be right. About the depression, I mean. It hit me hard, Craig leaving.'

'Bound to. But in spite of what's happened lately, you look much brighter these days. Now, on to something more positive. Do you really mean what you told me the other day?'

'What about?'

'Fighting back against the world.'

'Well . . . I intend to try.'

'Not the right attitude,' Jane said at once.

'Whatever do you mean?'

'You sound as if you're expecting to fail before you even start, as if you don't believe you *can* hold your corner and fight back.'

Molly looked at her in surprise. 'I . . . Do you know, you're right.'

'It's not enough to *say* you'll fight back. That's far too vague. What are you going to actually *do*?'

'I was planning to buy a house in the country and make a peaceful new life for myself. Only I can't do that until I sell this house.'

'Peaceful! Sounds rather boring to me. How old are you now?'

'Forty-eight.'

'That seems quite young to me. Surely you don't want to retreat to a cottage and sit there quietly until you die. *I'm* not looking for a peaceful life and I'm thirty years older than you. By all means move to the country, but find yourself a job, take up new interests, get out and about, look for a new man, if there are any suitable ones around.'

Molly shuddered. 'The last thing I want to do is get married again, or even live with someone. Men take too much looking after.' She paused to think. 'But a job . . . That might . . . No, who'd want to employ me? I've been out of the workforce for years.'

Jane looked at her severely. 'Anyone with sense would be glad of your help. I've seen you organise a dinner party for twelve people, cook all the food for it – gourmet food too – and manage the staff hired for the evening. That takes considerable skill. I've seen you run round after Craig in all sorts of ways, sorting out all his minor problems from work. What you are, is a born organiser. Do you have any formal secretarial skills?'

'I suppose so. I did train as a secretary, got a diploma and everything, though I've not worked for years—'

'Except as Craig's unpaid assistant.'

'I suppose so. But I'm used to computers and I'm still pretty quick at touch-typing. I can do spreadsheets, too.' She looked at Jane in surprise. 'I've kept up with technology, haven't I?'

'Yes. You even taught me to use a computer, and you were an excellent teacher.'

Molly could feel herself relaxing a little. 'You're very good for my morale.'

'I'm only telling the truth. What I'd suggest is you register for office work temping. You can give my name as a character reference, if you like. One of my granddaughters did some temping and she said she learnt a lot about people, as well as about business from going to so many different places. She really enjoyed it, too.' Jane let her glasses slip down her nose and looked over them at Molly. 'When was the last time *you* thoroughly enjoyed your life?'

She didn't even have to think about that. 'When the children were small, before Craig got so utterly career-oriented. It's never been quite as good since.'

'That's a long time to be unhappy, dear.'

'I haven't been unhappy, so much as . . . well, faintly anxious.' She looked at Jane in surprise. 'Goodness, I never realised that. I never seemed to do anything well enough to suit Craig, you see. And in the last few years we were together, it got much worse. He became so scornful.' She looked down at herself. 'I'm not good with clothes, I wear glasses and can't wear contact lenses, so I don't do him credit. There was nothing he didn't criticise about me.'

'And you believed what he said.' Jane let that sink in, then said with a smile, 'He's right about clothes. You're not very good at choosing them. I'd have helped you with your wedding outfit, but Denis isn't very well just now.'

'I'm sorry. He does look a bit . . . pale.'

'Yes. Let's focus on you, though. You should get right away from here.'

'I want to, but now that I can't sell the house I'll have to stay. If I tried to get work, I'm sure Craig would find some way to prevent me, I just know he would. Look at how he's ruined the auction. I'm sure it's him who's harassing me.'

'I agree.'

Molly looked at her in surprise.

'I never liked him, dear, and he felt the same about me. But it won't do you any good to go and cower in a country rut.' She frowned. 'Actually, I think I might be able to help you. Have you thought of letting the house for a time, rather than selling it?'

'And have Craig arrange for the tenant to be harassed? It wouldn't be fair to them.'

'You think he's that bad?'

Molly looked at her in surprise and it was a moment before she could pull her thoughts together. Another surprise. 'Yes. Yes, I do. He wasn't like that when we married but now he's a . . . a shark!'

Jane patted her hand. 'Then one solution might be to rent your house to my son and get on with building a new life elsewhere.'

Molly stared at her in surprise. 'Stuart? Why would he want to live here, with those yobs causing trouble?'

'He'd enjoy the challenge of sorting them out, if I know Stuart. It's a bit hard retiring, when you've been in the army all your life. If anyone knows how to deal with stroppy youths, my Stuart does. Since he and Wendy got back from touring Australia in a camper van, he's looking for somewhere temporary to live because, like you, he needs to sort out a new life for himself. He says he isn't buying a house till that's settled.'

'You've plenty of room for him and his wife in your house. Why would they want to live next door?'

Jane laughed. 'Stuart and his father are too alike to cohabit comfortably. Ooh, the rows they used to have before Stuart left home! And still do from time to time. No, I couldn't stand that. I'd have to spend all my time playing peacemaker, and I've better things to do with my life.'

She grinned and her eighty-year-old face turned suddenly into a little girl's mischievous one. 'Stuart and Wendy have got their youngest son intermittently at home while he finishes university and they have lots of army friends still who like to visit, so they want more than space for themselves. They always keep open house. Denis would hate to have strangers coming and going here, especially now. Look, I can tell Stuart the whole story, if you're considering renting it out, and then we can let him decide. Are you interested?'

Molly didn't even hesitate. 'It'd be a godsend. It'd let me try life on my own without committing to anything.'

Jane studied her. 'You know, I think dealing with this might be the making of you. If I can presume to offer you some advice . . . ?'

'Please do.'

'Go out and face the world boldly, whether you feel bold inside or not. Take the first step by making a vow to be more assertive. Say what you think and do only what you feel is right. That's a fairly manageable first stage, don't you think?'

Molly looked at her uncertainly. 'It's not always polite or sensitive to say what you think.'

'How far has being polite and sensitive got you so far?'

'Hmm. Not very far. Though I do have some good friends.'

'Of course you do and I hope you count me as one of them.'

'Of course I do.'

'Another thing, Molly, don't let your family know where you're going. Let them worry about you, for a change.'

'They won't care, let alone worry.'

'They might not at first, but as time passes, they will. Tell them they can contact you by email only.'

She gave Molly a quick hug. 'You can do it. I know you can.'

Her neighbour's kindness stayed with Molly all day, making her feel warm and cared about. She didn't know whether she could be more assertive but she could definitely try, couldn't she?

When a missile broke another window in the middle of that night, she didn't weep, she got angry, furiously angry, and it only firmed up her resolve to stand up to whatever the world – or Craig – threw at her.

He was *not* going to get the better of her. Why should she let him get her house from her at a knock-down price?

She'd take Jane's advice, and hold her ground, rather than backing away from confrontations from now on, verbal or otherwise.

* * *

Euan went into the office early the following morning so that he could check the previous day's building work before office hours. Outside, in the sunny but cool spring air, men were whistling as they erected the wooden framework for the next row of six lodges, accompanied by a chorus of birdsong and the sharp staccato sound of drills putting in tek screws.

The houses always looked so fragile at this stage, like a child's assembly kit.

He stopped to chat, because he liked the men working there to know he was keeping an eye on things *and* that he understood what they were doing. But he also stopped to chat because he enjoyed their wry comments on life. He'd worked with the foreman before and trusted Dan to keep things on track – and to maintain the quality of the work.

But however much you trusted your staff, he believed it still paid to be visible, not an absentee boss.

He was back in his office before eight o'clock. When he heard a sound outside, though no one had called out good morning, he went out to find one of the cleaners kneeling down, taking things out of the bottom drawer of the reception desk.

'Are you looking for something?'

She gasped and jumped to her feet. 'Oh, I—it's just – Penny rang and asked me to clear out her bottom drawer. It's only her personal things.'

He looked at the muddle of objects on the floor: a box of tissues, a half-eaten bar of chocolate, a packet of women's tights, a magazine – yes, these were personal. But there were also quite a few papers, the top one displaying the company heading.

'I've got a box to put them in, Mr Santiago. I'm sorry for disturbing you. It won't take me more than a minute or two to finish.'

'I'd rather check those papers first, if you don't mind. It looks as if business stuff may have got mixed up with Penny's things.'

His former secretary walked in just then, and while the cleaner hovered nearby looking distinctly uncomfortable, he explained what had happened.

Avril looked at the mess on the floor as if it was crawling with maggots, and said to the cleaner in a chill tone, 'I don't think it's your job to go through the desks in here. And when dealing with a mess of personal things like those, you ought to be wearing rubber gloves. You've put yourself at risk doing it, in more ways than one. If anything's missing, you might be accused of stealing, even.'

The cleaner backed away, looking terrified. 'I haven't taken anything away yet. I was only doing a favour for a friend. Look, I'll leave it and let Penny collect it herself.' She turned and hurried away.

'Just a minute!' Euan called, amazed when she started running. After a startled glance at Avril, he took off after her.

She bumped into another cleaner on the corner and ricocheted off the wall, sending cleaning materials flying.

He went to bar her way. 'Are you both all right?'

'Yes, no harm done,' the other cleaner said cheerfully.

The one he'd been chasing said nothing. He peered at her name tag. 'Are you all right, Karen?'

She nodded, shrinking away from him.

'Why were you running away?'

'I thought you'd be angry. Penny said you used to frighten her and I can see why.'

Euan realised suddenly that he might just have given Penny more evidence – if she was out to sue him – if he hadn't made a mistake about that. Oh, hell! 'When I found you going through the desk drawers, I was worried that you'd been pilfering,' he said quietly. 'And then you ran away. What was I to think?'

The other cleaner looked at him in shock. 'I'd better call the supervisor, Mr Santiago. She's also the union rep. It's her job to sort problems out.'

'Good idea. Do that. We'll all wait here for her.'

'I'm just finishing my shift,' Karen protested. 'I have to go and pick up my children from school.'

'Not till the supervisor's spoken to you. I want confirmation that you weren't stealing.'

She burst into tears but the other woman didn't try to comfort her. She put her mobile phone back into her overall pocket and said, 'Liz will be here in two minutes. She said we were all to wait.'

'Good. Suits me.' Euan leant against the wall.

Liz came hurrying round the corner in under two minutes. He'd seen her around because she was in charge of the cleaners for the hotel as well as for the suite of offices, but he hadn't spoken to her. She was wiry, looked as if she'd had a hard life and seemed ready to be aggressive with him. But when she heard what had happened, her annoyance shifted from him to Karen.

'You know very well you're not supposed to open any drawers or cupboards, Karen, and only to touch what you need to clean.'

Sobs were her only answer.

'We'll go and have a look at the things she took out of the drawer, Mr Santiago, if that's all right with you.'

'It's fine with me and thank you for coming so promptly, Liz. I wasn't sure what to do for the best, but I don't want confidential business information going out of here.'

When they got to the reception area, they found Avril sitting at the desk, looking as if she belonged there. 'Liz! Long time no see.'

'Are you back with us, Miss Buttermere?'

'Only temporarily. I'm helping Euan out because Penny decided to leave without notice. I seem to have walked straight into trouble.' She flicked one finger towards the mess on the floor. 'I decided it'd be best not to touch that lot without witnesses. Would you help me go through it, Liz?'

'Be glad to, Miss Buttermere.' She turned to Karen. 'You'd better stay. Do you want to ring someone to pick up your kids?'

Avril looked at Euan. 'And perhaps you'd like to get on with your work, Mr Santiago? I know how busy you are. Liz and I can investigate this and I'll bring you up to date about it later.'

Dismissed, he thought, hiding a smile.

What a relief it was to have Avril back in charge of the office!

The next morning, Jane came round to see Molly. 'I rang my son last night. Stuart would like to come round to see the house today, if that's all right with you.'

'That's fine. But—' She hesitated.

'I heard another window smash last night. They didn't hurt you?'

'No. I didn't put a light on in the room I was occupying and they chose to target my previous bedroom again. I've got the glazier coming round this morning to repair the window for the second day running. I still can't believe this is happening.'

'People can go overboard when they want something badly. The main thing is that you've not been hurt. And don't worry. I told Stuart about your little problem and it didn't put him off, rather the contrary. He hates bullying and cheating with a passion.'

Molly wasn't so sure about it. Stuart might be all right with the situation, but what about his wife? And what would they feel like once they'd moved in, if whoever it was carried on smashing windows, day after day?

She rang up the police, then her insurance company, and the person on the phone was very disapproving of the same window being broken two days running.

'Have you thought of hiring a security firm? If this goes on, you'll have to pay an increased premium, you know,' a young-sounding woman said. 'Please make sure you inform the police about this.'

'I've done that already.'

'And what did they say?'

'They don't think they can do much to prevent such incidents, but they'll send patrols round a couple of times a night.'

Towards the end of the morning, Molly kept watch from the corner bedroom window for Jane's son arriving, while the glazier fitted another window in the room next door. When she saw her husband drive past, she stiffened. No mistaking that profile or the personalised number plate. What was Craig doing here? This wasn't a road that led anywhere he was likely to go. In fact, it didn't really lead anywhere, except to a further tangle of streets.

He could only have come here to gloat! she decided. When he drove past a short time later, going in the other direction, slowing down again to smile, she was certain that was why he was here.

A few moments later the doorbell rang and she realised she hadn't even seen whoever it was approaching, so lost had she been in her own thoughts. She ran down to open it, to find Jane and her son standing there. He was as upright as she remembered, but he'd lost most of his hair and had shaved his head, which made him look very different. His smile was still as warm as his mother's, however.

'You remember Stuart, don't you, Molly? And by the way, did you see your ex driving past just now?'

'You saw Craig as well?'

'Yes. No mistaking that personalised number plate, or his face, come to that.'

'Oh, good. Would you mind writing down the date and the time you saw him? I'm keeping a diary of everything that happens. Pleased to see you again, Stuart. Do come in. The glazier's just finishing. Your mother did explain what's been going on?'

'About the harassment? Yes.'

'Doesn't it worry you?'

He bared his teeth in a grin that would have frightened her if she'd been a guilty person brought up before him. 'It'll be a fun little project to catch them, Molly.'

'If only you could!'

'I think I've got a fair chance.'

Jane moved towards the door. 'I'll leave you to show Stuart round in peace. I have an important phone call to make.'

She looked so sad as she said that. Molly glanced quickly at Stuart; he was watching Jane go. And he looked sad, too.

As she was finishing showing him round, Jane came back and Molly took them into the kitchen for some coffee.

'Well, what do you think of the house?' Jane asked her son.

'It's perfect for our needs and the harassment doesn't worry me. But I do need to find somewhere *quickly*, so the deciding factor will be how soon we can move in. We're staying with Wendy's sister at the moment and she's driving me crazy with her fussy ways, plus I have friends coming back from a tour of duty in Afghanistan in a couple of weeks. I need somewhere with spare bedrooms so that I can spend time with them.'

Another chance to be positive, Molly thought. 'I can be out of the house within a few days. I'll just have to find somewhere to store my furniture. Oh, and we have to discuss rent.'

He held out a piece of paper. 'These are the prices and descriptions we've been given of houses in this area. That one,' his finger stabbed at the sheet, 'sounds closest to yours, so that would seem to be a fair rent.'

She hoped she'd hidden her surprise at how much it was.

'Four weeks in advance suit you?'

'Yes.'

'Or you could rent the place to us furnished and we'd pay a little extra? We're careful tenants.' He grinned at his mother. 'If we weren't, Ma would soon be after us. Our stuff's in storage and that'd save uncrating and re-crating it if I decide to work overseas for a while. Do you need all this stuff?'

'No, definitely not.' She thought rapidly. 'I shall need a bed, I could take the furniture in the conservatory, my computer desk and a bookcase, as well as some of the crockery and stuff like that. But I've got plenty of cookware, so you'd still have enough left. I can't see me giving any more dinner parties for twelve.'

He stuck out one hand. 'Done! You're a woman after my own heart. No shilly-shallying and know what you want.'

She was a bit surprised by his compliment but pleased, and saw Jane beaming and nodding approval at her. 'Won't your wife want to see the house first, though?'

'One of the grandchildren's ill, so she's gone rushing off to help. We've already discussed what sort of place we need, and she trusts me and Mum to find somewhere to suit. I'll write you a cheque now, shall I, Molly? And I've got a rental agreement somewhere in the car that an agency gave me. I'll give it to you and we can fill it in together next time I come. If you trust me, that is.'

'You're Jane's son. Of course I trust you.'

He smiled and gave his mother a quick hug. 'There you are, Ma. I knew you'd come in useful one day.'

She pretended to hit him.

As they walked off, he put one arm round his mother's shoulders and Molly had to swallow a lump in her throat. She didn't think Brian had even looked at her properly lately, let alone shown any affection.

She walked slowly round the ground floor, feeling as if a load had been lifted from her shoulders. It took her a few moments to realise that the bright new feeling creeping into her head was hope.

How long had it been since she'd felt hopeful? Or even vaguely positive?

Galvanised, she went upstairs to start packing her personal possessions, then changed her mind and did some searching on her computer. She found a storage place, the sort where you hired a lock-up space, and phoned to book a unit. She'd put her things there till she settled somewhere.

While she was at it, she decided to ring Brian's mobile to tell him he had two days to remove his boxes of toys, then she suddenly realised that if she did, he'd probably tell his father she was leaving. And who knew what Craig would dream up then?

Instead she would ask Stuart if she could leave the boxes in the garage for her son to pick up – with a time limit, of course. She tried to remember what Stuart's wife looked like and could only dredge up a vague picture of Wendy. But she'd trust him with her home. Well, he was Jane's son.

Thinking of Stuart reminded her how she no longer trusted anything Craig said or did. She'd worried about his business methods for years, or rather the way he went about getting promotions by discrediting the opposition as well as by what he achieved.

And, if she was honest, she'd known something was wrong with their marriage before he asked for a divorce, but had been too cowardly to rock the boat.

She wasn't proud of that! Wasn't proud of a lot of things. Was going to make sure she did better from now on. However hard it might be.

Avril appeared in the doorway of the office. 'Do you have a moment, Mr Santiago?'

'Certainly, Miss Buttermere.' He noticed that Liz was still there, as was Karen. 'Is there a problem?'

'Perhaps you can tell us.' She indicated a pile of crumpled papers on her desk. 'Wendy and I sorted these out from Penny's things.'

He picked up the first one and frowned. A copy of his budget figures. One by one he picked the papers up and put them down. 'I don't understand what she's doing with confidential information like that. She didn't type this material up; I did. I don't even know how she got hold of it. That section of my computer is password protected.'

The two women looked at one another.

'There's something else. This was hidden in the toiletries bag.' Avril held out a thumb drive and he stuck it into the computer. What he saw made him whistle in shock. 'I think I'd like to call in the police.'

Karen wailed and began to sob.

'Be quiet! If you've done nothing wrong, *you* have nothing to fear.' Avril turned to Liz. 'Do you agree to calling in the police about Penny?'

'Yes, and I'm satisfied that you've followed the preferred procedures by involving me as soon as you knew there was a problem. I'd like to ring the union about it, Mr Santiago. I don't understand the importance of the information on that thumb drive, so I'll have to rely on your judgement until they send someone.'

He gestured towards the phone. 'Be my guest. I want to be fair to everyone.' He looked at Karen. 'What about your children? Have you found someone to collect them from school?'

She nodded. 'My sister.' She looked frightened now. 'I thought I was just picking up Penny's things, truly I did.'

He believed her. She was such an unlikely conspirator. She looked very upset, so he repeated, 'Then you have nothing to fear. Miss Buttermere, do you think you could organise a cup of tea for everyone? And perhaps you could keep all this material in full view of us all for the moment. Would that be fair, Liz?'

'Yes.' She took out a mobile phone, walked along the corridor a little way and keyed in a number. 'Hello? We have an incident . . .'

Her voice went quiet as she explained, then she cut the connection and returned. 'They're sending someone straight away and if it's all right with you, Mr Santiago, I'm to stay and keep an eye on these things until then.'

'Fine by me.'

He went to wait inside his office, hating the mess that greeted him, but very glad Avril had come back to help him. If she hadn't, how would he have coped with this?

In the middle of it all, a couple turned up to view the houses. He'd not realised he had this appointment, because it wasn't in his diary. Yet another example of Penny's inefficiency.

He summoned up a smile and took them round the houses, patiently answering the questions whose answers they could have perfectly well have found for themselves in the neat little brochure.

When he got back to the office, the police and the union official were there.

By the time they left two hours later, he had a raging headache.

Avril looked at him. 'Not a good day.'

'No. Enough to send you running for shelter from my troubles, I should think.'

'On the contrary. But there are some things that need to change here. It's early days to pass judgement, but I think you need at least one more member of staff, a sort of general factotum, someone who could take over the sales work and admin, as well as relieving me on reception, whatever was needed.'

'You're right.'

'And another thing: what sort of hours are you working each day? You came back here last night after you'd spoken to me, didn't you? I saw the time on those files you gave me to photocopy. You look exhausted.'

She began to gather her things, then stopped. 'I think you should make sure there's a security officer on duty tonight. I'd organise it myself, but I have an urgent appointment.'

'I was going to stay myself.'

'Can you manage without sleep nowadays? How clever of you.'

He gave in, knowing that tone of voice. 'No, I can't. You're right. I'll get someone in to keep watch.'

That took another couple of hours, so he grabbed some fish and chips on the way home, and felt so tired he went straight to bed.

He didn't expect to sleep but sheer exhaustion did the trick.

Chapter Five

Molly rang her cousin. 'Helen, I know it's last minute, but isn't the family reunion you told me about taking place this coming weekend? Oh, good. Look, my circumstances have changed . . .' She explained then asked if she could still attend it.

'It'll be great to have you. I'll see if they've got a room free at the hotel, and if not you can share mine. They do a lot of weddings there, you see, so they're often completely booked out. Everyone will really enjoy catching up with you. It's been ages.'

'I don't think most people will even remember me.'

Helen chuckled. 'Of course they will. They may not have seen you since you were a kid, but you were very noticeable then; a real tomboy, into everything. Remember the time you got stuck up that tree and your mother had to call the fire brigade to get you down? Or the time you led us kids on an expedition to the country and we all got lost for hours?'

'I'd forgotten that.'

Helen's voice became gentler. 'You've had a rough time lately, losing your parents and then Craig going off the rails. Have you got plans for your new life?'

'No. Not yet.' She struggled to keep her voice steady. 'Look, I'll tell you where I'm at when I see you.'

'Come to my house first. Come and stay for a few days.'

'Oh. Well, I don't want to be a bother and—' She stopped, hearing Jane's voice telling her to speak the truth. She'd love to visit Helen, so why not say it? 'Well, actually I'd love to stay with you, just for the night before the reunion, though. Emailing isn't the same, is it?'

'No, but better than nothing. I'm glad you've kept in touch, Molly. It'll be great seeing you without Craig. My Les didn't take to him at all.'

'No. I remember the awkward silences. I should be clear here by Friday. I'll be there in the afternoon.' Now she came to think of it, Craig had made little attempt to get on with any of her family. They were probably too ordinary to be of any use to him. Why hadn't she seen earlier how ruthless that drive for business success was? Was love always blind? Hers had been.

'Great. I'll send Les out for a drink with his mates that night, then you and I can have a good old catch-up. Do you still like Merlot?'

Molly laughed, suddenly feeling more cheerful. 'Yes, I do. But let me bring a bottle.'

When she put the phone down, she took a deep breath.

Friday, then. She was going to be clear of here by Friday morning, whatever it took.

She couldn't get a reply on Stuart's mobile phone, so went round to ask Jane to tell her son everything was arranged for the handover, then started on the packing. Good thing she'd had a thorough clear-out for the house viewing.

As she packed, her mind wandered to her children. Her daughter hadn't tried to contact her since that one call, hadn't even sent a postcard from the honeymoon. That hurt. Just as her confrontation with her son had hurt and *he* hadn't been in touch since then, either. Maybe one day the huge gaps between them would mend. You should never give up hope.

No one threw rocks through her window that night, but she still kept jerking awake, thinking she'd heard something outside.

On the Wednesday, Stuart rang to ask if he could put in security gates across the drive.

'I can't afford that, I'm afraid.'

'I've had a good deal offered me in return for a favour or two, so you don't need to spend a penny. It's just that in my line of business, which is installing security systems, I like to make sure people can't get to me easily.'

'Well, if you're sure it won't cost me anything, you're welcome to make any changes like that. Security is important.'

'Thanks. I'll bring a letter round for you to sign, giving me permission. And I promise I won't put anything unsightly in.'

'I don't think Jane would let you.'

'She's a terror, my old mum.' He chuckled; such a nice fat chuckle.

The memory of it made her smile several times.

On the Thursday evening, her two closest friends came round for a farewell drink, bringing takeaway Indian food.

'What's with the big gates?' Di asked.

'My tenant had them put in. I can't believe he got it done in twenty-four hours.'

'Must have cost him a bomb.'

'He's in the security business, got them cheap. Now, let me pour you some wine. Good thing your husbands are picking you up.'

'Where exactly are you going?' Nicki demanded after they'd all taken an appreciative sip or two.

'I don't know.' Molly laughed, feeling light and free, as if she'd shed years. 'I'm just heading off into the wide blue yonder and who knows where I'll wind up?'

'Good for you. Welcome back.' Nicki raised her glass.

'What do you mean?'

'It's the old Molly now, the one I used to work with, not the one Craig trampled into submission. Will you still be picking up your emails?' Molly nodded. 'Good. And we've got each other's mobile numbers. We'll keep in touch.'

'Oh. I've changed my mobile number. This is my new one. New start. I don't want Craig to be able to contact me. Please don't give this number to anyone else.'

'Your kids will tell him the new number.'

'They don't know it either. If they want me, they can email.'

Her friends didn't comment but she could see the surprise on their faces, followed by pity. She changed the subject and soon they were all laughing and reminiscing again.

When Nikki and Di had left, their goodbyes seemed to echo around her and it felt as if the house was adding its goodbye to theirs. She'd always loved her home, even as a child, but now . . . now it didn't feel like hers any more.

'Goodbye,' she said aloud. Whatever happened, she didn't think she'd ever live here again.

But where would she live? That was quite an exciting thought. She was totally free to go anywhere she chose. Or to move on again if Wiltshire didn't suit her.

'You ought to contact your mother now that we're back, you know,' Jamie said.

Rachel scowled at him across the table. 'We've already had this discussion and I haven't changed my mind. No way.'

'You can't hold a grudge for ever.'

'She got drunk and was late for my wedding. You saw her. It was embarrassing and it was the only thing that went wrong the whole day. How could she do that to me?'

'How do you know she was drunk?'

'Dad told me.'

'I heard differently from a friend who was there.'

Rachel dumped her knife and fork on the plate, folding her arms. 'What do you mean?'

'I heard she collapsed and was taken away in an ambulance during the wedding reception.'

'She couldn't have done. Dad would have told me, or Tasha.'

'You're not going to like this, but I have to say it. I've heard them embroider the truth before when they talked about your mother.'

Rachel stared down at the food then pushed the plate away from her. 'You're right. I don't like it. So let's drop the subject. Do you want a coffee?'

His shook his head, his usual smile missing. 'If anyone tells you bad things about me, I hope you'll have more trust in me, or at least wait to check out what's true and what isn't. And even if what your father said about your mother is correct, I feel sorry for her and I wouldn't blame her for seeking Dutch courage. You all treat her so scornfully.'

'I said: let's drop the subject or we'll be having our first row.'

He shrugged and began to butter another piece of toast, but he didn't chat any more and left early for work.

She didn't mention her mother again, but couldn't help thinking about what he'd said. And worrying about the disappointment in his eyes.

No, her father and Tasha wouldn't lie to her. They just . . . wouldn't. And she'd never forgive her mother for spoiling her special day. Never.

She sighed. Life was very boring when you didn't have

a wedding to look forward to and Jamie was a bit fussy about the place being tidy. She went to the spare bedroom and glared at the pile of boxes and bags that had been dumped there, thanks to her dear mother. She'd had no time to clear them up.

It was mean of her mother to send them here when she hadn't even sold the house yet. Just plain mean. She could have easily kept them in the garage. How could Jamie expect to keep the flat tidy with these piled up?

She glanced at the clock and let out a shriek. She was going to be late for work if she didn't hurry.

On Friday, Molly hugged Jane, handed over the keys to Stuart and set off. Her car contained clothes, her computer and a few personal bits and pieces, but it was by no means loaded. The rest of her possessions were in storage.

She felt liberated as she drove along the M4, stopping for coffee and a snack because she'd been too excited to eat much that morning.

She arrived at Helen's house mid afternoon, and when her cousin opened the door, they stood staring at one another before hugging.

'You don't seem anything like your age,' Helen said. 'How do you stay so young-looking?'

Molly couldn't return the compliment because her cousin looked a lot older than the last time she'd seen her. 'Oh, being fat fills up the wrinkles,' she joked.

Helen held the door open. 'You're not fat. You're not even plump. Whatever made you think you were? Come in.' When they were sitting in the kitchen with a cup of coffee, she said abruptly, 'I'd better tell you, because if I don't someone else will tomorrow. I had breast cancer four years ago.'

'No! You never said! Are you clear now?'

'Yes. Three years since treatment finished and counting towards the magic five. But cancer changes you, makes you realise what's important.' She fixed Molly with a steady gaze that made her look like their grandmother. 'I'll be upfront about it: I wasn't upset when you and Craig split up. I'd been expecting it for a while. I think you'll do better and be happier on your own.'

'Everyone seems to have been expecting it – except me. They say the wife is always the last to know.' Molly shrugged. 'It's taken me a while to get used to it.'

'Why have you decided to leave your old home? I thought you loved it. We had some great times when my parents brought me to visit. I thought you'd get a job nearby, meet someone else – you're definitely the marrying sort – and make a new life.'

Molly explained about the difficulty of selling the house and her cousin was suitably sympathetic. 'It must be Craig behind it. Who else could it be?'

'Try telling that to people. Everyone except Jane next door thinks I'm crazy.'

By the time Les came home from work, they'd had their first glass of wine and were deep in reminiscences. He gave Molly a hug, then ran upstairs to change and was out of the house within quarter of an hour.

She was definitely tiddly by the time she went to bed, but she hadn't laughed as much for years and that felt good.

Stuart Benton helped the two men carry the cartons and miscellaneous smaller possessions into the house, then stood for a moment in the conservatory. He really liked the feel of this house, which was much larger than his parents' home next door, though of the same era: Edwardian.

Wendy came out from the nearby kitchen to join him. 'She's left the whole place immaculate. What a great house this is!'

He pulled her to him for a quick kiss and grinned down at her. 'Told you I'd find us somewhere nice.'

'I thought it was your mother who found it.'

'Same difference.'

Her face grew sombre. 'How bad is your father?'

'That's one of the things I want to find out. They're both being very cagey about it, but he's looking . . . fragile. And she's looking sad. I can understand them not wanting to broadcast the fact that he's got cancer, but I'm their eldest child, their only son. Surely they can tell me what's going to happen? Surely there's something you and I can do to help Mum?'

'Just being here will help them, I should think.'

'I hope so. Now remember, pretend we don't know what we'll be doing next year.'

'You'll have to tell people eventually.'

'I'm not sure I will. It may be helpful for the company to have an invisible partner, given that it's dealing in big security projects, at least while we're setting things up and can't afford to hire a lot of staff.'

'You could just retire, you know. We could afford to do that on your army pension.'

He made a scornful noise in his throat. 'I'd go mad with nothing to do but play golf. I can't see myself ever wanting to retire completely.'

'Well, don't ask me to work with you. I'm going to do my own thing too from now on.'

He plonked a kiss on her cheek and stepped back. 'I know. Go for it. Do whatever it takes to get your creations off the ground. You've supported me for long enough.' He looked beyond her. 'Mum! Come to have a good old nose round?'

Jane joined them, smiling. 'Of course I have. I'm also curious about that big gate. Was it really necessary?'

'You can't be too careful in my business. And before you ask, I paid for it, not Molly. We do have a year's lease here, after all.'

'Well, you know your own business best. Now, show me round. I never got beyond the kitchen and sitting room, hardly even that when Craig was living here. He didn't encourage poor Molly to waste time gossiping with the neighbours. She came across for a coffee with me usually.'

'What's he like?'

'Don't get me started. Arrogant, selfish, treated his wife like a doormat. Denis can't abide him.'

'And now he's trying to stop her selling the house to anyone else.'

'Seems like it. Nothing can be proved, of course, but

I've seen him drive past a couple of times and this road isn't a shortcut to anywhere, so he'd certainly not be passing by chance. I note it down now every time I see him pass. He's definitely keeping an eye on the place, and why would he want to do that when he's got married again and is living several miles away?'

'Let him keep an eye on it, Mum. By tomorrow, I'll be keeping an eye on whoever drives past. And with that personalised number plate of his, I can set my new electronic toy to keep a watch for him.'

'You and your toys!'

He smiled. 'Given the vandalism, no one should question my need to use it here. Maybe I'll have a word with the local police as well. You did say Molly reported the crimes to them?'

'She did, but they weren't major crimes, and there wasn't much to go on, so they more or less shrugged it off by saying they'd drive past occasionally. We'll have the whole world driving past at this rate!'

'In the future, there will be more and more need for people to take personal security precautions like these, or so I think. And talking of that, Mum, I'm going to be fitting some security gates and surveillance equipment at your place, and you really should get double glazing put in.'

She pulled a face. 'I don't see the need. We've nothing worth stealing. And I like my old-fashioned windows. Leave it be, Stuart. No one's targeting me.'

'You never know. Besides, even having a security system puts some people off.' He hesitated, then added,

'And Dad's not exactly fit to tackle intruders, is he?'

Her face grew sad. 'No.'

He put an arm round her and gave her a big hug. 'Want to talk about it?'

'Not really. It's terminal and untreatable. I'm glad you're going to be close by. This is one time when I'll come to you for help if I need it – though Denis and I have organised everything as well as we can.'

'How long has he got?'

As she bent her head, he saw a tear roll down her cheek, so he waited.

'Up to six months. They're not sure.'

Stuart sucked in breath and gave her another hug.

The following day Craig couldn't resist driving past the house again. He was wondering which window to have broken next, maybe the other hall window. No, not that one. He wished now that he hadn't arranged for the hall window to be broken, as it was a valuable feature. But needs must break a few eggs when dealing with someone as stupid and stubborn as his ex.

He stopped the car further down the street to make sure she wasn't out in the garden. He had every right to drive wherever he wanted, but still, it was better not to be too much in her face. Though he could always tell people he was doing it because he missed his old home dreadfully. And he did miss the prestige of living on Lavengro Road, not to mention resenting that a stupid bitch like her had the house.

From the end of the street he could see a man strolling

round the front garden, a bald chap who looked as if he pressed weights or something. He looked vaguely familiar, but Craig couldn't place him. Had she got herself a lover, then? No, not Mrs Meek and Mild. Who'd want a fat sow like her?

And it looked as if she'd put some sort of security gate across the drive. It was open now, so he couldn't see it clearly. What a stupid bitch she was, spending money on that sort of thing! She should just have cut her losses and got out.

Stuart went out to examine the creeper that covered part of the front wall. It was pretty but he'd have to trim this part to give a clear vantage point for his new electronic device. He automatically glanced up and down the street and saw a car parked there, a BMW with *that* number plate. He immediately glanced away and strolled back into the house, then ran up the stairs and went to the landing window, where he'd left a pair of binoculars.

It was Craig Taylor's car, no doubt about that: a showy silver BMW with a personalised number plate. And although its windows were tinted, they weren't dark enough to hide the person driving it, not when Stuart was wearing his special glasses.

'Well, well, Mr Taylor,' he muttered. 'You can't keep away, can you? Stupid, that.'

He would, he decided, wait until after dark to set up his surveillance equipment. No need to advertise what he was doing.

He watched the car start to move slowly forward and stop for a few minutes outside the house, so that the driver could look directly into the garden. Bad security, that, to have such an open entrance. If this was his house, he'd put up a visual barrier or two. He might do that anyway. He was sure Molly wouldn't mind. A decorative wooden fence could be put up quite cheaply and could hide all sorts of other devices, if necessary.

He waited till the car had driven away then, whistling cheerfully, he went out to buy the bits and pieces he needed for this house and his mother's from a very discreet shop he loved visiting.

On Saturday morning the two women went shopping and Helen bought a new skirt, while Molly couldn't resist a novel by her favourite author. It felt good to dawdle around town, chatting, stopping for a coffee.

After an equally leisurely lunch, they drove to the hotel where the reunion was to be held, a smallish place in Wiltshire with very friendly staff. The view from Molly's room was over the golf course to one side. People of all ages were earnestly hitting balls or waiting patiently for their turn to start playing. Craig had played golf, not for love of the game but because it was a good way to make contacts. She'd never been attracted to it.

Looking to the other side, she could see some building work going on down the slope from the hotel and wondered what it was. It looked like a residential development. So close to a golf course? That surprised her.

After she'd unpacked what she needed, she looked in the folder of information provided for guests and found a brochure detailing the leisure village that was being built next to the golf course. It sounded a great idea, offering a community lifestyle rather than just a dwelling. She'd heard of such places but never visited one.

She went back to stand by the window, loving the view. That had been the one thing her old home was missing, a view. She could see sunlight glinting on water in the distance. Plans of the new development showed a few tiny lakes dotted about. There were mature trees and sweeps of grass between the houses and the golf course. This place didn't look as if it was being developed by eco-vandals.

It might be a good idea to look for a similar place for herself once she'd sold her house, if not here then elsewhere. She didn't fancy living in isolation. The big old house had felt very lonely for the past few months, with Brian and Rachel home so rarely. And she'd felt very vulnerable after the vandalism started.

After finding out the opening hours from the brochure, she decided to go and look at the show houses before she left the following day, to get some idea of what might be available if – no, *when* she sold her old home. She had to keep reminding herself to think positively!

Then she forgot about her future as she went down to the room set aside for the Peel family reunion, and was immediately surrounded by relatives exchanging reminiscences. Those people she didn't know were happy to meet 'Patsy's lass', and those she did know were eager to catch up with her news and share theirs.

She wouldn't neglect her extended family again, she decided. They'd asked about her children. To her shame, she'd never introduced Brian or Rachel to any of them except Helen. Craig had kept her so busy supporting his career, and had arranged for the children to do after-school activities which would enable them to meet the right sort of people.

Why had she let him take over her life so completely? She'd read books about abused wives after he left her, and while he'd never hit her, he'd controlled her in an unconscionable way, which the books said was another form of abuse.

She suddenly felt extremely weary, so she waved to Helen, who was still talking earnestly in one corner, mimed a yawn and slipped out of the function room.

As she walked across the semicircular reception area, a burly young man in a dark suit sitting behind the desk smiled and nodded to her. When she turned the corner to the lifts, she bumped into another man coming from a side passage. 'Oops, sorry.'

'My fault. I wasn't looking where I was going.'

He moved on, glancing back with a slight frown as if he thought he'd recognised her, then shaking his head as if to banish the idea.

She watched him go. He was attractive, about her own age, one of the most attractive men she'd seen for ages. Dark hair, greying at the temples, trim body, a very elegant suit with a tie that was awry and made her itch to straighten it. But he looked tired. Did he work here?

She definitely hadn't met him before, but she felt as if she knew him. She wished she did.

Smiling, she got into the lift. How long was it since she'd even looked at a man in that way, let alone fancied one?

It felt good, a sign of the new Molly.

Chapter Six

The following morning Molly met some of her relatives for a leisurely buffet breakfast, then said goodbye to her cousin Helen. She refused a warm invitation to stay with them for another few days but promised faithfully to keep in touch, giving Helen her new mobile number.

It was, she felt, important to be independent right from the start of this trip, even though she was nervous and uncertain about what she would do next.

She was supposed to check out of the hotel, but suddenly changed her mind and decided to stay for another day, possibly longer. It would be a useful centre for her search; it was such a lovely part of England, with lush, rolling countryside and picturesque villages. She'd forgotten just how beautiful Wiltshire was.

Why not look for a job near here?

The receptionist changed her booking, but said she could only have the room for another two nights because the hotel was completely booked out for a big wedding.

She pointed out the rack of tourist brochures and Molly selected a handful. But she already knew what she wanted to do first: go and look at the show houses. She'd peered down the hill at them several times from her window, liking the style, feeling they were modern and yet classical in their symmetry and balance.

Since the show houses weren't open for another half-hour, she decided to lie on the bed and relax with her new book.

She woke an hour later, amazed at herself, because she didn't normally sleep at all during the day. She stretched lazily, feeling better than she had for ages, then strolled down the hill to the sales office. The man she'd bumped into near the lift the previous night was sitting behind the desk, speaking earnestly to a fit, tanned couple, who were in their sixties at a guess. A younger couple was looking at the photos and floor plans on the wall and even as Molly watched, they glanced impatiently towards him.

A sign on his desk said *Euan Santiago*. He looked up with a professional smile of welcome, while listening to the woman. He nodded and turned to Molly. 'Would you like to—?'

'I've just come from the—' she began at the same time and they both stopped with a smile.

'Oh, thank goodness!' he exclaimed. 'The agency said they might not find anyone, but if ever I needed help, it's today. If you'll just wait at the other desk for a few minutes, I'll explain the set-up and you can start straight away. Could you please give brochures to anyone who comes in?'

She opened her mouth to protest that he was mistaking her for someone else, then closed it again. He looked frazzled, and she had plenty of time to spare. No harm in helping a fellow human being, especially one so attractive.

He finished dealing with the first couple and moved across to the others, who were looking rather impatient now.

Just then the phone rang and after a moment's hesitation, she put out her hand as if to pick it up and looked at him questioningly. When he nodded and pointed to a name on the wall, she smiled to show her understanding. Picking up the phone, she said calmly, 'Marlbury Leisure Village. May I help you?'

'Is Euan there?' a woman's voice asked.

'Who's speaking, please?'

'His secretary. I gather he's busy?'

'Yes. Look, I'm new here. Your name would be . . . ?'

'Avril Buttermere. Could you ask him to ring me at home when convenient? I'll be here all day.'

'Certainly. And your number is . . . ?'

'He knows it, but you're right to ask.' She reeled it off.

Molly put the phone down then sat listening with interest as he explained about the development, before sending the couple off to view the show houses on their own.

He turned to her. 'Thanks for jumping in. I'm Euan Santiago, by the way.'

'Molly Peel. And before I forget, your secretary wants you to ring her at home when convenient. I have the number.'

'Avril? No worries. I know her number by heart.' He grinned and perched on the edge of his desk, looking suddenly like a schoolboy dressing up as an older man. 'I can't tell you how glad I was to see you. The agency have earned their money today, I can tell you.'

'I'm not from the agency.'

He looked at her in shock. 'Ah. Sorry for the mistake and thanks for your help.'

She took a deep breath, reminding herself to be brave. 'But I am looking for a job, so if you're short of staff, even temporarily . . .'

'Are you, now?' He gave her an assessing gaze. 'Tell me about yourself.'

She'd written out a summary and learnt it off by heart, at Nikki's suggestion, so that she wouldn't fumble for words when she needed to make a good impression. Taking a deep breath, she launched into her spiel. 'I'm recently divorced and looking for work. I originally trained as a secretary but haven't been in the workforce for years. However, I've been acting as unofficial secretary and organiser for my hus—my *ex*-husband, who is a high-powered executive, for many years. I know my way around a computer, am used to dealing with people of all sorts, I'm a good organiser and can whip up a dinner party for twelve at the drop of a hat. I'm—'

He finished it for her, 'Quick on the uptake, kind and have an excellent telephone manner.'

The compliments threw her and she could feel herself blushing. 'Oh, well, I'm glad you think so.'

He frowned, looking as if he was thinking over what

she'd said, so she didn't try to speak, simply waited. When he looked up, she braced herself for a refusal.

'I can only offer you part-time work for the moment, so if you need to support yourself totally, I'm afraid this job wouldn't be much use.'

'I have a small income, but I can't sell my house yet so I need to work. I'm intending to find a small flat to rent. Money would be helpful, but more important would be some experience to help me get back into the workforce.' She looked at him questioningly.

His smile was warm and his voice gentle. 'You're supposed to ask me next what the job entails.'

'Oh. Yes.' She could feel herself blushing. 'You can tell I'm not used to this. What does it entail?'

'All sorts of things. What I really need is a general factotum. I'm going to hire a full-time secretary and a part-time assistant for her, but I also need someone who can deal with sales enquiries, show people round, answer queries about the new buildings when I'm away, whatever comes up.'

She was going to say she could try, but caught herself in time. 'I'm sure I could do that, Mr Santiago, as long as you brief me carefully about the specifics.'

'And if I asked you to organise a small dinner or a buffet?'

'I could do that, too. As long as you have the cooking equipment.'

'I don't. The hotel can handle the big stuff, but occasionally it'd be good to have a small gathering in my house – I'm going to be living in one of the show houses.'

'I'd need to find somewhere to live close by. Are there plenty of rental properties round here?'

'I suppose so.' He snapped his fingers. 'Or I have a caravan that I could have hooked up on site, if you're interested. It's old but in good condition and as it sleeps four, it's not too cramped.'

Excitement was welling up in her. 'That sounds fun.'

'Let's give it a month's trial. If you use the caravan you'll not need to risk finding a flat in the neighbourhood, and either of us could say if we weren't happy about continuing at the end of the month. How about that?'

'Sounds a perfect way for me to re-enter the workforce. Oh – I also forgot to ask about pay.'

'Hourly to start off with. We'll get Avril to find out a fair rate. She's my ex-secretary, come back to work temporarily to get me out of a hole. I'd trust her to act fairly. In fact, I'd trust her with my life. Do we have a deal?'

'Yes, we do.'

He stood up and held out his hand.

When she took it, she sucked in her breath in shock. It was more than a handshake; it was a connection humming between them. She let go of his hand immediately and stepped back, feeling flustered.

He looked at her in similar surprise, then cleared his throat and said hurriedly, 'That's . . . er, settled, then. Uh-oh. The Temples are coming back. Will you be all right minding the phone while I chat them up?'

'Yes, of course.'

But she was glad that the phone didn't ring, because it

gave her time to pull herself together, then listen to him talking about his development.

She hadn't realised it was such a personal venture, and though he didn't say that, the way he talked about his leisure village gave him away. He'd invested more than money into it; he'd invested love and hope, and a concern for the environment.

She'd love to live in a village like the one he described, one with a sense of community, with houses that didn't gobble up power. Was it really possible to create such a thing? Surely communities evolved over time?

After the couple had gone, Euan let out his breath in a whoosh of relief. 'I think they're interested.'

'They're definitely interested, Mr Santiago. But they're not sure you can deliver, especially the sense of community you talk about.'

'Do call me Euan. I don't stand on ceremony. I think I can deliver the community feeling by building carefully and providing some amenities for residents.'

'Do you have rules for the residents as well?'

He frowned at her. 'Wouldn't that be presumptuous?'

'We-ell, whenever we've stayed in villas in France or Spain, there have been rules about not making a noise after ten at night, or before six in the morning. That seems fair enough, but some people do need it spelt out. And what about children?'

'What about them?'

'They're noisy.'

'I can't stop them coming as visitors, but since it'll be mainly older people, children won't be permanent residents.'

'Even older people have grandchildren.'

He leant back in his chair, steepling his hands and staring down at them, then up at her. 'You've got a point. You know, you're definitely earning your money even on your first day here.'

She blinked in shock. 'I didn't realise I was already employed.'

'I'm taking up your time today. It seems only fair that I pay you.'

'Oh. Well. Thank you.' She tried not to let him see how thrilled she was, but the way he looked at her, she reckoned he'd guessed. He had such a lovely, understanding smile and she couldn't help smiling back.

He stared into space for a moment or two. 'We'll put it in the rules, then: children not to run around shrieking, or play ball games, except in designated play areas. How does that sound?'

'It sounds reasonable, but perhaps it could be phrased more tactfully?'

'We'll make drawing up the draft rules part of your job.' He looked at his watch. 'Right then, I'd better ring Avril.'

He walked outside to make the call and Molly tried not to listen, because she guessed they'd be talking about her among other things. She went along the wall rack, taking a copy of each brochure. She'd have to learn everything she could as quickly as possible, not only about the leisure village but about the surrounding area.

Euan came in as she was sorting through the pile of brochures. 'Homework,' she said.

'Good. Um . . . Avril wants to meet you. She's intending to vet every single person I hire for the office work, doesn't trust me after the fiasco we've just had. Avril doesn't want to have to come back to work for long, you see.'

'I'm happy to meet her.'

'She's invited us both to tea at her house. Would you mind?'

'Not at all. It's very kind of her.'

'Look at the time. Have you had lunch?'

'No.'

'Then why don't you go and get something at the hotel? I have a client coming to see the houses at two o'clock, so if you could hold the fort here then, it'd be great.'

'Have you already had lunch?'

'No, but I can wait.'

'I could easily bring you something back.'

He grinned. 'Now I know Avril will like you.'

Molly tried to work out the connection and failed, so looked at him in puzzlement for an explanation.

'My last secretary found it beneath her to get me lunch, even when I was busy. Of course, she didn't say that at the interview. She didn't actually refuse to do it, but she made her displeasure plain so I stopped asking.'

'What happened to her?'

His expression darkened. 'I'll tell you about her later.' He glanced at his watch. 'Better get off for your meal quickly. And any sort of sandwich will do me.'

Molly walked briskly up the slope to the hotel, excitement fizzing along her veins. She had a job, a real job. Part-time at first, but with prospects.

At least, she would have a job if this Avril person approved of her. Surely she would? She'd sounded reasonable enough on the phone.

Brian decided to go and retrieve his boxes of childhood toys, because he'd been told some of them were quite valuable and he didn't want his mother giving them away.

He arrived in Lavengro Road and made his usual turn into the drive, only to jam his brakes on hard, barely stopping in time. 'What the hell!'

The entrance was blocked by high, wrought-iron gates. What maggot had got into his mother now? Such a waste of money to fit new gates when you were trying to sell a house. These must have cost a fortune. Dad was right. She didn't have a clue about money.

He got out of the car and tried to open the gates, but they were locked in some way he couldn't fathom out. There was a doorbell and intercom to one side, so he pressed it, then got angry and kept on pressing it.

'You can take your finger off the bell now.'

It was a man's voice. Brian frowned. Had she acquired a live-in lover? He couldn't imagine it. 'I've come to see my mother.'

'What's your name?'

'What's yours? What the hell are you doing in my mother's house, anyway?'

'I'll come out to the gate.'

Brian waited, foot tapping impatiently. A tall man who looked vaguely familiar came striding along the drive, used an electronic remote to open a small gate set into one half of the larger ones, and stood looking at him.

'Yes, I remember you now. Brian, isn't it?'

He nodded. 'And who are you?'

'I'm the new tenant.'

Brian gaped at him. 'Tenant? Is my mother taking in lodgers?'

'Certainly not. She's rented the house to me.'

'You mean, she's not living here any longer?'

'Exactly. Now, you'll have come for those boxes in the garage. She told me you would. I'll help you carry them out to your car.'

'It'd be easier if you let me drive in, then we could load them straight into the boot.'

'If they're too heavy, I'll carry them out for you.' He chuckled and strode off towards the garage. He might be bald, but he looked extremely fit and healthy.

Scowling, Brian followed. 'I didn't catch your name.'

'I didn't give it to you. It's none of your business.' He opened the garage door, which also seemed to have a new operating system, and led the way to the back, getting one box down as if it weighed nothing. He thrust it at Brian. 'There you are. I'll carry the other one out.'

Not knowing what to say, Brian followed him, and when the boxes were in the boot, the man turned to go back inside the garden. 'Hey! Just a minute. Do you have Mum's forwarding address?'

'No.'

'But you must have some idea where she's gone?'

'I don't, actually. She wasn't sure herself. All I have is her email address and surely you have that too?'

'Yes, but—'

Brian was left staring through the bars into the garden as the man strode along the path and vanished into the house without looking back. He couldn't believe his mother had just upped and left. She wasn't the sort to do something like that. And where could she have gone anyway?

Guilt shot through him. Was she so short of money she had to rent her house out? If he'd known that, he'd have made a bigger effort to pay her rent and housekeeping money. Only, from what his father said, he'd thought she was loaded with money.

To his surprise, not knowing where she was made him feel uneasy. He'd ring his father up tonight. If *he* didn't know, he'd soon find out.

The afternoon flew by and Molly, nervous at first of being left on her own, found she was coping just fine. When she couldn't answer a question, she explained this was her first afternoon working there and promised to get back to them.

It seemed as if the leisure village had stirred up a great deal of interest.

It was five o'clock before she knew it.

'Intending to stay here all night?' an amused voice said from the doorway.

She looked up to see Euan leaning against the door frame, looking relaxed and far too attractive for a man of his age. 'Oh! You startled me.'

'You were lost in your notes. Could I ask what you're doing or is it private?'

'I'd not do private work in your time. I was jotting down some notes about the residents' rules. I found some on the Internet for another leisure village, which gave me a start.'

He smiled and his voice softened. 'I didn't think you'd cheat me. You have a particularly honest face. That was very enterprising of you. Now, I have to go round and lock up the show houses, which includes checking that all the windows are closed. Want to come and help me? I can give you the grand tour at the same time. You've not seen the interiors yet.'

'I'd love that. I came down here to look them over as potential homes for myself. Once I've sold my present house, I'd like to find somewhere smaller and easier to keep up.'

'Had your house on the market for long?'

'No. But there were problems with my ex. I'll explain another time.'

'Yes, of course. None of my business anyway.' He led the way round the three show houses, explaining the prices and showing off the fittings with imperfectly concealed pride.

Then he looked at his watch. 'Damn! We're going to be late. I'll just call Avril.' He made a quick call to say they'd been delayed and would be setting off in five minutes, then turned to Molly. 'We'll go in my car. It's closer and I know the way.'

His car was a sleek Mercedes convertible. She felt like a princess being swooshed away to a ball as he drove away. Even Craig hadn't been able to afford a car like this one. It reeked of big money. And, more important to her, it was wonderfully comfortable.

She beamed as they drove along, then caught him smiling at her. 'What's so amusing?'

'It's a pleasure to drive someone who's enjoying it. You snuggled down in the seat like my mother's cat does in her furry rug.'

'Oh. Well, it is a lovely car.'

'Yes. I like it. Very useful for impressing the richer clients, too.'

'Will rich people want houses this small?'

'No. But I have some other designs for individual houses that can be custom built.'

'How wonderful to create a whole village like that!'

'It is. It's years since I've enjoyed my work as much. It's a bit of a change for me and—oh, here we are.'

Brian decided to call in to see his father, rather than phone. That way, he might get a free meal. Otherwise, it'd be fried eggs and baked beans again, one of the few things he could cook, if you could call it cooking. He really missed his mother's wonderful food.

Geneva opened the door and glared at him. 'What do *you* want?'

'What do you think? To see my father. I'm not going to stop seeing him just because I have to put up with your sour face as well.'

'I'll see if he's available.' She slammed the door in his face.

He was furious at this reception but had no choice except to stand outside and wait.

His father came to the door. 'Geneva's still very angry with you, so Tasha doesn't want you coming in and spoiling our meal. And you might try ironing your clothes after you've washed them. No wonder Geneva said you looked like a tramp.'

'And of course you took their side, Dad. You always do. So, if I'm not welcome here, I'll keep the news to myself and you can find out about Mum some other way.'

'Wait! What's this about your mother?'

'See you around.'

'Oh, come in, you fool! But make sure you keep a civil tongue in your head.'

In the hall his father stopped again. 'Well? What about your mother?'

'She's left.'

His father looked at him as if he were speaking a foreign language.

'She's not living in the old house any more. She's rented it out to some stranger and left.'

'Are you sure of this?'

'I was speaking to him this lunchtime.'

'Who is he?'

'He wouldn't tell me his name. He looked vaguely familiar, but I can't remember where I know him from.'

'Didn't you have the wit to ask for her forwarding address?'

Brian had never found his father so hard to deal with and suddenly felt a stab of sympathy for his mother, who had put up with years of this sort of treatment. 'Of course I did! He said he didn't know where she'd gone.'

'He's lying. She must have left a forwarding address for the mail.'

Tasha came to the door of the dining room. 'Is this going to take long? Dinner's ready.'

She ignored Brian completely. His mother would never have treated a guest like that.

'Could you set another place, please, darling? Brian's brought some interesting news.' His father, who was more prone to bark out orders, always spoke to Tasha in a conciliatory tone. Wow, she had him right under her thumb. Who'd have thought anyone could do that?

She pulled a face, but shrugged agreement.

Brian followed his father into the dining room, 'Hi, Tasha; Geneva.'

Geneva sniffed and ignored him; Tasha gave him a scornful look. 'Next time you visit, ring first and make sure it's convenient, and wear something half decent. I don't usually open my house to tramps and layabouts.'

Suddenly Brian felt angry enough to defy her. 'I'm not making appointments to see my own father. If I'm not wanted here, I'll leave and—'

His father's voice cracked out like a whip. 'Shut up and sit down!'

And as he had done a million times before, Brian swallowed his anger and did as his father told him.

The food was superb, as always, but the helpings were small. He could have eaten twice as much. Did his father only marry women who could cook? he wondered suddenly. Yes, of course. That would be quite important. His father did a lot of entertaining and networking. He frowned as he realised that his father didn't actually have any long-time friends, only current business acquaintances.

In between mouthfuls, he answered questions, explaining in more detail what had happened.

'Let me know if you remember where you've seen this fellow,' his father said. 'And now, if you've finished scraping the plate, Tasha and I have some important things to discuss tonight.'

Brian took the not-so-subtle hint and thanked his stepmother for the meal, then nodded to Geneva, who sniffed and tossed her head. 'Can't we even be friends now?' he asked her, forgetting the others.

'I'm not staying friends with a slob like you.'

He felt angry all the way home. He wasn't a slob. He was just . . . a bit untidy.

But when he looked round the tiny studio flat, he couldn't deny that Geneva was right. It was a right old mess. And he'd forgotten to buy any cleaning materials, even though he'd put them on the list. Of course, if you didn't take the list with you when you went shopping, it wasn't much use, was it?

Even he didn't want to live like someone dirty, so he went out to the local supermarket. He was amazed to find a whole aisle devoted to cleaning materials. He tried reading the labels, but they all claimed to work miracles and he was utterly lost as to which to buy.

'Can I help you, sir?'

He turned to see a neat young woman in the store uniform. 'Would you? I've just moved into a flat and I need to clean it, only I don't know what to get.'

She questioned him and gradually loaded his trolley with items, the cost of which shocked him rigid. At this rate, the money his father had given him wouldn't last till his next payday.

'I can't afford all that!' he blurted out. 'I've got to buy food as well.'

'Hmm.' She looked into his trolley and began unloading it, leaving only a few items plus a packet of cleaning cloths.

'I'm really grateful,' he said when she stepped back. 'Can I buy you a coffee?'

'No, thank you. I'm on late shift tonight.'

He saw then that her name label read Carol, Deputy Floor Manager. 'Another time, perhaps?'

'There's really no need. It's all part of the service. Now, if you have everything you need, sir . . . ?'

'I'd better get a cookery book. Cheap and easy.'

'There's a free one if you buy certain frozen foods. It's quite good, too. I'll show you.'

He bought some frozen vegetables and potato wedges, looking at the book doubtfully as he put it in the trolley. He'd never so much as opened a cookery book before.

'If you can read, you can follow instructions and cook,' she said with a smile. 'It's far cheaper to cook for yourself than to buy ready meals, unless you try to cook expensive stuff.' She stepped back. 'And now I really must get on.'

He watched her walk away. She had a nice manner, a lovely smile and he liked her face too. Not glamorous, but wholesome and healthy-looking. Well, you could keep glamorous from now on. Geneva might have looked stunning, but she'd been a high maintenance chick and had cleaned him out of money.

Honesty made him add mentally as he queued at the checkout that though she'd encouraged him to spend money, he'd not been reluctant.

He'd have to find out about the value of his toys; see if he could sell them. He had very little household equipment or furniture. He was using a friend's camping stuff, a blow-up mattress and pillow, and an old sleeping bag, plus a yellowed plastic garden chair that he'd found on someone's verge waiting for the rubbish collection.

It was a far cry from the comfort of his mother's house. And he'd better iron a shirt for tomorrow. He'd been forced to buy ironing equipment early on because he had to look decent for work. He didn't know what he'd do if he lost his job.

As he smoothed the shirt carefully with the iron, terrified of scorching it, he wondered where his mother was. She'd be all right, of course she would.

But still, he wished he knew. She annoyed the hell out of him sometimes, and she'd made a fool of herself at the wedding, but she *was* his mother.

Molly followed Euan to the front door of a cottage that looked picture-book pretty. It opened before they got there, and he gave Avril a hug before introducing them.

Secretary indeed! Molly thought. Avril was more like an aunt and looked at him just as fondly.

She gave Molly a very thorough appraisal in thirty

seconds flat, relaxing visibly. 'Do come in. I've got everything ready.'

'Apple pie?' he asked.

She rolled her eyes. 'Of course. And yes, I'll bring some in for lunch tomorrow.' She said confidentially to Molly. 'He's not hard to please. Are you any good at making apple pies? If you're going to work for him, it's useful to know how to soften him up.'

'I enjoy cooking.'

'Good.' She gestured to a chair at the table. 'I hope you don't mind eating straight away, but since you're a bit late, everything's ready and I don't want it to overcook.'

It might have been a purely social gathering, it was so pleasant, except that Molly was aware of Avril leading the conversation with a masterly hand and finding out a lot about her in the process.

Somehow she didn't mind answering these questions, because they weren't asked with malice by a person likely to come back and worry at your weak spots afterwards. This was a woman determined to protect Euan Santiago, a man who ought not to need protecting, but somehow, it seemed, did. How intriguing!

It was probably because this project was his dream, Molly guessed as the conversation continued. You only had to listen to the way he spoke about it. The words were out before she could stop them. 'I really envy you, Euan.'

'Why?'

'Because you have a dream and you're making it come true.'

'Don't you have any major dreams?' Avril asked.

Molly shook her head. 'When I was married, Craig was trying to get his career established and we put everything into that. I simply didn't have time to daydream. Now . . . I haven't got my own act together yet. That's why I've come away. Even after we split up, he was there, either in person or getting at me through our children.'

'How long have you been divorced?'

'A little over a year.'

'You'll have to tell me about it sometime – just general things – if you don't mind, that is. My niece has just split up with her husband and she's having a hard time. I'm not sure how best to help her.'

'She has to help herself. It took me a while to figure that out.'

'Is that what you're doing?'

Molly shrugged. 'Starting to. And about time too. Now, tell me more about the leisure village and what gave you the idea for building one, Euan.'

They allowed her to change the subject, thank goodness. She wasn't yet ready to air all the dirty washing from her marriage in public. And besides, she didn't think she came out of it well. She'd been so . . . spineless! And even now, wasn't as strong as she'd like to be.

While she was helping Avril wash the dishes, the other woman said abruptly, 'Don't forget to stand up for yourself in your new job.'

'Who against?'

'Everyone. Euan, for one. He sometimes lets his needs run away with everyone else's time, though he's mostly very caring about his employees.' She patted Molly's forearm with one soapy hand. 'And think about finding some dreams of your own, my dear. Everyone needs them.'

'My main dream is learning how to stand up for myself.'

Another pat. 'That's a good start. But it shouldn't stop you working out what you want to do with your life, how to find joy again. They're not mutually exclusive.'

Avril's sympathy gave Molly the courage to say, 'Unfortunately, I don't have any particular skills or even any hobbies, except for reading. I'm just . . . ordinary. A housewife, really. I'm not even good at choosing clothes for myself. You should have seen how awful I looked at my daughter's wedding. Craig used to send one of his staff out shopping with me when there were big events. I've got a wardrobe full of formal clothes in storage.'

But she'd given her wedding outfit to a charity shop. She never wanted to see it again, even though she'd lost enough weight in the past few weeks to make it fit properly. Strange, that. She hadn't been trying to lose weight. She realised Avril had said something. 'Sorry, I was just thinking about something.'

'I said, if you need help shopping, come to me. I love choosing clothes. Not for fashion statements but to make the most of people. And I'm quite good at it too. All my nieces come to me for help with important outfits. Now, let's take Euan's coffee through.'

He was asleep on the sofa, all his weariness showing in his face.

Avril set the tray down with a sigh. 'I hate to disturb him, but he needs to go home to bed.'

'If you want to let him sleep for a while, I can catch a taxi back. It's not far.'

'Oh, no. I'm too fond of my privacy. And how would he respect my authority if he saw me wearing my tatty old dressing gown with my hair in its morning tangle? Let him run you back, then make sure he goes straight home. Do not allow him go back to his office.'

As she went to the cloakroom, Molly wondered how she was supposed to make sure a powerful man like Euan Santiago went straight home. Though he didn't look so powerful when he was asleep. Or when he was sitting on a desk swinging his feet and laughing about something.

When she went back into the cosy sitting room, Euan was yawning and stretching. 'Sorry. I must be more tired than I'd realised.'

'I'm just sorry you've had to come out this evening. You should have had an early night.'

Neither of them said much on the drive back, but as he pulled up at the hotel, Euan touched her arm to stop her getting out of the car. 'Avril approves of you, so if you're still willing to work for me, could you please go into the office and give her your employment details tomorrow morning? I'll show you where the office is now. I've got a bit of paperwork to catch up on before I go to bed. We have an office suite just off reception. There is a separate entrance, but we mostly keep it locked after office hours, because it's easier and safer to use the hotel entrance at night.'

She couldn't think of a tactful way to say it, so blurted it straight out before she lost her nerve. 'You shouldn't go back there now. You need to get some sleep.'

'I can manage without much sleep.'

'It's obvious you need more than you're getting. Besides, I have instructions from Avril to send you straight home after you've dropped me. Are you really going to disobey *her*? I wouldn't.'

He stared at her in surprise, then burst out laughing. 'No. I wouldn't dare either. And I am tired. Perhaps . . . Oh, very well, I'll go straight home. I can always come in early tomorrow.'

'Not too early.'

'Yes, ma'am – or do I mean, No, ma'am?'

After they'd got out of the car, he hesitated, as if wondering whether to do the kissy-kissy thing.

Molly took a step backwards. She hadn't grown up with all this kissing stuff and never felt comfortable having such close contact with complete strangers. And she especially didn't want meaningless air kisses from Euan. She wanted . . . employment. A professional relationship. And that was all. She'd had enough of high-flyers from the business world, however attractive they were physically. 'I'll see you tomorrow. I'll just watch you drive off.'

'Don't you trust me?'

'Not where work is concerned.'

He chuckled and gave her a mock military salute. 'Yes, ma'am.'

She stood there for a few moments, watching the

big silver car purr away, then went inside to find the clerk at reception studying her with interest. Nodding a greeting, she headed for the lifts. The clerk could think what he chose. She was dying to get to bed. It had been a long, busy day.

It wasn't till she was lying in bed that she let herself think of what she'd achieved. She'd found a job! She really had.

Or rather, it had found her.

Well, it amounted to the same thing. She beamed into the darkness, vowing to do whatever was necessary to keep the job and prove to the world – no, to herself first and foremost – that she really could stand on her own feet.

What do you say to that, Craig Taylor?

To her surprise, for the first time in many years, she realised she didn't care what her ex said or thought. She was enjoying taking the first hesitant steps towards . . . what? Freedom was such a cliché. So was making your dreams come true. Independence, then. That was what she was seeking.

It'd be best if no one from her family knew where she was, so they couldn't come and harass her. Especially Craig. She'd never dreamt he'd go so far as to try to rob her of what her house was worth. All the years they'd had together seemed to mean nothing to him, and she'd never forgive him and Tasha for the wedding fiasco.

He hadn't always been so ruthless. Why had he changed? She didn't know; didn't understand him these days. She wasn't even sure she understood herself, either.

Perhaps she ought to send Jane next door a couple of postcards to forward to Brian and Rachel – no, she wouldn't do that. Let them worry about her, as she'd worried about them over the years. She wasn't even going to send them an email to remind them that they still had a way of contacting her.

She was going to build a new life alone and try to find a little quiet happiness.

And anything else would be a bonus.

Chapter Seven

Craig looked across the table at Tasha. 'What do you suppose the silly bitch is doing now?'

'Who cares? It's about time you let Molly go.'

'You were the one who wanted to live in a better address, among older money. My old house is perfect for us.'

Her voice grew noticeably sharper. 'It's *her* house now. I repeat: let it go, let *her* go. We can find somewhere else to live.'

'It's still the best address in the area,' Geneva put in. 'All my friends joke about how the old snobs live in Lavengro Road, but really they'd like to live there too. They were jealous when Brian used to take me there. And it's a lovely house, Mummy. Or it could be if it were redecorated with your flair. You should see it. Big rooms, but not just squares. I loved it.'

'Out of the mouths of babes . . .' Craig said with a smile.

But Tasha merely sniffed and continued to eat her morning yoghurt and fruit slowly.

'I'll be out tonight,' Geneva said. 'I'm going clubbing with my girlfriends.'

'No, you're not.' Tasha put another half spoonful into her mouth.

'But you've let me go clubbing with Brian.'

'He's a tall, strong guy and I trusted him to look after you. You are definitely not going to a club with that drunken bunch you call friends. They don't even have the sense to elect a driver who can stay sober and get them back safely.'

'I can catch a taxi back.'

'Drunk? I think not.'

'Hello! I *am* twenty-one. If I want to get drunk, I can.'

'And you're dependent on me till you've finished your studies.' Tasha laid her spoon down neatly beside her empty yoghurt carton. 'And do not think you can deceive me about where you're going or the state you get into.'

Craig watched his wife turn a basilisk stare on her daughter, who scowled down at her own breakfast but didn't argue back. He had to confess that he didn't argue with Tasha, either, when she got that look on her face. He decided to change the subject. 'What's the agenda for this weekend?'

'Look in the engagement diary. That's what it's for.' Tasha got up, cleared away her things and left the room. Her heels clicked along the white marble tiles of the corridor, stopped and clicked back again. 'And do not leave your breakfast dishes lying round. Either of you. I don't appreciate slovenly clutter in my kitchen.'

When her mother had gone, Geneva rolled her eyes at her stepfather, but he wasn't getting into any exchange of comments about Tasha. His stepdaughter shrugged and went to get ready for college.

Craig finished the breakfast Tasha had prepared and got himself an extra slice of toast. He sat thinking about his stupid ex. It was all right Tasha saying let it go, but why should he? He had to keep an eye on Molly, under the guise of helping her out, for his children's sake, or goodness knows what messes she'd get into and maybe drag them into as well. He didn't want his name blackening because of her.

It'd be a long time before Rachel forgave her. He'd made sure of that.

Where could Molly have gone? And why had she rented out the house when she'd sworn before a legal officer of the court that she loved it too dearly to leave? He'd better have a drive past on his way to work and see if he could spot the tenant. Maybe he'd recognise him, if Brian thought the fellow looked familiar.

There had to be some way to get the house back. Craig had a rule for his personal life, stemming from when he'd been bullied as a child, that no one ever got the better of him – ever! – without payback. Even if it took years. And his ex wasn't going to be the first to do that. He had a moral right to that house. Anyway, Molly didn't *need* it and he did. He'd paid for its maintenance for years, hadn't he? And it was perfect for a rising man, just as Tasha was the perfect wife for him at this stage of his career.

She was a bit too perfect, perhaps, but it was better than being plump and dowdy. Far better. He was proud to be seen out with Tasha, who was a sleek, elegant creature, and he knew that he was envied by other business acquaintances.

On Monday morning Stuart strolled round the garden, admiring the roses. He'd just stepped behind a holly bush to pick up some rubbish when he heard a car draw up further down the road. It needed servicing, had a faint ticking sound to it that you couldn't mistake – well, not if you knew anything about cars. He risked a quick glance through the gates and smiled as he confirmed that it was Craig Taylor's car. Again.

He risked a peep and blessed the excellent long-distance vision you got as you grew older when he recognised Taylor staring at the house through a pair of binoculars. Grinning, he ducked back behind the bush and waited. The hidden camera would catch the car and he'd pick the visual details up from it later. He glanced at his watch. Eight-thirty.

He listened hard, but didn't hear the car drive away, so stood in the bushes for ten long, quiet minutes. Birds sang around him, leaves rustled in a slight breeze and one branch kept brushing his head. Well, he could outwait Taylor. He'd had a lot of practice in waiting patiently. The army certainly taught you to do that.

Wendy came to the door, shading her eyes with one hand as she looked round for him. He signalled with one hand for her to get back inside and she did so without showing any reaction to him. An observer would think she'd failed to find someone. The only problem was, would Taylor remember Wendy? He'd met them both once or twice, so he might, though her hair had gone completely silver now.

Stuart would rather keep the fellow guessing.

It was another few minutes before the car drove off.

He strolled into the kitchen and gave his wife a smacking kiss on the lips.

'What was all that skulking in the bushes about?'

'Taylor was outside in his car, watching the house. I didn't want him to realise who was renting it.'

'Does it matter? He's bound to find out. He must remember us, surely?'

'His son didn't. Anyway, I don't want to make it easy for Taylor. Even if he does recognise us, he won't find out from me where his ex is. Molly said she'd be in touch once she'd settled somewhere. Until then, I won't even email her. Let her find her feet in her own time. Mum says her ex is a bully and has been sapping her confidence for years, so I reckon the poor lass deserves some peace and quiet.' He glanced at the wall clock. 'I'll just nip over to Mum's and see how they are.'

'I'm going shopping soon. Don't forget to take your keys.'

His mother greeted him with a strained smile.

'How's Dad?'

'He had a bad night. I think we'll have to ask for the pain medication to be increased.' She looked at him in anguish. 'Fifty-eight years we've been together. Oh, Stuart, I know it was bound to end sometime, but even the thought of losing him hurts.'

He pulled her to him and held her. The fact that she let him spoke volumes. She wasn't one to dwell on problems. But this . . . Well, they were all struggling with it now that he knew how bad it was. His father was being incredibly brave. Stuart had seen a lot of men die in the army; good men, too. His own father, though. That was so much harder as to be almost unbearable. Except you had no choice but to bear it.

She pulled away. 'No use giving in to it. What can't be cured . . .'

'. . . must be endured,' Stuart finished. He was glad he'd decided to stay in England; would have changed his plans if he hadn't, because she was going to need him. He suspected he'd find it helpful to be needed . . . afterwards, because for all their differences, he'd miss his father greatly, too.

Doing something, anything at all, always helped in times of trouble, he'd found.

While Molly was enjoying the view from her hotel window early on the Monday morning, she saw a four-wheel drive vehicle towing a caravan make its slow way past the hotel and down the slope to one end of the building site. Two men were waiting to help manoeuvre it into place, then they lifted a manhole cover and began work on some connection or other. Electricity, perhaps? She watched, fascinated.

One went off and came back towing a small trailer, which he set up at one end of the caravan. What was that?

The phone rang. She hesitated, hand over the receiver. She'd changed her mobile phone number, but still felt nervous when she picked it up, kept expecting Craig to find out her new one and start harassing her again. 'Hello?'

'Have you looked out of the window lately, Molly?'

'I have, Euan. I'm standing there at the moment, actually, watching with great interest.'

'Want to come down and inspect the inside of your new bijou residence?'

'I'd love to.' She put the phone down, so excited she waved her hands in the air and shouted 'Hoorah!' before grabbing her handbag. This room felt very cramped. She wasn't made to live in hotels; wanted her own space; enjoyed preparing her own meals.

Euan was waiting for her outside the caravan and smiled as she ran the last few yards across to him. She stopped and looked at him uncertainly. Was he laughing at her? Was it ridiculous for a woman of her age to get excited about living in a caravan?

'Come on! Let's tour the stately home.'

He held out his hand and without thinking, she took it, then looked up at him uncertainly.

'Don't think. Enjoy!' he said quietly. 'It took me a long time to learn that lesson.'

'It's taking me even longer.'

His expression grew sad. 'Not much longer, I think. From the happy expression on your face today, you're well on your way.' As she opened her mouth to speak, he put one finger lightly on her lips. 'Shh. No thinking or analysing, just enjoy.'

He pulled her forward without even waiting for her answer and she went with him willingly. This was the new Molly, wasn't it? She was taking on the world, meeting new people. She was even managing to feel happy again. Was impulsive too much to ask for as well? She used to be impulsive. That trait might be a lot harder to slip back into, though.

The caravan had seen a lot of life. Its pale blue paint was faded, the white trims were missing here and there, and three or four small dents decorated it at knee level and below.

'I had a few bumps,' he said. 'But the inside's in much better condition.' He unlocked the door and stood back to let her go first.

To her surprise, the inside was immaculate. She turned to see him standing in the doorway with a fond smile on his face. 'You love this caravan, don't you?'

'Yes. It was the first home of my own; a place not shared with slobs, not filled with loud music that I didn't enjoy, and kept clean and tidy most of the time. My grandmother bought the caravan for me when I was working in construction and moving around the country a lot. I've always been grateful for that. We lost her soon afterwards, and my father was furious that she'd spent so much money on me instead of leaving it all to him. He's bitter now that I've made good, but if it wasn't that, it'd be something else. He always finds something to complain about.' He sucked in his breath. 'Sorry. Don't know where that came from.'

'I'm honoured by your confidences and touched that you're lending such a prize possession to me.'

He looked at her, head on one side. 'It's strange, that. I've never lent it to anyone before. Never. I usually keep it on a plot of land I have, and I go and sit in it sometimes, when I need to think. I've had the appliances upgraded and the upholstery redone.'

'Why don't you show me how everything works? I've never stayed in a caravan before. Craig would have died rather than take a holiday in one, even when the kids were small.'

It was a small space, only about fourteen feet long, and she was at first much too conscious of Euan's lean body, bending and stretching as he showed her all the cupboards and other details. That reaction to him was disconcerting at her age. Then she got mad at herself. Her age! She wasn't old. Why did she keep thinking about herself as past finding a man sexually attractive?

A double bed was formed by lowering the table and combining it with the seat benches, but there were two bunk beds one above the other at the rear end, so if she didn't want to bother making up the double bed each night, she could use one of them. The cooker had two burners and a tiny oven/grill. Well, there would only be herself to cook for now, so that would be perfectly adequate. The fridge was bigger than she'd expected, thank goodness, with a small freezer next to it.

'I put in a few modifications to make life easier,' he said.

There was a knock on the door and one of the men stuck his head inside.

'Got her fixed up now, Euan lad. If you open up the bathroom, we'll attach the module. How about a pot of tea? It's thirsty work.'

'Can do. I've just been showing my friend round. She'll be living here, so will you keep an eye on her? Molly, this is Dan, the best foreman in the trade.'

Dan was frowning. 'We can keep an eye on her in the daytime but what about at night? No one will be around then. It'll be a bit lonely down here for a woman on her own. And since the new houses have just been fitted out with white goods, they'll be especially attractive to thieves.'

'I'll be living in the end house of this row by Thursday or Friday.' Euan chewed his thumb as he had a quick think. 'But I may not always be here overnight, so I think we ought to put in a panic button or siren connected to the hotel's security service.'

'Surely there's no need for that,' Molly protested.

'Probably not, but I'd rather be safe than sorry. Apart from anything else, you might see people nosing around who shouldn't be here and you could press the button to save me from vandalism and theft.'

'Oh. I see.' She smiled. 'So I'm a night watchperson as well.'

'Only incidentally. But I'd advise you to keep your door locked at all times after dark. As you can see, the door in the caravan's bathroom now connects to the shower block, which comes in two halves. I had the van modified for that add-on. I do like my comforts, I'm afraid. We'll make sure the outer door of the block is locked as well. I'm afraid the workmen will be using the other half of the shower block during the day. Will that bother you?'

'Not at all. I'll probably be out working for you, or exploring the area, or visiting my cousin.'

'That's all right, then. I've had insect screens put on the van's windows and they're stronger than they look, made of a special steel security mesh which can't be poked through. You'll be quite safe leaving a window open. I put them in because I didn't want intruders when I was camping on building sites or out in the wild, but it's good to keep out insects, too – unless you adore moths and midges.'

'I don't. You seem to have thought of everything.'

'Well, I wanted to be comfortable when I was using the caravan and I hope you will be too.'

'I'm looking forward to it. It'll be so much better than a hotel room. Now, how about I make the guys' tea under your tuition, as a practice run? I presume you have tea bags and milk here?'

'I have everything I need for my sudden visits. Feel free to use anything you find – though I don't think my spare clothes will be much use to you. I'm a trifle taller than you.'

'Like about six inches!'

'If you need the extra space, I'll take them away.'

'We'll see how we go. I've not got a lot of stuff with me. And I'll replace any of the food I use, of course.'

'That's not necessary.'

'It is to me. I really value my independence.' It was the only dream she had at the moment, and two lovely older women had encouraged her to pursue it more actively than she might have done on her own. She didn't intend to let them down – or herself.

She set about making the tea, then stood outside to drink hers with them, listening to Euan chatting to the foreman and his sidekick. She didn't say much but she learnt a lot about the development – and saw how Euan treated his staff, which wasn't like Craig, who talked scornfully about his base level staff, as if he considered them lesser beings.

Afterwards, as she washed the mugs and Euan dried, she had a sudden thought. 'I wonder what I can do about getting online? Do you think they'd let me go up to the hotel each day?'

'I'll give you access to my wireless network at the site office.'

'That would be great but you must let me pay you for it.'

'No need. It'll not cost me a penny extra to have you on board. Just consider it a perk of the job.'

'Oh. Well, thank you. You're being very kind and you don't even know what sort of employee I'll make.'

He smiled at her. 'I've had a lot of practice judging people and I'm not often wrong. I think you'll be a treasure.'

Warmth flooded through her at this compliment. A treasure! What a lovely thing to be called!

He looked at his watch. 'Have you had breakfast yet? I haven't and they'll be closing the hotel dining room soon.'

'No. I forgot in the excitement.'

'Then let's go and eat.'

She was thoughtful as they walked briskly up the slope. Surely employers didn't usually spend this much time with temporary staff or provide for them so generously? He was behaving as if they were old friends, and sometimes it felt as if they were. Did that mean he was hoping for . . . personal favours? No, surely not. She'd met a good few sleazy men during her years as executive wife and could usually recognise one on the prowl. Not that they'd prowled after Craig Taylor's dowdy wife.

They went for a buffet breakfast and spent most of it talking about the leisure village. That was safe territory, at least.

But she was still disturbingly aware of him as a man and that was beginning to worry her.

When they got up to leave, she looked at the clock. 'If you don't need me right now, I can check out before ten o'clock and move into the caravan. That'll save me another day's hotel bill.'

'Good idea. Do you want the whole day off to move into the caravan?'

'Well, I do need to do quite a bit of shopping to set

myself up for food and everything. Or do you need me this afternoon?'

'No. The sales office isn't open on Mondays so this is actually the best day for you to move in. You should report to Avril tomorrow morning, say at nine-fifteen, to get the paperwork in order, then come down to the sales office.'

'OK. And Euan . . . thank you.'

'My pleasure.'

But she could see that he'd already moved on mentally to his next task. Good, so would she. She couldn't help looking back at him as she walked away, though. And found he'd turned to watch her. Why was he frowning? Was he regretting how much he'd done to help her?

Oh, stop worrying, Molly Peel, she told herself. *Just get on with it! If he doesn't like what you do, he can sack you.*

But she hoped he wouldn't, hoped he'd continue to think her a 'treasure'.

Craig arranged with the same young thugs to lob more rocks through the windows of the house on Lavengro Road, then settled down to enjoy an evening at home. He wished he could see that fellow's face when a window shattered.

After Tasha had cleared away, she joined him in the sitting room and said abruptly, 'Why are you looking so smug?'

'Am I? Must be the excellent food.'

'You were looking smug before I fed you.'

'I was anticipating the meal.'

'Stop lying to me, Craig. I'm not Molly.'

He looked at her cautiously. 'What do you mean?'

'I mean, you're not pulling the wool over my eyes about anything. I can always tell when you're embroidering the truth, or lying outright. So, tell me why you're looking smug tonight.'

He felt indignant at that. 'How the hell can you tell when I'm ly—er, fudging the truth?'

'I'm not revealing all my secrets. Come on, what are you plotting?'

He shrugged. 'I told you Molly's got a tenant in the house at the moment. I'm taking steps to make sure he's not comfortable there.'

'Oh.'

'What do you mean by that?'

'Well, is it wise? I didn't really like you doing that last time. It wasn't fair and if it was found out, it'd be embarrassing.'

'It's the same guys taking care of it. They do what they say they will. And *they* aren't going to give me away, are they?'

'Nonetheless, I don't think I care enough about moving to Lavengro Road to put our good name at risk. You could lose your job for this.'

'Did anyone suspect me last time?'

'Molly must have. She can't be as stupid as you say.'

He chuckled. '*She* won't do anything about it, and even if she tried, she'd get nowhere. Her own children don't believe her.'

'I still feel guilty about you telling Brian and Rachel their mother was drunk at the wedding.'

He drew her into his arms. 'Trust me, it was necessary. I don't want her interfering in their lives, mucking theirs up as she's mucked up her own.' He kissed her then pulled back a little and smiled down at her. 'You're thinking too much tonight, my love. Let's forget Molly.'

Tasha melted into his arms, as always. She was needy in bed and that really turned him on. He'd never met anyone before who could match him for that.

In the middle of the night, the sensor buzzed and Stuart sat up in bed, instantly awake.

'What is it?' Wendy asked, her voice fuzzy with sleep.

'Nothing you need to bother about. I'll see to it.' He ran downstairs and slipped out through the conservatory door, which couldn't be seen from the street. As he moved from one patch of shadow to another, he could see a youth straddling the top of the wall, speaking to someone below him on the other side and reaching down for something.

As the youth hefted a heavy object in his hand, clearly about to throw it, Stuart pre-empted him by firing the paintball gun. Years of weapons training had given him the skill to hit the intruder smack in the shoulder with dye that was indelible and would spray all over his face and hand.

With a yell, the youth tumbled from the wall and there was a jabber of low voices. Stuart ran forward and stood on a rock to shoot over the wall at the other one. He heard a yelp and then running footsteps.

Bit of luck, there, he thought with a grin. They were slow on the uptake, overconfident. He'd not expected two bullseyes. One of his sensors was set to give warning when someone started to climb the wall, and that lad had probably thought everyone was asleep so there was no need to hurry.

Stuart waited quietly for ten minutes but they didn't come back.

When he went in, Wendy was awake, which didn't surprise him. She hadn't put the bedroom light on. He'd never stopped being thankful that he'd married a smart woman.

'What happened, Stu?'

He explained and she asked eagerly, 'What colour did you use?'

'Yellow. Rather a bright shade actually, same as those highlighter pens.'

She chuckled. 'I'd love to see him try to scrub it off.'

'Them. I hit two of them. I wonder how they'll explain that to people.'

'With difficulty. Is what you've done legal?'

'Who knows? I'm sorry, Your Worship. I don't think I hurt them in any way. I certainly didn't intend to. I only wanted to frighten them away. You see, they'd driven away the owner with similar tricks and my wife was getting nervous.'

She punched him in the upper arm. 'You'd say that with a straight face, too.'

'I would indeed. I don't believe in giving crims, even the minor sort, a fair chance.'

'What other tricks have you installed?'

'Wait and see. I'm hoping they won't be necessary.' He settled down in bed with a happy sigh. 'And there are more gadgets to come. I had to order some from overseas.'

That evening Molly settled down in her new home, feeling lazy but satisfied with her day's shopping. The caravan was now well stocked for her current needs and the only thing missing was a television set. She'd decided not to buy one, and had bought a book and one of her favourite magazines instead, but now, sitting surrounded by silence, she wished she had a television.

If she'd had one of those fancy mobile phones, she could have got hold of some music, but Craig had taken her fancy mobile with him when he left, saying it was a business expense, his backup phone. She hadn't known whether he was telling the truth or not, hadn't protested or found out.

What a fool she'd been! She cringed to remember how she'd given in to him over all sorts of mutual possessions. She'd bought a cheap smartphone but she missed the other one. It occurred to her, not for the first time, that she hadn't had time to wipe the personal information off it.

She fidgeted around, unable to settle. After all the evenings she'd spent alone in the past year or two, you'd think she'd be used to silence by now, but she wasn't, not complete silence like this anyway. She'd had such a busy social life until Craig left her that being on her own for much of the time was still difficult. When the children were younger, there'd been all the school functions to attend, always something going on. She enjoyed being busy.

That'd make a strange dream to tell Avril about, wouldn't it? To be busy all the time. But if it made her happy, why not? Once she settled somewhere, maybe she could do some voluntary work with old people. Most people found kids' charities more appealing but older folk deserved help, too. She loved listening to their stories of when they were young.

She should be thankful for the progress she'd made, getting a job and a temporary home so quickly. Taking out her one and only bottle of wine, she poured herself a glass. 'To my new home,' she said aloud, raising it in a salute.

Just then someone knocked on the door and she jerked in shock, causing wine to splash from her glass on to her hand. She hadn't heard anyone approaching, so was glad she'd locked the door. She grabbed her brand new tea towel and wiped her hand, calling, 'Who is it?'

'Only me: Euan.'

She unlocked the door at once.

'I'm glad to see you're security conscious. I came to check that everything was all right before I went home.'

'It's fine. More than fine. I love your caravan. Come in, do.'

'I'm not disturbing you?'

'Not at all. I was just having a drink to celebrate being here. Would you like a glass of wine?'

'Better not. I missed dinner again. I don't like drinking on an empty stomach.'

'I've got some quiche and salad, a nice crusty roll, too.'

'But that's probably your meal for tomorrow.'

It was, but she didn't care. She'd far rather have his company. 'Only my lunch and I can easily buy a baguette at the hotel café. Do come in.'

'Thank you, then.' He entered and shut the door behind him, locking it. Then he saw her looking surprised. 'Habit. I always did lock this door on the world. Do you want me to unlock it again?'

'No. I probably share your habit these days.' She poured him a glass of wine in one of the cheap glasses she'd bought for less than a pound for four, then busied herself getting him the quiche and salad.

When she turned, he was sitting at the table, looking very much at home. He ate the food like a man who was ravenous, so she got out the rest of the quiche.

'I'm taking all your food.'

'Oh, I bought a few other things as well. And it's a poor person who can't offer food to a friend.'

He raised his glass again. 'Here's to new friendships, then. May they last till they become old ones.'

She clinked her glass against his and sipped, leaning back and trying not to watch him eat, which was bad manners. Instead she focused on his hands, which were long-fingered and surprisingly graceful for a man. Not manicured and soft, like Craig's; hands that worked physically, judging by a long scratch on the back of one. Yet still attractive.

When he'd finished eating, he made a satisfied noise then stared down at the plate. 'Would you feel demeaned if I asked you to keep my house stocked up with quick, easy foods like this, once I've moved into the village? I'll pay you at the same hourly rate as the rest of your job for doing it.'

She chuckled. 'Why would I feel demeaned? I'm employed as a general factotum, aren't I? That means doing anything legal that you need, as far as I'm concerned.'

'My last so-called secretary objected to doing anything that wasn't connected to her desk and computer, then she tried to set me up for a harassment claim when she left.'

'What?'

'Not sexual harassment, job harassment. Fortunately, we found suspicious copies of my accounts in her personal drawer, and I'd called the union representative in, so it was all cleared up and she didn't have a leg to stand on. But it could have been messy – and very bad PR for my development.'

'What a good thing you stopped her!'

'Isn't it? Avril's going to find me the next secretary and I trust her judgement much more than my own where that's concerned. She thinks a friend of hers would come in part-time for a while and she'll fill in the rest herself till she's sure she can safely leave me.'

'She's very fond of you, isn't she?'

'And I'm fond of her. She's seen me through some difficult times.' He hesitated, then stared down at his hands, as he said, 'My wife died suddenly a few years ago – a stroke. Karen was only thirty-seven and it was totally unexpected. I rather went to pieces, I'm afraid. My sons were shocked rigid and at a vulnerable age. Something like that should bring you closer to your children, shouldn't it? Instead, they clung to one another and now they're closer than some twins, and I withdrew into myself.

'Then Avril became our universal auntie and I don't know what we'd have done without her. The boys keep in touch with her more than they keep in touch with me, though they do condescend to send me emails now and then.' His fond smile said that it was more than just a cool relationship now.

'Tell me about them.'

'Jason's twenty-four. He's in IT. Grant's twenty-two. He's just finished university and is backpacking round the world. Heaven knows where he is at the moment. It's a bit worrying generally, but even more so when they get to the Far East.'

'It must be.'

After another sip of wine, he looked up and gave her one of his warm smiles. 'What about your children, Molly?'

'I have a son and a daughter and . . . and they're not s-speaking to me.' Suddenly she was weeping, found herself in his arms and wept harder against the comfort and strength of his chest. It was as if a dam had burst. He said her name a couple of times in a gentle, caring way, patting her back. Gradually, she managed to stop.

'Tell me how it happened.'

She explained about the wedding, then how Craig had tried to get her house at a knock-down price. 'It could only be him arranging for the harassment. No one else's house was targeted, just mine.'

'Well, your tenant sounds as if he can take care of himself.'

She pulled away, scrubbing her eyes, embarrassed.

'Have another glass of wine and we'll drink to a better future, whatever it may hold.' He reached across for a tissue and dabbed her cheek.

She looked at him, caught her breath and knew he was feeling the same surge of attraction. When he pulled her towards him, she went willingly. As he lowered his head to kiss her, she raised hers to meet him halfway and then lost herself in a kiss that was gentle and yet compelling.

He pulled away and stared at her. 'I didn't expect that.'

'No. I didn't, either. But it made me feel good, wanted. Towards the end, Craig made me feel old, worn out and unattractive.'

'He's a fool to abandon a treasure like you.'

She gave him a wry smile. 'You don't know yet that I'm a treasure.'

'You feed a hungry man at the drop of a hat. You waken feelings in me that have been dormant for years. No, not the sexual attraction, the other attraction, to the whole woman. I've dated since Karen died, of course I have, but I've never wanted to stay at home with them and just . . . be cosy. That's how I feel with you tonight: cosy. It feels good, too. We were happy together, Karen and me. I not only miss her, I miss being part of a couple.'

She studied his face as he spoke. Could he really be so honest and truthful about his feelings? Could she trust him?

He stood up. 'I think we should become good friends before we try anything else, don't you? We've both got scars and yours are rather raw still. There's no need to rush into anything – though there's no need to rush away from it either, I hope?' He looked at her enquiringly.

She nodded. 'I agree. You can't have too many good friends.'

He stretched, rotating his shoulders wearily. 'I'd better go home now. I've got to sort my things out for the packers. I'm moving into the end house on Thursday.'

'If you need any help, I'm a demon packer. I've had a lot of practice lately.'

'I'll remember that.'

She went to the door with him, watched him walk off into the darkness, till only his silhouette could be seen outlined at the top of the slope against the faint glow from the hotel. Then she locked the door carefully, cleared up and went to bed.

The weeping had exhausted her, but it had also shifted the heavy lump of unhappiness that she had felt lodged in her chest.

And she was surprised at how comfortable, how *right* she felt with Euan.

He hadn't hesitated to talk about their reaction to one

another. She liked that. Let's face it, she liked him. Why deny it? Why not see where the attraction led?

She smiled into the darkness at the thought that she could still attract a man like him.

Chapter Eight

On Tuesday morning, the post arrived early at the block of flats. Rachel studied the letter. 'Who's this from? Oh, it's that cousin of Dad's who came to the wedding, Sally something or other. Boring old creature. What's she writing to me for?' She dropped the letter on the coffee table unopened.

'Aren't you going to read it?'

'It can wait till tonight. I don't want to be late for work.'

But that evening she continued to ignore the letter, claiming she had to do some ironing.

'You really should open it,' Jamie said.

'You do it. I can't be bothered. It won't be important. She's an old fusspot and we'll probably never see her again.'

He read the letter with a mutter of annoyance.

'Throw it in the bin.' She reached for another top.

He stood for a minute, reading it again, then walked across, slapped the letter down on the ironing board and took the iron out of her hand. 'You need to see what it says.'

Pulling a face at him, she read it through then shot him a quick glance. 'I don't believe her. Dad wouldn't lie to me.'

'He lied to your mother. Often. We've both seen him do that.'

Rachel screwed the letter up and hurled it across the room, missing the wastepaper basket and leaving it on the floor as she turned back to her ironing. 'Sorry, but I prefer to believe Dad's version of events.'

He picked up the letter and smoothed it out, putting it on the coffee table. 'Well, I believe Sally. And she's clearly quite worried about your mother. You should at least set her mind at rest about that. After all, she did give us a wedding present.'

She pulled a face at him. 'I'm too busy and I don't do snail mail.'

'It'd only take five minutes.'

'I am *not* writing to her. I don't believe her.'

'I do. And if you won't write, I will.' He took the letter and walked out without another word.

She heard the musical tone of his computer starting up and blinked her eyes rapidly. They were starting to quarrel with one another and she didn't like the feeling of being estranged from him. If he loved her, he'd take her side in everything.

After she'd finished the ironing, she poked her head into the spare bedroom and asked, 'Want a cup of coffee?'

'No, thanks.' His voice was cold and he didn't turn to look at her.

She began to feel angry. 'Who's more important to you, a distant cousin or me?'

'It's not that. It's how you treat your mother that upsets me. It's the one thing we disagree about. I warn you now, if you ever speak to *my* mother half as rudely as you speak to your own, there'll be trouble.'

'I don't. I haven't.'

He looked across at her, his expression stern. 'Then why do you treat your own mother so badly?'

'You don't know what she's like.'

'I've known you for two years, and met her lots of times. That gives me a pretty good idea, don't you think? She's a really nice person and it upsets me that she's been treated so badly by all her family. I've mentioned that it upsets me before, but you ignore me. The only one who can get through to you is your father. He pulls all your strings and you'd believe him if he told you elephants could fly.'

With a huff of annoyance she left him to it, switching on the television. But she didn't see much of the programme because she was too upset. Jamie wasn't the sort to quarrel, but he was really hung up on this thing about her mother.

He couldn't be right about what had happened at the wedding . . . could he?

Even if he was, what did he expect her to do about it now? She wasn't going to upset her father. She'd learnt to avoid doing that when she was a very small child.

Anyway, her father was fun; her mother wasn't. She tossed her head and tried to watch what was usually her favourite programme, but a little niggling doubt kept creeping into her mind.

And Jamie didn't come to bed till late. She gave up trying to stay awake, turning her dampened pillow over.

The next day went really well at work. Molly found Avril efficient and informative about Euan's business. He had other financial interests, but Avril didn't give details, only hinted that they were successful. And yet, he was about to trade in his expensive convertible for a four-wheel drive. Not a brand new model, either. Was he short of ready cash? Or just being prudent?

She stood outside the hotel for a few minutes, enjoying the sun and the narrow fringe of gardens that were a riot of flowers at this time of year.

The thought that Euan might have more money than she'd realised was a warning to her not to get emotionally entangled with him. She had learnt to be wary of high-flyers, however charming they seemed. Craig could charm the socks off a statue once he got going, but look at how he'd treated her. And some of his colleagues were similar, with wives who never said anything controversial and were very decorative, many of them second wives, younger than their husbands.

Not that she'd put Euan in the same category as Craig. No way. He was a much nicer person. Anyone Avril Buttermere spoke about so warmly couldn't be treacherous, she was sure. But still, he wasn't an ordinary man. He was . . . special. Very. And she wished whatever he'd woken in her would calm down again.

No, she didn't. He made her feel like a desirable woman for the first time in many years. That was such an ego boost, whether anything came of it or not.

She forced herself to concentrate on her job as she walked down to the sales office. She'd studied all the brochures and felt far better primed to work there. She could do it.

Euan was on the phone. He waved cheerfully and pointed to the second desk, then continued to talk, patiently explaining the concept of the leisure village and the sorts of houses he was building. How many times must he have gone over that?

When he put the phone down, he shook his head in irritation. 'They have a brochure, but they still wanted everything explained in detail.'

'Yes, but . . .' She hesitated.

'What?'

'Well, the information in the brochure is a bit dense. I don't think people want to know that much until they're seriously thinking of buying. I wouldn't. And anyway, most people are on the Internet these days. That's where they should be able to get further information if they want it.'

He looked at her in such surprise she wondered if she'd gone too far. Fancy criticising your employer on your first full day there! She was so stupid. His next words made her sag back in relief.

'You know, you're absolutely right, Molly. I never thought of it that way.' He picked up a brochure and flapped it at her. 'OK then, apart from answering the phone and showing people round, I'd like you to work on those residents' rules and on redesigning the basic brochure. You'll soon find out what folk want to know.'

'Me? Euan, I don't know anything at all about designing brochures.'

'Oh, we'll get a graphic artist to finish it off. What I want you to do is sort out the information needed. Pretend it's the first time you've heard about the village and put down what you'd want to know.'

'Well, I'll try. But don't be annoyed if I mess it up.'

'It'll be a team effort, Molly, and I don't think you'd mess it up, even if you did it on your own.' He frowned and added, 'And I'd never get annoyed with someone who was genuinely trying to do their best.'

She realised she'd been wimpish again and got angry at herself. 'OK, then. I'll enjoy having a go.'

'Great. That's another job off my shoulders.'

'Can I go and explore the show houses before I settle down here? I'll keep my eyes open for people coming to view the houses and rush back if I'm needed. I feel I should get to know the houses thoroughly, don't you? I've only had a lightning tour so far.'

'Good idea. Go for it.'

She picked up a notepad and walked out, seeing Dan working on one of the new houses and returning his wave. She found it amazing that she was being paid to enjoy herself.

This time she explored the houses thoroughly, looking into each cupboard, studying each detail, even how the kitchen drawers self-closed, and writing notes to herself on the pad she'd brought with her. Then she went outside and studied the back and front, trying to relate these houses to the artist's impression of the finished village on the brochure. It wasn't at all clear from the brochure which groups of houses had already been built and which hadn't.

By the time she got back to her desk, she had a few ideas, but the phone was ringing and Euan was already speaking to someone, so she picked it up, 'Marlbury Leisure Village. Molly speaking. Yes, you've come to the right place. What would you like to know?'

The whole morning zipped past and she was surprised when Euan said, 'About time you took your lunch break. Can you work till five today? I have to go out.'

'Yes, of course.' The phone started to ring again.

'I've got it,' he said cheerfully and made shooing motions with his free hand.

She walked briskly up to the hotel and bought a chicken and salad baguette from the coffee shop, sitting in a corner to eat it, enjoying a few minutes of peace. The coffee shop wasn't very busy and that didn't surprise her at all. The food was rather ordinary, sandwiches and pies mainly, yet this was an age of interesting food and women who were on a diet would want salads not huge sandwiches.

She wasn't on a diet, though she had lost a little weight, but one of these every lunchtime wouldn't be good for her waistline. She decided as she ate that she'd go shopping again tonight, not only for more food and wine, but also for a small television.

She'd ring her cousin Helen, too, and have a bit of a natter.

And maybe she'd look at her emails. She'd avoided the laptop since she left home. It'd hurt so much to find no emails from her children.

Don't go there! she told herself. *Concentrate on the good things.*

Brian decided to visit his sister that evening. He'd been wondering how Rachel was coping with married life, amused at the thought of her doing the cooking and cleaning. Heaven help poor Jamie, because she wasn't at all domesticated and had refused point-blank to learn to cook anything when she was living at home. She hadn't even done her own washing most of the time.

Nor had he. He found that he wasn't proud of that, and wondered if Rachel had changed her attitude now as well.

He found the newly-weds sitting over the remains of their tea and it seemed to him that both of them were rather relieved to see him. 'Any leftovers for a hungry brother?'

Rachel waved one hand towards the two dishes in the centre of the table, one with stringy-looking meat in a thin gravy and another with lumpy mashed potatoes. He'd bet anything the latter were from an instant packet. She didn't appear to have cooked any green vegetables, not even frozen peas. He hoped his brother-in-law knew something about cooking or the two of them would be in big trouble healthwise.

'Learnt to cook now, have you, brat?' Then he saw Jamie's glassy-looking expression and shut his mouth on a forkful of meat. It was tasteless and tough, but it was food, so he chewed and swallowed. 'What's this supposed to be?'

'I was trying to make Mum's casseroled steak,' Rachel said. 'But I must have got the other ingredients wrong.'

'Why don't you email her and ask for a few recipes?'

Her face went rigid and she collected the dirty plates, taking them to the kitchen and banging around a bit.

Jamie looked at Brian. 'Have *you* been in touch with your mother?'

'No. Has she been in touch with you two?'

'No, she hasn't, but your father's cousin Sally has. She wanted to know how your mother was because she got a "This number is no longer in operation" message when she tried to phone Molly. She said she was sorry she couldn't visit your mother in hospital.'

Brian stared at him. 'Mum had to *stay* in hospital? Not just be treated in casualty?'

'Yes. Concussion from a vehicle accident. I got a friend who works there to check the records. Must have happened on the way to the wedding.'

'Mum wasn't drunk, then?'

'No. She collapsed and was taken to hospital.'

'Oh.'

'Rachel still insists on believing your father's version of events. Are you more open-minded?'

Brian swallowed hard. 'You're sure of this?'

'Oh, yes. We were just discussing it when you arrived,

or I was trying to discuss it and yet again Rachel was refusing to accept the truth.'

That accounted for the fraught atmosphere. 'Well, I've got some more news about Mum to add to the mix. Bit of a shock, really.'

Jamie raised his voice. 'Rachel! Your brother has some further information about your mother.'

'I told you: I don't want to talk about *her*.'

He stood up. 'We'll join her in the kitchen.'

His brother-in-law's voice was chill and Brian suddenly wished he hadn't come tonight. He didn't want to get mixed up in a quarrel, let alone make it worse. He trailed after Jamie and stood in the kitchen doorway, feeling uncomfortable.

Rachel immediately tried to walk out, but Jamie caught hold of her arm. 'I don't know what Brian has to say, but you're going to listen. We have to deal with this.'

She scowled at her brother. 'You not only came to mooch a meal off me, you came to make trouble. Well, Dad wouldn't lie to me. He wouldn't!'

'He lies to everyone. Even I know that.'

Her lips wobbled and tears brimmed suddenly in her eyes. 'Not to me, he doesn't.'

Jamie tried to put an arm round her but she shook him off and went to lean her hips against the working surface, folding her arms. 'Well? Get on with it, Brian. What else has Mum done?'

'Left home.'

'What?'

'She's rented out the house and left.'

'Where's she gone?'

'I don't know. I asked the fellow who's renting the house and he—' Brian suddenly snapped his fingers. 'That's who he is, Mrs Benton's son. I knew I'd seen him before but he had hair then. Now what the hell is his first name?'

'Stuart. This is for real, right? He's living in her house, the place she told the arbitrator she couldn't bear to leave?'

Jamie intervened. 'She didn't actually tell him that; she told him the house had come to her from her parents, and she felt she had a moral right to keep it.'

'Whatever. Brian, how come you were talking to Stuart Benton?'

'I went to pick up my boxes of old toys and he was there. He refused to tell me his name or give me Mum's forwarding address.'

Rachel made a huffing noise. 'What's got into her? First she refuses to sell the house to Dad, then she rents it out to someone else and just . . . disappears. She *is* losing the plot and I am so not going to be part of trying to cheat Dad.'

Jamie intervened again. 'Your father told me how much he was offering for the house. He boasted he was going to get it at a knock-down price. Rach, his offer was way below market price, like about fifty per cent below.'

'Well, it probably needs a lot of work doing to it.'

'You know it doesn't. Your mother has always made sure it was kept in good repair.'

Brian intervened hastily as they glared at one another. 'I'll go and see Mrs Benton next door. She'll know where Mum is. I always got on quite well with her.'

'Let us know too,' Jamie said.

Rachel made another scornful noise. 'Don't bother!'

Jamie spoke to Brian. 'Look, I'm seriously worried about your mother and I feel guilty. I shouldn't have let you all treat her like that at the wedding. She was the mother of the bride and deserved to sit in the correct place, not by herself at the end of the table, with no one talking to her. My mother gave me hell for it afterwards, said she wished she'd known. If she had, she'd have insisted on being seated near Molly.'

'Mum was still on the top table; it's no big deal,' Rachel said.

But Brian remembered how unhappy his mother had looked and she'd been very pale, now he came to think of it. Why hadn't he paid attention to it, then? Because he'd been sloshing down the booze, that was why.

He stood up. 'I'll go and see Mrs Benton straight away. Thanks for the meal, Rach.'

His mother's tenant opened the door at the next house and greeted him with, 'Oh, it's you again.'

Brian kept his voice polite with an effort. 'Can I see Mrs Benton, please?'

'Not now, lad. My father's just collapsed and we're waiting for the doctor.'

Lad! Who did he think he was talking to? Then Brian realised what Stuart had said. 'Sorry about that. I hope Mr Benton gets better soon. Look, I just wanted Mum's forwarding address or her mobile phone number.' He whipped out his business card. 'If you know them, could you email me? Her old mobile number doesn't work and I'm getting a bit worried about her.'

'So you damned well should be. Where were you when she was being harassed by that group of yobs?'

'What?'

'Rocks thrown through windows during the night, trouble caused every time someone came to view the house. No wonder she couldn't sell it.'

Brian stared at him in shock. 'I didn't know about that.'

'How come? Didn't you ever go round to see her?'

'Well . . . not lately. I've been too busy trying to find somewhere to live. I was camping out at a friend's place and I've only just found somewhere of my own. Things were a bit hectic at work, lots of overtime and I really needed the money.'

'Shows where your priorities lie, doesn't it? If she were my mother, she'd be more important than my job and I'd take better care of her, too. Ah, here he is . . . This way, Doctor.' He turned back to Jamie. 'Why don't you try emailing your mother? I told you last time: her email address is working perfectly well. She hasn't changed that.'

'I wanted to talk to her.'

'If I were her, I'd not want to speak to anyone from the family. No wonder she changed her mobile number.' He shut the door without another word.

Brian walked down the drive looking sideways at his old home as he passed, wishing he was still living there. He hadn't realised how easy he'd had it in those days, hadn't even paid his rent most weeks, felt ashamed of that now. He'd mooched a meal off his sister tonight, but he'd mooched a lot more from his mother.

Now he couldn't afford to go out for a drink with his mates, couldn't even afford to get an Internet connection, so would have to take his laptop to work and ask permission to email his mother from there in his lunch hour. They were a bit sticky about you using their email system in work time, but he'd tell his boss how skint he was and promise only to hook up to the network outside working hours.

He cringed at the memory of how scornfully Stuart had talked to him. And his brother-in-law had been disapproving, too. He'd never seen Jamie look like that, so icy and disapproving. He was only a couple of years older than Rachel, but many years wiser.

The trouble was the two men were right. He hated to admit it, but they were. Even if his mother was mad at him, he still wanted to know she was safe . . . and happy.

Rachel didn't seem to care about Mum, though. Well, she'd always been Daddy's little princess, hadn't she? But surely even she couldn't go on believing the lies their father told her? If she did, his sister was far stupider than he'd thought. Actually, he didn't know what Jamie saw in her. He'd never fancy a spoilt brat like her, however pretty she was. Geneva was one, too, and she'd been hard to live with, even temporarily.

He'd acted pretty badly. He'd been spoilt too. What would any woman see in him? The one he'd met in the supermarket had dismissed his invitation to coffee out of hand. She might already have a fellow, of course, but she wasn't wearing a ring. No, she hadn't even shown a flicker of interest in him. Probably thought him a clueless oik after he'd needed help with such basic things.

He was useless at looking after himself, but he was doing something about that, at least. A man ought to be able to care for himself.

He went into his flat. It had been advertised as a studio flat, grand words for one small room with a sink and two-burner cooker, and a minuscule bathroom. At the moment the place looked like a campsite. He burped. Rachel's food was sitting very heavily in his stomach and he couldn't even afford a can of beer to take the greasy taste away.

The only thing Brian was certain of at the moment was that he had to hang on to his job. He'd become Mr Eager Beaver and was working harder than he ever had before, because times were chancy and people were being laid off everywhere. His boss had complimented him last week on a job well done.

He wasn't getting into any more debt, either. Look where his spending spree had brought him! He was living like a tramp.

He'd look up some of his boyhood toys on the Internet tomorrow. If he could sell one or two online, he might scrape together enough money to buy a bed, at least. Sleeping on a narrow, old-fashioned air mattress in a tatty old sleeping bag was the pits.

It suddenly occurred to him that his sister hadn't even asked where he was living. Selfish bitch! Well, she'd had her big day as Princess of Wedding World. Now she had to come down to earth, just as he'd had to. He burped again and grimaced, making himself a slice of bread and jam to try to get rid of the taste. She was a lousy cook. So was he. But if he couldn't do better than that tough meat of hers, he deserved shooting.

He hunted through a pile of old newspapers for the free cookery book he'd been given at the supermarket and sorted out the stuff as he went. It occurred to him that if he didn't let the place get untidy in the first place, he'd not have so much to clear up. When he'd finished sorting the papers out, he sat down and looked through the list of recipes. Plenty of stuff he liked here.

He read the introduction and chose a simple dish – well, they said it was simple. Pulling out his mobile phone, he began to list the ingredients he'd need to buy tomorrow.

Actually, now he'd got started, he was quite looking forward to having a go at cooking. How hard could it be if you followed the recipes carefully? And he did have a frying pan, at least.

When he'd finished that, he didn't know what to do with himself, so played card games on his laptop.

He couldn't even scrape together enough for a TV, because he'd maxed out his credit card. Perhaps he should join the library. Books were still free, weren't they?

He looked round the room and groaned. If his workmates could see him now, they'd fall about laughing and he'd never live it down.

But he was managing, wasn't he? Independent. And about time too.

He hoped his mother was managing too. He'd definitely send her an email tomorrow.

But would she reply?

Later in the afternoon, Molly looked after the sales office on her own while Euan went to show a couple round the houses. She started to go through the stationery supplies and the jumble inside the two cupboards. She'd ask permission before she touched Euan's drawers, though.

At nearly closing time, he'd still not come back so she phoned through to ask Avril if she should lock up the office, since she didn't have a key to open it once that was done.

'Lock it up. You're not paid to work all the hours God sends,' Avril said. 'I'll make a note to get you a key.'

Molly went shopping, buying some more bottles of wine and a very small TV. It had been nice to have Euan visit her last night, but she'd be on her own most evenings, so this wasn't an extravagance. Of course, she could visit Helen occasionally, or invite her cousin to visit her, but that would still leave a lot of empty evenings. They were the hardest part of single life, she found, those evenings. No one to chat to.

When she got back, she couldn't be bothered to cook the steak she'd bought, so settled for a cheese toastie and an apple. Then she got out her laptop and went online, relieved to find that Euan had been right. His Wi-Fi network did extend to where the caravan was and the password he'd given her worked.

She found emails from her friends, but nothing from

her children. That made her feel sad but it was no use dwelling on it. She replied to Nikki, sent off a cheerful email to her cousin Helen and closed the laptop.

Television reception with the small indoor aerial recommended by the salesman was adequate, but not brilliant. She found a couple of programmes to watch.

She was managing just fine.

In the middle of the night she woke up abruptly. She lay in the darkness wondering what had disturbed her sleep, then heard it again – the sound of breaking glass.

She went to the open window and stared out through the security mesh. There was some moonlight, enough to see if someone was around. There was no sign of anyone at the front of the houses, but that had definitely been breaking glass, so she phoned through to the night security guy at the hotel.

'I'll be down straight away,' he said. 'It's probably nothing, but I could do with some fresh air.'

She hurriedly put on some jeans and a top, then continued to watch through the window. The security man came down the hill quietly, not needing a torch, but it could only be him, surely? She saw him move along the front of the finished houses then disappear behind them.

Suddenly there were yells and shouts, and she didn't know what to do. The security man was on his own. What if he'd had two or three intruders to tackle? But she was small and would be no help in a fight.

Two figures appeared suddenly from behind the house, running up the hill, pursued a few seconds later by another figure. The first one was thin, looked like a youth and ran so fast he pulled ahead of his companion. The second was bigger, not running quite as easily, but still pulling further and further ahead of the security man, who wasn't the slimmest fellow on the planet and who was pounding along heavily behind them.

The two men disappeared into the hotel car park. She heard an engine start up and a vehicle pulled away with a screech. Had they escaped? She doubted he'd have caught them, but perhaps he'd got their registration number. She did hope so. She hated thieves and vandals. What right had they to steal or spoil other people's hard-earned possessions!

The phone rang. The security man, sounding breathless.

'They got away but I saw their car reg, so I've called the police.'

If the police were coming, she'd keep her clothes on and not go back to bed. She decided to make some drinking chocolate. Milk was supposed to help you sleep. Closing the curtains, she took out her book.

While she was sipping her drink, there was a knock on the door which made her jump. She went to look through the little spyhole and saw Euan standing there.

'Just wanted to thank you. You disturbed some thieves and saved me quite a bit of money. They were after the appliances and had disconnected them ready to remove. They had a transit van waiting in the hotel car park. I suppose they were going to bring it down here when they were ready. I don't know whether we're going to become a target for organised theft, but I think it's time to put automatic gates across the entrance to the village and lock them at night. It's on my list of to-dos but I didn't think it was urgent yet. I'll give you a remote, of course, so that you can get in and out any time. I'm sorry you were disturbed tonight.'

'You must have been disturbed too, if they rang you at home.'

He ran his fingers through his rumpled hair. 'Tell me about it. I'd not long been asleep.'

'Would you like some drinking chocolate while you wait for them?'

'Don't you want to get back to sleep?'

'In a few minutes. Anyway, the police might want to talk to me as well.'

It felt good to have him sitting opposite her again. Too good. She was sorry when the police arrived and he went to talk to them.

She got annoyed at herself for feeling like that. This was just a fleeting attraction and she mustn't read more into it, either on his side or her own. It happened all the time, a man and a woman met, were attracted, then life moved them apart or there weren't enough things right to keep them together.

It didn't usually happen to her, though, she had to admit. Once married, she'd taken her marriage vows very seriously and not even looked at another man. Since Craig left her, well, she'd not been ready to look at men in that way.

But she was ready now. And Euan was well worth looking at.

Someone knocked on the door and she went to answer it. 'The police would like to talk to you, Molly.'

'Bring them in.' She smiled at the two uniformed officers. 'Would you like some drinking chocolate?'

She got them drinks, answered their questions and after Euan had gone, she yawned and got into bed again, smiling. Who'd have thought she'd meet with such excitement in a quiet place like this?

On his way home from work that evening, Craig made another detour into Lavengro Road. He'd not heard from the lads he'd hired and wanted to make sure they'd done their work before he paid them.

To his disappointment, there was no sign of damage to the house, though someone had spilt paint on the footpath in front of it. He should really have driven past this morning. The broken window could have been repaired by now. Those security gates looked very strong. Must have cost a packet. She was stupid to go to that expense, but maybe the tenants wouldn't take the house unless she put them in, given the trouble there had been. He smirked at the thought of how easily he'd stopped her selling.

And whatever Tasha said, he was going to continue his campaign.

He wished the fellow renting the house would come outside so that he could see what he was like, but there were no signs of life. It was such a pretty house. And big. He'd always liked living here.

After a while he drove off. He and Tasha had a charity

event to attend tonight, useful people, but a pricey affair. He was only going because he'd had it on good authority that the chairman would be attending. He just hoped it'd be worth it.

Tasha looked superb and he enjoyed the praise and envious remarks from other guys. But as the evening wore on, it became clear that the chairman wasn't going to turn up, so Craig had wasted a good sum of money.

There was a guy at the top table, however, whom he thought he should recognise. It took a while for the penny to drop. Could it be . . . ? Yes, it was. Surely it was – the tenant? 'Who's that fellow?' he asked his neighbour. 'The bald one next to the fat old woman with white hair.'

'That's Stuart Benton, and his wife isn't fat. She's just a normal size.'

Craig didn't argue, but in his opinion that woman was well overweight. 'Of course! I knew I'd seen him before. I used to live next door to his mother.'

'Rising fellow, Benton. He's left the army now and word is he's helping set up a big international security company. It's all very hush-hush at this stage, though, and no one can get any details. I'd invest in it like a shot if he went public. He knows his stuff.'

Craig made a sound that could have been agreement, but wasn't. He watched sourly as Benton smiled and chatted. Normally he'd go over and say hello, renew the acquaintance, but he and the neighbours had never got on. They were not his sort of people. Nothing useful to be gained from associating with them.

Funny how he wasn't enjoying tonight. He usually

revelled in functions like this. He was glad when Tasha signalled she was ready to leave.

'What's got into you?' she demanded as the taxi pulled away. 'You've had a sour face on you all night.'

'Got a bit of a headache. And the chairman wasn't there, so no use staying late.'

'A lot of other useful people were there. I met several women who asked where I got this dress. They'll be coming into my boutique this week.'

'Good.' But he was glad to get to bed and for the first time in ages he didn't want to make love, just go to sleep. Which didn't please madam at all.

Well, too bad. He was a man, not a sex machine.

Chapter Nine

On Thursday, Euan rang Molly at seven-thirty in the morning. 'I didn't wake you, did I? You said you usually got up early. Oh, good. Would it be asking too much for you to come here and help me finish packing? I'm never going to be ready to move house tomorrow otherwise. Would you mind?'

'Of course not. I've already had my breakfast, so I can come straight away.' She was supposed to have the morning off and hadn't been looking forward to it, because there wasn't much to keep you occupied in a caravan, and there was only so much shopping to do when there was just yourself to feed.

She followed the directions to Euan's house and stood admiring it for a moment or two – old, beautiful, built of stone, with picturesque gables, in a lovely village setting. She couldn't imagine why he wanted to leave this to live on what was little more than a building site.

The front door was open and when she rang the bell, a voice yelled, 'Come in!' The hall was wide but was full of boxes and oddments of furniture, two dark oak chairs, a small table, a bookcase. She edged her way cautiously past these obstacles and followed the voice upstairs, finding Euan frowning at a bare mattress topped by piles of folded bed linen. He looked so frazzled, her heart went out to him.

'Thank goodness you're here, Molly. I seriously underestimated what needed doing and it's taking far longer than I'd expected.' He waved one hand around. 'This used to be my grandparents' house, and my grandmother left it to me when she died. I knew living here would just be temporary, so I didn't get round to clearing out all the cupboards.'

'Did you never think of living here permanently? It's a beautiful house.'

His expression darkened. 'It may be but it doesn't have good memories for me. I spent a few summers here with my grandparents. My father didn't get on well with his parents so he didn't stay. All I have left from that side of the family now is this house and the name, Santiago. My grandfather's family came from Portugal, and I think he and my grandmother were stuck in a time warp when it came to raising children. They were very strict and not at all loving.'

She could hear the unhappiness in his voice and blessed her own normal childhood.

'Anyway, I've been more busy than I expected setting up the leisure village. Now, I'm finding so much stuff that needs sorting out that I'm panicking. I know I could throw things away but they're not worn out and that seems wrong, and some are family mementoes, while others are probably quite valuable.'

'Hmm.' She inspected the piles of bedding, most of which was in excellent condition, then let him show her the five large bedrooms on this floor, all with cupboards and drawers full of items. They looked sad, with the beds stripped.

'There's another floor,' he said, 'and there's still more stuff up there, too.'

She followed him up to some smaller bedrooms with dormer windows. Most of them were unfurnished but a couple had beds and wardrobes, though these were very plain, unlike the beautiful furniture on the floor below.

Narrow stairs led above them to a long, thin attic running across the length of the house under the highest point of the roof.

'Thank goodness this was clear of everything except these pieces of worn luggage,' he said. 'I can just throw these out, at least.'

She went over to look at them. 'This is antique luggage and I'd guess it's worth quite a bit of money.'

He came to stand beside her. 'What? Are you sure? I was going to get a skip delivered and chuck this lot into it.'

'Very sure. I'm interested in antiques. I've watched a lot of those programmes on TV.' Molly opened one suitcase and found it full of old clothes. She pulled out a dress and held it against herself. 'Nineteen-thirties. Isn't it gorgeous?'

'I suppose that's worth money too.'

'Bound to be.'

'I can't throw this stuff away, then.'

'You could sell it online.'

'I wouldn't know where to begin.'

She hesitated.

'You know how to do it, don't you?'

'Well, I have bought and sold a few things online. Craig wasn't interested, so I never talked about it to him, but I enjoyed it and I usually made a profit.'

'Sell this lot for me and we'll split the proceeds fifty-fifty,' he said promptly.

The old Molly popped her head up and she nearly said she wasn't sure she could get him the best deal, then the new Molly took over. 'All right.'

'What about the rest of the furniture and the other things?' he asked as they went back downstairs.

'There's no way you can be packed in time for tomorrow, even with my help. Don't forget we have the sales office to open later today.'

'I have to have the house clear by tomorrow so I can't cancel the removalists. Tomorrow's exchanging contracts day.'

'Why don't you ring the removal firm and see if they have a packing service and could send someone straight away to help you? Have you hired storage space for the things you aren't sure about?'

He nodded. 'One of those self-store places.'

'Hire some more space, then. Hire one area just for possible resale stuff. You'll be able to go through your grandmother's things at leisure, then.'

'Or you could do it for me. Molly – do you think you could work for me full-time? Still as a general factotum, not just in the sales office. It'd be a big help if you could go through this stuff with me, for a start.'

'I'd love to do that.'

He held out one hand and they shook solemnly, then he took his mobile phone out and spoke to someone at the removal firm. Next he rang the storage complex and asked for more space, giving her a triumphant signal of success with his free hand.

Once he'd finished, he leant against the wall and beamed at her. 'I feel better just to have you here. I'm good at the big stuff, but not at the details. I've had back-up teams before and I didn't realise quite how much they took off my shoulders. You're good at details, aren't you?'

'Am I?'

He frowned. 'You keep doubting yourself. Don't. You're clearly an extremely capable woman. You've made everything seem simple and logical today.'

'Logical maybe, but it isn't simple. I've recently had the experience of going through a house full of memories and getting rid of most of the trivia. It takes time.' And it hurt, but she didn't say that. 'I've got my personal stuff in storage too, waiting until I can sell my house and find a new home.'

He leant forward and plonked a quick kiss on her cheek. 'You're an even bigger treasure than I thought, Molly Peel, and I don't know what I'd do without you.'

She felt flustered. 'Oh. Well, that's all right. I like to

keep busy. Shall we . . . um, start sorting out what you want to take with you to the village?'

'There won't be much, mainly clothes and personal stuff. I've got modern furniture going into the big house at the end of the row today, specially designed to make the place look like a million dollars. I'm moving it from the other big house, which I've just sold.

'I'll have to show customers through until I get a similar house built, but just the fact that I live there myself says something, don't you think?'

'It certainly does.' And he'd be a neighbour of hers. She liked the idea of that.

The two of them worked steadily, helped by the removalists' team of packers, who turned up a short time later.

At half past twelve, Euan said, 'One of us needs to go back and open the sales office. Do you think you can hold the fort there on your own? I really need to stay here. Here's my key in case yours hasn't arrived yet. OK?'

'Fine. Do you have any appointments?'

'No. I kept today clear on purpose.'

'So you'll be in your new house tonight?'

'Yes. We'll be neighbours. I'll take you out to dinner at the hotel to celebrate.'

'That'll mean getting smartened up. Let me make us something quick and easy instead, then we can stay scruffy. If you want that house perfect, you'll need to get your things put away quickly.'

He gave her an appraising look. 'You know, sometimes you remind me of Avril.'

'What a lovely compliment! But I'm not in her league.'

He grinned. 'You're close. But you're much prettier.'

She felt her cheeks heating up.

'I love it when you blush.'

'Let's just . . . keep things businesslike.'

'They aren't. And you can't close Pandora's box.'

He didn't touch her, but he might just as well have. One of the packers came to ask him something and he turned away, so she went into another room before he could say anything else like that.

The effect Euan had on her was disconcerting and yet she loved being with him.

She ought to work out a way to keep her distance from him. A man like him wouldn't stay with a woman like her, and she wasn't the sort to hop into bed with anyone just for a temporary pleasure – was she?

Did she even know what sort of woman she was now?

Brian confided the full extent of his recent troubles to his boss and asked permission to pick up his emails at work during lunchtime.

Mr Simmonds looked at him thoughtfully. 'I'm glad you've told me that. We all learn some things the hard way. Certainly, your work has improved lately, which is a good sign.'

Brian smiled ruefully. 'I hope so.'

'And yes, you can go online with our system. Set your laptop up in our interview room. In your own hours only, though.'

'Of course.'

Brian went to pick up his emails at lunchtime, but had difficulty writing to his mother. It upset him even to try. Where the hell did he start to apologise for treating her like that? She was the one who was good with words, not him. In the end he kept it simple.

Dear Mum,
I've been trying to contact you. I didn't even know you'd gone. Are you all right? Where are you?
Can you let me have your new mobile number? I'd like to talk.
I'm getting myself sorted out, gradually.
And Mum – I'm sorry for being so selfish, and all that. Really sorry.
Brian

It wasn't quite what he wanted to say, but he figured it was better than nothing, and after a quick glance at his watch, he clicked on the 'Send' button and went back to his desk.

The afternoon was busy, with several people coming to look round the development. Molly could have done with someone else to help, but luckily most of the visitors were only looking and didn't mind being sent off on their own. One older couple called Sarcen seemed serious about buying, however, so she took them round the houses herself, answering their questions patiently, envying the easy way they showed their affection for one another in small touches and quick smiles, as well as by holding hands.

She left the office unattended with a sign on the desk saying she'd be back in a few minutes and people should help themselves to brochures. She ran the sign off on the computer in a large font but it still looked amateurish. They needed to get a proper sign made for busy times, a stand-up one on glossy white card, not a floppy piece of paper stuck to the lid of the box the brochures had come in. She made a quick note of that on her list of things to do.

It took longer than she'd expected to show the houses to the Sarcens, who asked a lot of shrewd questions. This might be her very first sale, and Euan had said she'd get commission on sales she made on her own. What a lucky thing she'd come here that first day!

As she got near the office she stopped dead, and all her happiness evaporated abruptly, because she recognised the two people inside going through the brochures, even with their backs to her – well, she recognised their car as well. There couldn't be two Citroëns with that idiotic pink fluffy animal in the back, nodding at the world.

'Is something wrong?' Mrs Sarcen asked.

Molly backed to one side, out of sight, and admitted, 'I don't want to meet those people in the office. They're friends of my ex-husband and I don't want him to know where I am.'

Mrs Sarcen looked at her sympathetically. 'Abusive, was he?'

'Not physically.'

'Why don't you nip down to your caravan and we'll say we're waiting for you to find us some information? I'll come and get you when they've gone.'

'I shouldn't. And it'll mean you hanging about waiting for them to go.'

Mr Sarcen patted her shoulder. 'We've got plenty of time and you've been very patient with us today. If people can't help one another, they're poor sorts.'

Molly glanced towards the office again and heard Ginny Mercer's strident voice saying, 'I think we've got all the brochures. Let's go and look at the houses now, Ralph.'

With a quick 'Thank you!' she dashed down to her caravan and hid. It might be cowardly, but the last thing she wanted was Craig finding out she was here.

It was a full half hour before Ralph and Ginny finished looking round the houses. At one point they came close to her caravan because he insisted on looking over the plots that were not yet built on. He even walked along streets, which at this stage consisted only of pretty signs and plot numbers on small posts.

'This development is a good idea, especially if we buy a house in France when I retire. I've played at the golf course here a few times and it's one of my favourites.'

'I'm not at all sure about this, Ralph. I don't think I want to live overseas and leave all my friends.'

'Well, we don't have to go to France, it was just a thought for a holiday home. We could buy one of the houses here instead. I can't think of anywhere nicer to come for little holidays or weekends. We'll soon make friends if I play golf here.'

'But I don't play golf. What will *I* do here?'

'You don't have to come every time.'

Their voices faded into the distance as they walked back to the car parking area. Molly could imagine that sour expression Ginny always wore when something didn't please her, but Ralph was very much in charge of such decisions – as Craig had been.

When their car had driven away, she went cautiously outside and Mr Sarcen beckoned to her from the sales office, grinning broadly. She couldn't neglect such charming customers, so hurried across to join them.

It took her only a few minutes to provide them with cups of coffee and supply them with relevant house plans, then she answered more questions about prices and building schedules.

'We mustn't keep you any longer,' Mr Sarcen said. 'Thank you for being so patient with us. We're definitely interested and we'll get back to you about which of those two plots of land we prefer.'

Molly stood at the door waving as they drove away. They were just the sort of people Euan wanted to attract, unlike Ginny, who wouldn't be an asset to any community and was only tolerated because of whose wife she was. Oh, please! Let the Mercers not buy here!

Phew! What a close shave she'd had today!

As they drove away from the leisure village, Ralph said, 'We'll go and have a cup of coffee at the hotel and get a feel for the amenities here. I'd like to have another look at those brochures before we go, in case there's anything else I need to check.'

'Good idea. I'm parched. Strange that they didn't have someone on duty. A poor way of running things, that.'

'They're only just starting up.'

After they'd finished their coffee, he said, 'I think I'll just run down to the village again. I want to check that plot of land near the end of Honeysuckle Close. I rather like the outlook. I notice there was one house already being built there. I wish we could have got that end block.'

'You're really keen?' she asked.

'Yes. I'm very keen.'

'Oh.'

He drove down and they arrived in the car park just as Molly was taking another couple into one of the houses.

Ginny grabbed his arm. 'Isn't that Molly Taylor, or whatever she's calling herself these days?'

He squinted across. 'Looks like her. Do you want to go and say hello?'

'Heavens, no! Can't stand the woman. I wonder what she's doing here.'

'Selling houses, it looks like.'

Ginny grimaced. 'Heaven help her employers, then. No wonder there was no one to attend to us today, if she's the one on duty. Craig Taylor is well rid of her, if you ask me.'

'His new wife is certainly an asset socially, and a very attractive woman.'

As they drove past the hotel, Ginny said, 'I need to use the ladies'.'

He stopped. 'I'll wait for you here.'

Inside the hotel, she went to reception. 'I wonder if you can help me. I think I just saw an old friend down at the leisure village. Her name's Molly.'

'Oh yes. Molly Peel. She's working there.'

'I'll have to catch up with her. Thanks for your help.'

She walked out, not saying a word to Ralph. She'd guess Molly must have seen them when they first arrived and hidden somewhere, perhaps in that ugly little caravan.

A smile crept across her face as she wondered if Craig knew where his wife was.

Rachel hadn't seen her father for ages, so rang him after she got back from work.

'Princess! How are things going?'

'Oh. All right, I suppose.'

'What's wrong?'

'It's such hard work, cooking and washing and all that stuff.'

'You would marry a poor man. You should have waited and let me find you someone with a bit of money.'

She didn't answer, didn't want to discuss that. He meant an older man and that was gross. 'Brian came round last night. He looks to be living in squalor.'

'Not good with money, our Brian. I'm sure he'll learn a lot from this experience. Has he seen your mother?'

'No. He's a bit worried about her, actually.'

'Aren't we all? I still can't believe she rented out that house, rather than selling to me.'

'It was mean, wasn't it? But it's Mrs Benton's son who's renting it. Brian remembered where he'd seen him.'

'Military fellow, rather stiff-necked?'

'That's the one.'

'I saw him at a function. Look, darling, got to go now. Faces to see, places to visit. We must have you round to dinner soon. I'll get Tasha to give you a ring. Things have been frantic lately.'

She sighed as she put the phone down. She missed seeing her father. Tasha seemed to keep him busy elsewhere and didn't often invite her round. And Jamie didn't like Tasha anyway.

It was all very complicated and she wished she had married a rich man – a young, rich man as attractive as Jamie. Then she wouldn't have to go out to work and come home to the problem of thinking of things to eat. She hadn't realised how much Jamie ate or that he'd insist on a cooked meal every single night, instead of just grabbing a sandwich or going out to eat.

He wanted to save money to buy a house, but you needed so much. She'd been hoping Daddy would front up with the deposit, but when she'd hinted, he'd said he wished he could, but he had a big mortgage of his own to pay off, thanks to her selfish mother.

Her mother should think of others for a change.

Rachel sighed. She'd thought it'd be fun to be married, but it wasn't.

* * *

At five o'clock, Molly rang Euan on his mobile phone to check how things were going at the house.

'Really well, thanks to your intervention.'

'Do you need any more help there?'

There was silence, then he said, 'You've already done far too much.'

'I'd be happy to go on helping, but this evening will be in my own time as a friend, so I won't want paying.'

'I can't resist the offer. You *are* a treasure! And yes, please.'

Smiling at the compliment, the treasure locked up the office, went to change into jeans, which fitted her much better than they had before, and drove out to the little village where Euan lived. She was tired, but he desperately needed help, and she owed him a lot for giving her this job.

Denis Benton died early the following day, simply gasped and stopped breathing as his wife was sitting with him.

She stared at him in shock. The look of death was unmistakable but still, she checked for breathing with a mirror. As she'd expected, there was no breath misting up the surface. 'Oh, Denis! I'm going to miss you so much, my darling.'

He'd pleaded with her not to go in for any heroic resuscitation, so she didn't hurry to call for help. He'd wanted to slip away quietly and had been granted his wish, thank goodness.

She closed his eyes, stroked a lock of silver hair back from his forehead and sat down again beside him, wanting just a little more time with him. She'd thought she was prepared for this, but were you ever?

After a few minutes she picked up the phone. 'Stuart . . . It's your father. He's . . .' She couldn't force the words out.

'I'll be right over, Mum.'

She went to meet her son at the front door and fell into his arms, weeping. 'He's dead! He just . . . died. Between one breath and the next.' She let her son hug her, let herself cling to his strength for a few minutes, then pulled herself together. 'Sorry.'

'What for? Being human? Weeping for the loss of the man you love.' He held her for a while longer, then set her back from him gently. 'I'd better go and look at him. Do you want to call the doctor or shall I?'

'I'll do that.' She phoned and stumbled through an explanation to the receptionist, then spoke to the doctor, whose voice grew hushed and gentle as he realised what had happened.

When she went back to the bedroom, Stuart was standing looking down at his father. 'He hasn't looked so peaceful for a long time, has he? He must have been in a lot of pain.'

'Yes, he was. He was very brave about that, but I could always tell when he was hurting badly.'

'I'll do what's necessary when the doctor arrives, Mum. How about you go and make us a cup of tea?'

'Thank you. And . . . I don't want to see Denis again. I know it's cowardly but that—it isn't him, somehow. He's changed already. There's no expression left on his face.

My Denis was always fired up about something, if it was only the headlines in the newspaper.'

'He used to get fired up about what I was doing, too. We didn't always get on well, considering we were father and son, did we?'

'You were too much alike, I think. Both dominant men.' She touched her son's arm. 'I'm so glad you're nearby.'

'I'll just nip back and tell Wendy, then I'll have that cup of tea.'

Children were a huge comfort. As she made the pot of tea, her mind skipped from one idea to another, anything to avoid thinking of Denis.

Molly's son, Brian, had apparently come round to see her, wanting his mother's contact details, but Stuart had sent him away. She did hope that meant Brian was going to reconcile with Molly. A woman shouldn't be estranged from her children . . .

Jane didn't intend to move from this house afterwards. It was her home. She was staying put, whatever anyone said about it being too big . . .

She was so glad Denis had been spared helpless dependence . . .

She wished Stuart could stay on next door. It'd be such a help and comfort to have him nearby. But she wouldn't tell him that, of course. She didn't want to chain him down; could stand on her own feet if she had to. Mostly.

Ah, here he was. She turned to greet him. 'I'll give you the big mug. You always did drink a gallon of tea in the mornings.'

He patted her shoulder. 'And you always did cope with whatever happened, even when you were upset.'

She nodded, held the tears at bay and concentrated on what she would have to do on that sad, sad day.

Euan watched Molly park her car and come into his grandmother's house. She looked alert and happy.

'Have you had a good day?'

'Really good. I think I've sold a house for you, and to such nice people.'

'That's marvellous. You do realise you get a hefty commission for each sale.'

'Yes, but most of all, I'm happy to have succeeded.' She held out the carrier bag. 'I got us some takeaway. It's fish and chips from a Chinese shop, so I don't know how good it'll be.'

He grabbed her and gave her a hug. 'How did you guess I'd be ravenous?'

'Maybe because I am too. Craig always used to say I ate too much and should try to eat less to lose weight.'

'The man sounds a fool. You're a perfect weight.'

'I'm a bit overweight by today's standards.'

'You're just right for a normal woman. Who wants to make love to a stick insect?' Their glances caught and he suddenly thought to hell with it. He pulled her into his arms, not giving her the chance to resist him, kissing her as he'd wanted to do all week. She was soft and feminine, not at all fat. Her ex must be a lunatic.

At first she tried to pull away, then he suddenly felt

her start to return his kiss and the warmth of their coming-together wrapped round them like a soft, invisible blanket.

'Don't say you didn't enjoy that,' he said as they both came up for air.

'How can I? I joined in wholeheartedly.' She looked down at the carrier bag, which she'd dropped on the floor. 'Oh dear, I hope it hasn't spilt. We'd better eat it while it's hot.'

'The follow-up is only postponed,' he said, trying not to show how aroused he was.

She looked at him, then gave a tiny nod and a half-smile.

The food was good and they both cleared their plates.

'More?' He offered her the container.

'No. You finish it.'

'All right. And you must tell me how much I owe you for this.'

'Nothing.'

'But I—'

'Nothing. I'm not a pauper, Euan, and we are, I hope, friends now.'

'Then thank you.' He finished the rest off.

They worked all evening and at one point Molly found herself telling him about her close encounter with one of Craig's colleagues.

'Did you really have to hide from them? It seems . . . a bit unnecessary.'

She looked at him sadly. 'It's not. Craig is absolutely ruthless when he wants something. He's already stopped me selling my house. Worst of all, he took away my self-confidence and came between me and my children for years. If he finds out where I am, he'll probably hire some people to set fire to the caravan. He's absolutely determined to force me to sell that house to him.'

'High-flyers in business don't usually take risks by breaking the law like that.'

'He'll find a way. He boasts that he never lets people get the better of him without paying them back, and he thinks I got the better of him in the divorce settlement.'

'Won't his new wife stop him?'

'Who knows? She seems just like him. Mrs Perfect. Slender, not a hair out of place, dresses like a model. All gloss, and you wonder if there's any heart to her.'

She looked down at herself. 'You can't go wrong with jeans and a top, but you should have seen how awful I looked at the wedding. I don't have much dress sense, I'm afraid.'

After a short silence, he smiled wryly. 'I noticed.'

She could feel herself blushing. 'Is my appearance that bad?'

'No. It's just . . . you don't make the most of yourself. Your office clothes are—'

She finished for him. 'Dowdy. And even when Craig got me good clothes, I didn't wear them with style.'

'We'll get Avril on to it. She'll know what to do.'

Molly looked at him doubtfully, not knowing what to say to that. He'd said 'we' again. He said it so easily. Was it charm, or was he simply acknowledging the growing connection between them?

'Now what's going through your head?' he asked softly.

'I feel uncertain – about everything.'

'Ah. Of course. And that includes me. Let me tell you something: I was happily married to Karen. I know what makes a good relationship and I think it might be possible between us. There's a certain sort of warmth, hard to put into words, as if things are . . . right. I really like you as a person and I fancy you as a woman, too.' He grinned at her, then added, 'Dowdy clothes and all. I'm willing to wait until you've regained enough confidence to let yourself relax with me, then we can both see what happens.'

'You may get tired of waiting. I'm not very confident about anything.'

'I won't get tired, Molly. A treasure like you is worth waiting for. But I also won't push you into anything. You must walk into a relationship with me freely and happily.' He looked at his watch and sighed. 'Time is against us at the moment. If you'll help me finish this room, I'll get up early in the morning and dive in again.'

'*We* shall get up early.'

'Thanks.'

They worked till ten o'clock, then Molly yawned and said, 'I've had enough. I'm going home and you should go to bed as well. You can set the alarm for really early. You'll work more efficiently if you get some sleep.'

'All right. But I'll walk you out to your car first, and you must check that there's no one around before you get out of it at the caravan. Promise me?'

'I promise.'

She drove home and was out of the car and standing at the caravan door before she realised she should have checked for people lurking. She looked round, feeling vulnerable, and fumbled with her key, dropping it on the ground. How stupid!

Her heart began to pound as she scrabbled under the edge of the caravan for it.

At last she got the door open and locked it quickly behind her, with a loud sigh of relief. After using the bathroom, she couldn't resist lying on the bed for a moment or two before she got undressed. She was so tired all she wanted to do was close her eyes.

She woke once during the night feeling cold, pulled the covers over herself and went back to sleep.

The dawn chorus of birdsong woke her – who said the countryside was quiet? Then she realised she hadn't even got undressed and laughed at herself. That hadn't prevented her from enjoying an excellent night's sleep. And she'd promised to go early to help Euan.

It wasn't till she was drying herself after a shower that she realised she'd been humming one of her favourite tunes as she got ready. Well, she had something to sing about now, a possible new relationship (she dared go no further than that) and a job.

She'd just wait and see what happened with Euan. Relationships weren't as straightforward as he made them seem. At least she hadn't found that. But perhaps they were with him?

She caught sight of her laptop. She didn't have time to check her emails this morning. Anyway, there'd be nothing important. The important things in her life were happening here in Wiltshire. Everything else was on hold.

Chapter Ten

'I can't find the letter from your father's cousin,' Jamie said on Friday morning.

'I threw it away when I was clearing up.'

Rachel hadn't cleared anything else up, but he tried to be patient with her. 'Do you have Sally's address? I'll reply to her.'

'There's no need and anyway, I don't have her address.'

He stood very still, looking at her, not saying a word. When he saw her wriggle and begin to fiddle with her mug of coffee, he knew she was lying and felt bitterly disappointed. 'I'll have to ask your father for it, then. She deserves a reply.'

'No! You can't go to him. Daddy will be furious when he finds out why you need her address.'

'Why? Because what she said proves him a liar?'

'He didn't lie. He just . . . got it wrong.'

'Then give me Sally's address.'

Sulkily, looking like a twelve-year-old rather than a married woman of twenty-three, Rachel dumped her mug on the table, sending splashes of coffee everywhere, and went to switch on her computer. He followed her into the spare bedroom, where the computers were set up.

Muttering to herself, she found the address, scribbled it down and flung the piece of paper at him. 'There! I hope you're satisfied now.'

'I'm not. I can't believe you're acting like this. Don't you care at all about your mother?'

'Not much.'

'What about your brother?'

'Brian's OK. I've not got much in common with him, though.'

'What *do* you care about?'

'You.' She burst into tears. 'Us.'

For the first time, he didn't take her in his arms and comfort her, because he didn't feel at all sorry for her. 'If you do care about us, then it's about time you started acting responsibly. You're a married woman now, not a dependent child.'

She stopped crying instantly and glared at him. 'Oh yes? And what about you? What about your loyalty to me? You care more about my mother than how I feel.'

'I care about being fair to people. I always have done. Surely you realise that? It's why I work in social welfare.'

'Well, you certainly don't work there for the money. Daddy says—'

'I know what *darling Daddy* says about my job and I don't want to hear it again.'

'Why are you being so m-mean to me?'

'*Mean?* What sort of word is that? It's a child's word.'
He bent to pick up the piece of paper she'd tossed at him
and scanned the address. 'You forgot the postcode.'

'I have to get to work.'

'You've time to find the postcode first. I'll write to
Sally in my lunch break.'

Rachel sat down at the computer, yelled out the
postcode, then switched it off and went to get ready.
'I'm going for a drink after work with my friends. I don't
know what time I'll be back.'

He watched her go, sadly. She was dressed as if she
was going out on the pull. She was the only one of her
group of friends who was married, and the others always
seemed to be looking for guys, though they never seemed
to keep the same one for more than a few weeks.

He'd asked her not to go drinking with them, but
she'd tossed her head at that. Then she'd agreed just to go
for a drink, not go on to the club.

During the few months before the wedding, he'd kept
telling himself it was wedding excitement which was
making her behave so childishly. Well, he'd been excited
about getting married, too. Once they were married,
he'd expected her to settle down but was now beginning
to worry that this wasn't going to happen. Even on the
honeymoon, he'd felt uneasy. She'd been utterly spoilt by
her father, of course, but still . . .

What if Rachel never grew up, never started to act
responsibly? They'd only been married for a short time
and yet already huge gaps were yawning between them.

And she always cast him as the villain. Nothing was ever her fault. There was no give and take from her, only take.

They were going for Sunday lunch with his parents this weekend. At least he'd get a decent meal then. And Rachel had better behave herself.

They'd have to have a serious talk about that tonight after she got back. Maybe his mother could write down a few easy recipes for them on Sunday. He'd email her tonight and suggest it.

Feeling more than a little worried, he left for work.

Molly went to hold the fort at the sales office on Friday afternoon, while Euan coped with the removal.

Avril came down at just after two. 'Oh, good, you're on your own. I've brought your wage slip.' She put an envelope on the table and sat down in the customers' chair. 'How are things going at Euan's?'

'Not so well. He's had to hire extra storage space and dump stuff there to be sorted out later.'

'He's like that: poor on planning the everyday details, good at big picture stuff. He rang me to beg me to let the men in and tell them where to put his things. Not that there will be many things, only his office furniture and personal effects. He's still tied up with clearing the house, apparently. Karen used to take care of that side of things. Rather as you did with your ex, I should think.'

Molly nodded, adding hastily, 'Euan doesn't seem like Craig in other ways, though. He's kind and thoughtful about people, doesn't use them.' She broke off suddenly, forced a laugh and added, 'Unless Euan's a brilliant actor.'

'He isn't. He cares very much about the people who work for him and especially about his sons. He hasn't made his money by trampling on other people or neglecting his family, I promise you. I'm glad he's got you to help him now, though, or I'd not be able to call my life my own.'

'You're very fond of him, aren't you?'

Avril smiled. 'Oh, yes. And I'm fond of his sons, too. But that doesn't mean I want to devote my whole life to looking after them all.' She changed the subject firmly. 'How do you like selling houses?'

'I enjoy selling these houses because they're lovely – well, the whole place is lovely. I don't think I'd like selling something boring, though. Craig used to say it didn't matter what you sold, it was just "product", but it matters to me.' She grimaced. 'What you do with your life should be important to you, don't you think? I loved being a housewife and mother when the children were small.'

'I never got the chance to do that. My fiancé was killed a couple of months before we were to marry. I never found anyone else to match him.'

'I'm sorry.'

'Oh, it's a long time ago now, and I've made a full life for myself, not to mention acting as unofficial aunt to the Santiago family.'

'What are Euan's sons like?'

'Charming. Now Jason's got the travel bug out of his system, I dare say he'll settle down and make a success of his life. I'm beginning to wonder if he's met someone important already, but you can't keep an eye on them when they're overseas. We'll have to wait and see. As for Grant, he's off somewhere travelling – Vietnam, I think at the moment – and that's worrying. But you have to let them experience life, don't you?'

'The only life my daughter's experienced has been clubbing and preparing for the wedding.' Molly could hear the bitterness in her voice and shut her mouth tightly against other words.

'She may settle down now she's married.'

'Perhaps.'

'You sound worried about her.'

'Yes. But I'm out of the loop now as far as Rachel's concerned, so I try not to dwell on it. Heaven help Jamie when he finds out she can't cook and hates housework. Unless she loves him enough to learn.' She wasn't sure Rachel cared about anyone except herself and her father. Her daughter had always seemed to treat Jamie like an accessory, rather than a life partner.

'And your son?'

'I don't know. Brian's more complex, more intelligent, too. He's had quite a few shocks lately. I threw him out and Craig wouldn't let him live with them. I don't know how he's coping.'

'Tough love sometimes works.'

'I hope so.'

Avril stood up. 'Here it comes!'

They both went to the door to see a modest removal truck bumping its way slowly down towards the leisure village.

Molly watched Avril wave to the driver and walk

briskly along to the detached house that stood on its own to one side.

Tonight, Molly would have a neighbour. She wondered if Euan would want to eat with her again. She had plenty of food. Or was that being pushy?

The phone rang and she hurried back into the office to answer it.

After that the phone rang so regularly that when it came to five o'clock, she was glad to shut up and go down to her caravan.

No sign of Euan yet, and she didn't know whether he needed more help or not. Surely he'd have called if he did?

Oh, she should stop thinking about him and get on with her own life.

But he stayed in her thoughts as if he belonged there.

When Jamie got home from work that evening, there was no sign of Rachel.

The phone light was blinking to show there was a message. It was his wife. Why hadn't she rung him on his mobile? In an airy voice, she said, 'Oh, hi, Jamie. Just to say I'm going clubbing with the girls, after all. See you later.'

He stared at the phone furiously. Women he worked with complained about their husbands spending a fortune going drinking with the lads on Friday nights. In his marriage, it was Rachel who did that, spending money on booze that they were supposed to be saving to buy a house – fifty pounds she'd spent last week – and then had come home by taxi and he'd had to pay twenty pounds for that.

He supposed she'd be slurring her words again when she got back and not remember most of the evening. She'd have a raging hangover tomorrow, too, and be grouchy.

They'd agreed last time that she was past that stage in life. Or he thought they'd agreed. It didn't seem to have got through to her.

As for tonight, he'd already checked the fridge, ready to start cooking a meal, because it was his turn, and found almost nothing to eat. She'd said she'd do the shopping if he cleaned the house, but she wasn't doing it. She didn't seem to have a clue, actually.

He'd better take her out to the supermarket and show her what basics she needed to buy. He'd start showing her how to cook, too. He was surprised her mother hadn't taught her more, because Molly was a superb cook. No, scrub that. Once Rachel dug her heels in, nothing would move her, certainly not a gentle person like Molly. He'd seen that with the wedding preparations.

A couple of times this week, Rachel hadn't bothered to plan a meal and they'd had to get takeaways, but he didn't want to live like that. He liked healthy food and salads, not greasy, heavily salted chicken and chips. It had never even occurred to him that Rachel would be totally useless as a cook or that she'd be such a slovenly housekeeper. She hadn't done any washing for days. Did she think clothes got clean by magic? There was a pile of her dirty clothes in a corner of the bedroom.

He gathered his own things together and put a wash

on. It took all of three minutes to do that. Not exactly hard work.

He wasn't old-fashioned about a woman's role and had expected to take his share of the housework. But he wasn't going to do it all, and he certainly wasn't going to pick up her dirty underwear. No way.

He went out to the local supermarket, buying food mainly, but also some toilet rolls, because they were nearly out of those.

After he got back, he fried a steak and cooked some low-fat chips in the oven, adding a nice, crunchy salad. He started to eat but felt so depressed, he pushed it away half-eaten. After staring at it for a few moments, he yanked the plate back and forced himself to finish it. He needed some decent food after this past week.

Brian checked his emails one final time, then got ready to go home from work.

'Coming out for a swift one?' someone called.

'Got something on today.' He didn't tell them he couldn't afford to go drinking. Only his boss knew about that.

He felt upset that his mother hadn't replied to his email. He didn't deserve a reply, he knew that now – but somehow, he'd still expected one. She surely didn't intend to take off and never associate with them again?

He'd hate that.

He stopped at the supermarket and checked out all the special offers. Two for the price of one on packets of carrots. He could chop them up and take them to work with his sandwiches.

At the end of the aisle, he bumped into the woman who'd helped him with the cleaning things. She was about to walk past, but he stopped her and said, 'I just want to thank you for helping me last Sunday.' He could see she didn't remember and he should have smiled and walked on, but she looked so healthy and nice, he added, 'With the cleaning materials and the cookery book.'

Recognition dawned. 'Did you try any of the recipes?'

He nodded. 'Three of them. And they were good, too. First time I've ever cooked. When I get on my feet again, I'm going to try more things. At the moment, it's whatever's cheapest.'

Which reminded him that he couldn't chat anyone up, because he couldn't afford to take her out. 'Anyway, I just wanted to thank you. You were a big help.'

'Lose your job, did you?'

'Not exactly. Got kicked out of home – and my mother was right to do it. I was acting like a spoilt brat. But it's going to take me a while to get myself sorted, and I had to put down a month's rent in advance, so I've not got much left to live on.'

She smiled. 'You sound like my brother. Mum kicked him out because he wouldn't even pick up after himself.' Her smile faded. 'We haven't heard from him since.'

'I'm sorry.'

She hesitated. 'Um . . . would you like a cup of coffee? I've just finished my shift. My shout. I've just won two hundred pounds on a scratch card and I've no one to celebrate with.'

He looked at her, wondering if she felt sorry for him, then

decided the reason for the invitation didn't matter. He'd like to get to know her better. 'I need to finish the shopping first.'

'I could help you, if you like. I know all the specials, since I work here, and I can probably give you a few hints about what to buy. Don't hesitate to tell me if I'm being pushy. My mother says I could organise for England.'

He smiled. 'Any help gratefully received. I've still got my L-plates on for this shopping stuff. I'm Brian, by the way, Brian Taylor.'

'I'm—'

'Carol Ryder,' he filled in. 'You were wearing a name tag last week and I remembered the name. I don't know any other Carols.'

She gave him what looked like a nod of approval. 'My friends call me Carrie, though. Right then, let's sort out some food for you.'

When they'd finished, he seemed to have more in his trolley than last week and yet had spent less. He'd definitely eat better, thanks to Carrie's help.

They loaded the bags into his car, then she led the way across the car park to a small café at the end of the row of shops. He'd never even noticed it before.

'This is my cousin's place,' she said. 'She's only had it a few months. She's a good cook if you're ever looking for a hearty meal.'

He decided to be utterly honest with her. 'I won't be able to eat out for a while.'

The coffee was wonderful, her cousin was another cheerful, healthy-looking woman, though not as pretty as Carrie.

When the café got busy, Carrie said, 'Just excuse me for a minute or two. Mel's getting swamped and needs a bit of help.' She went round clearing dirty cups and plates off tables and whisking them out to the back, so Brian followed suit.

In the rear, she said, 'Mel's kitchen hand didn't turn up tonight. I can't leave her like this.'

'Tell me what to do.'

'You don't have to work for your coffee.'

'I've nothing else to do. I don't mind.'

When Mel came rushing in and saw what they were doing, she hugged her cousin and then hugged Brian, too.

He'd never have considered clearing up a fun thing to do, but with Carrie and Mel cracking jokes and teasing him about how clueless he was, the time passed quickly.

Once the rush had died down, Mel came in and flopped on a chair. 'Phew! I don't know what I'd have done without you two. I'm going to have to find new help for Saturday nights and Sundays. I can't be doing with an unreliable guy.'

'You need a kitchen hand?' Brian asked. 'Just for those two shifts?'

'Yeah. I've got one for other times, but she can't work weekend shifts.'

'Look . . . I could do with some extra money. I might not be much use, though. Carrie can tell you how little I know about cooking and that sort of thing. But I'd promise to be reliable.'

Mel looked at him speculatively. 'The pay's not good. However, I can not only throw in a hot meal each night –

but you can take the unusable leftovers home with you.'

He beamed at her and stuck out his right hand. 'Done.'

'Can you continue working tonight?'

'Definitely.'

Carrie gave him another of those nods of approval. 'I'll leave you to it, then. I'll see you around.'

The café closed at ten, like most of the shops in the centre, which was a relief to Brian, whose feet were aching. But he went home with a stomach full of the leftovers of a cottage pie that he'd shared with Mel, and some other bits and pieces in takeaway containers, along with his shopping.

'It'd only be thrown away,' Mel said cheerfully. 'Nine o'clock tomorrow morning, OK? We get a lot of Sunday shoppers popping in for coffee and cakes.'

'I'll be there.'

He drove home feeling good about this. His father would throw a fit at him for taking on such a menial job but he rather thought his mother would approve.

At nine o'clock, Molly heard a car drive down from the hotel and stop nearby. She went to peer out of the window. It was Euan. As he got out, he stretched, easing his back as if it was aching.

Worry about him overcame prudence and she went to join him outside his house, only a minute's walk down the hill.

He turned to watch her come towards him, smiling and rotating his shoulders again.

'Is it done?'

'It is. Those packers were wonderful, and so was the cleaning team.' He turned to look at the house. 'Did my things arrive safely?'

'Yes. Avril saw them into the house. Um . . . Euan, have you had anything to eat?'

'No. And if you're offering to feed me again, yes, please. I'm taking shameful advantage of you, but I will make it up, I promise.'

'Come up to the caravan when you're ready, then.'

As she walked away, she heard him open the front door of his house and wished she could see inside, but it hadn't been opened for viewing yet. If this was his showpiece for the bigger, detached houses, it must be something special, because the others were beautifully built and finished.

He was up within ten minutes.

'Everything OK?' she asked.

'Perfect. Avril's even hung up my clothes. All I have to do is unpack my computer and set it up.' He sniffed. 'Something smells good.'

'It's just home-made stew. I'd have done something better, but I wasn't sure you'd want a meal, or when. You might have grabbed one on the way back.' She realised she was babbling nervously and stopped herself from saying anything except, 'Glass of wine or cup of coffee?'

'Wine, please. You're joining me, surely?'

She poured him a glass and went to take her own half-empty wine glass from the shelf. 'I was ahead of you.' She raised the glass. 'Here's to your new home.'

He clinked his against it. 'And to good friends who help out when you need them.'

It was great to feel useful again. She'd missed that dreadfully.

At eleven o'clock that evening someone knocked on the door of the flat and Jamie opened it to find two of Rachel's friends holding her up and laughing hysterically. Her head was lolling and she had no shoes on.

'Brought her home for you. She's absolutely legless.'

One of them giggled and added, 'We didn't let her go off with that guy, though. You owe us one for that.'

Shocked rigid, he took his wife from them. 'Where's her handbag?'

'Oh, nearly forgot.' One of them passed it to him. 'Sorry about the shoes. Couldn't find them.'

Rachel's eyes weren't focusing and she was mumbling something. He wasn't at all sure she'd even recognised him. 'Thanks.'

'Got to go. Taxi's waiting.'

He nudged the door shut with his hip and carried Rachel into the living area. It was the smell which alerted him to the fact that she'd thrown up all over herself. Grimly, he took her into the bathroom and stripped off her clothes, then his own. Although she squirmed and protested, he held her under the shower till she was, at least, clean, then wrapped her up in a bath towel.

'Sleepy,' she murmured and closed her eyes.

In case anything else went wrong, he put her in the

spare bed. He wasn't risking her vomiting over him during the night.

Then anger took over, such boiling fury that it was ages before he got to sleep. She'd been ready to go off with someone, had she? So drunk she didn't care, or was this something she'd done before? What price did she put on their marriage vows?

Handsome is as handsome does, his granny used to say. Well, Rachel might be good-looking, but her behaviour wasn't at all handsome. In fact, it sickened him.

Chapter Eleven

On Saturday morning, Molly woke up early, as usual. As she was sat enjoying her first cup of tea of the day, a figure in running gear trotted past her caravan. Euan. She smiled. She might have known he'd be into fitness and exercise. She enjoyed a brisk walk, but she wasn't into running.

The sales office wasn't open till ten, so she planned to go shopping first. Had Euan meant it about doing some housekeeping for him? She'd better find out exactly what he wanted.

He came back after half an hour, so she waited a few minutes, then walked down to his house.

He opened the door, looking rosy with damp hair, as if he'd just showered. 'Come in!'

'I only wanted to ask if you'd like me to do some grocery shopping for you when I do mine this morning.'

'I don't have any early appointments today. Let's do it

together. That'll be much more fun. When will you be ready?'

'Ten to eight? I don't think the local supermarket opens till eight.'

'Are you always up so early?'

'Yes. I wake up automatically soon after five. It used to drive Craig mad. He was a night owl, but dragged himself out of bed early a couple of times a week to go to the gym at work because the chairman is big on exercise.' And hadn't Craig been grumpy on those mornings!

'I love running and most sports. Do you play golf?'

'Heavens, no. I'm useless at ball games.'

'Once this village is up and running, I intend to play quite often.' He looked longingly towards the nearest green, where three men were watching intently as another made a careful shot from near the hole.

'Good luck to you. Um . . . before we set off, do you have any food in the house? We don't want to buy something if you have it already.'

'I've only got a few bits and pieces. Look, come in and I'll show you, then if you can take over keeping the basic supplies available here; it can be part of your job.'

She stopped in the hall to stare round. 'This house is very different from the row houses.'

'Yes. The detached places are quite a bit more upmarket. We'll do a proper tour another time, because you may have to show this one to people. See – formal lounge/dining, great room, utility room and home office downstairs. Two bedrooms on the middle floor, each with en suite, two more rooms on the third floor with a shared bathroom. What do you think?'

'I love the way the living areas are spacious and I'd love to go all over the house, but if we're to do the shopping in time, we need to get a move on.'

She studied his single shelf of supplies in the walk-in pantry in surprise, then peeped into the near-empty fridge. 'Is that all the food you brought with you?'

"Fraid so. I've been neglecting the home front lately, eating out most of the time.' He winked at her. 'My nearest neighbour here has been particularly kind about feeding me.'

'I haven't exactly laid on feasts. A few sandwiches and a bowl of stew are nothing. I can always cater for a friend.'

'Yes, you would be able to.' His smile was particularly warm as he said that. 'See you in ten minutes.'

Shopping with Euan was fun. She saw other women eyeing him, then looking enviously at her. She wished . . . *Oh, stop it, you fool! Just go with the flow.*

By ten o'clock, they were back and opening up the sales office.

At eleven, Euan's first appointment turned up; a man he knew already and clearly got on well with. He took him down to look round the houses.

Molly enjoyed the quietness. Well, it was mainly quiet. She could hear the men working on the new row of houses. A glance out of the window showed that they were making excellent progress. It wouldn't be long before they were finished. Two men were carrying fridges and cookers into the end two houses now, and the outside timbers were getting their second coat of paint.

At twelve o'clock, the noise stopped and soon afterwards, two vehicles drove past.

Euan came back and immersed himself in work on his computer. He looked up to say, 'Take a break and surf the Net or read a book. There's nothing you can be doing here till someone turns up.'

'Are you sure? It feels like . . . cheating.'

Another of those warm smiles. 'You'd never cheat, Molly.'

She was surprised when he suggested she go to lunch. She hadn't realised it was one o'clock already.

As she ate some cheese and crunchy vegetables with hummus in the caravan, she decided to pick up her emails. It had been days since she'd bothered, but she didn't get many these days so it probably didn't matter.

When she found a message from her son, her breath caught in her throat and she had to take a few deep breaths before she could pluck up the courage to open it.

For Brian, master of the terse word, it was a long email. What it said brought tears to her eyes.

She nearly answered straight away, but something held her back, told her not to rush into this. She wanted to think carefully about her answer, about whether she'd tell Brian where she was. And she wasn't sure she believed he was sorting himself out. He'd lived to drink and party, as had her daughter.

What worried her most was that he might tell his father where she was. She'd found the courage to do a lot of new things, but wasn't sure she'd ever find the courage to face up to her ex.

When she went back to the office, Euan took one look at her and said bluntly, 'What's upset you?'

She blinked, horrified to find more tears filling her eyes, and before she knew it, he'd come round the desk and put his arms round her.

'What's happened? Tell me.'

'My son's emailed. It's the first time I've heard from him since I threw him out.'

'If he's been saying something to upset you . . .'

'He hasn't. He's worried about me, wants to know where I am. And . . . he says he's sorry and is sorting himself out.'

'And that's upset you?'

'Mmm. Only . . . how do I know he means it? If he does, it's what I'd hoped for. If he doesn't, if he's pretending because he wants something from me – well, I don't know what I'll do. I don't think I can cope with any more . . . disappointments.'

'You're not sure about him? Not sure he's telling the truth?'

'Not sure at all. All three of them could always fool me easily. I was the original soft touch. And they were always so scornful towards me.'

He rocked her in his arms. 'Oh, my little love, you didn't deserve that.'

She gasped at what he'd said. 'What did you call me?'

'My little love,' he repeated, following this up by a gentle kiss on her lips. 'It's happened very quickly, but I seem to have fallen in love with you.' He brushed a strand of damp hair off her forehead. 'But you're not certain whether to believe me, or whether you dare trust me, so I'll give you time. How could your own family have done this to you?'

'How could I have let them?'

'There is that. Would you let them again?'

'No. Definitely not. But it took a lot to strengthen my backbone, so I'm not proud of myself.'

'Onwards and upwards. Now, about your son. Do you know where he's living now?'

'No. I only have his email address and his mobile phone number.'

'Why don't you give him a ring, then?'

But she shook her head. 'Not till I'm in better control of myself. I've been too weak in the past. I'm not hurrying to smooth things over.' She realised she was still in his arms and oh, she didn't want to move away.

He smiled and dropped another of those sudden kisses on the tip of her nose. 'I like hugging you. I like kissing you, too, and we need to talk about ourselves, but this is neither the time nor the place for it because, unfortunately, someone's just driven up and parked.'

'I didn't even hear the car.' She stepped hastily back. 'Thanks for the . . . the comfort.'

'My pleasure. Oh, and would you please come out with me tomorrow night? I'd say tonight, but I've a long time arrangement to see some old friends. Next time I go to see them, I'll take you with me.'

She couldn't pretend. 'I'd love to go out with you tomorrow night.'

'And wear something pretty. I know a great restaurant.'

She looked at him doubtfully.

It took him a minute to work out what the problem was. 'I'll come over and help you decide what to wear. I'm good at clothes. It'll be fun being your dresser.'

Stuart helped his mother plan the funeral, which left her tearful, so he didn't pursue the question of what she was going to do afterwards, saying only that he'd be over the following day for a chat about the future.

Since they were both early birds, he was at her house by eight o'clock. She looked tired and strained, as if she'd not slept well, and her eyes were reddened. His heart clenched with love and he swept her into his arms. 'You need a hug.'

She clung to him for a moment or two, then pushed away and gave him a watery smile. 'You were right. I did need that. Want a cup of something as we talk?'

'I've just finished a mug of tea, thanks.'

She led the way into the sitting room. 'I can still manage my life perfectly well, you know. I'm not a child nor am I in my dotage.'

'I know you can manage, but I don't like the thought of you being here on your own.'

'Well, that's how it is. I'm not moving anywhere and I'm *not* going into one of those retirement places. This is my home and I want to stay here till . . . the end.'

'I knew you wouldn't want to move, so I think it's about time I told you my news, though I'd be grateful if you'd keep it to yourself for the time being. Don't even tell the rest of the family. I'm going to be part of a big new company dealing with electronic security in an age of terrorism. It's international and though I'll be based in England, I'll be doing a lot of travelling all over the world.'

'Sounds exciting; just up your street.'

'It is. But Wendy's sick of travelling and following me around. Her wire sculptures are getting very popular – well, I love them myself. They take your eyes into so many soothing curves. I've held her career up for long enough, so we're going to buy a house and settle down properly, a house big enough for a decent workshop for her. In fact, the one we both want to buy is Molly's house. We love living here. Do you think she'd sell it to us?'

'I think she'd be glad to. She'd have sold it by now if it hadn't been for those louts harassing her. I do hope you've sorted them out.'

'The first round went to me. I think they'll be back, though, once her ex finds out I'm buying the house. He'll want to put me off the neighbourhood, as he did the other buyers. Maybe we can get round that by buying and selling secretly.' He waited. 'What do you think, Ma? Would you like me for a permanent neighbour?'

'I can't think of anything nicer. You and Wendy both.'

'Good. I'll email Molly once the funeral is over and ask if I can go down to Wiltshire to talk about the house. Now, do you need any help with the guest list?'

'It won't be a long one. Most of our friends have died or are too infirm to come. Old age is cruel. It steals your life from you one piece at a time. I'll rough out a list then check with you two. I rang your brother and he's flying here from Australia for the funeral. I wish he'd managed to get back for a visit before . . . it happened.'

'Yes, so do I.'

'What about your daughters, Stuart?'

'I'm sure they'll come down from the north for it. Wendy rang them last night.'

He left her and started back towards his house, then turned back, intending to tap on the kitchen window and tell her something he'd forgotten.

But she was sobbing bitterly at the kitchen table, head on her arms. He hesitated, tears coming into his own eyes at the sight of his mother weeping. But he moved quietly away, leaving her to her grief.

Some things you needed to do in private. And no one could weep for you.

Saturday morning dawned sunny and bright. Jamie woke early, in spite of a restless night. Something had woken him. What was it? He raised his head and heard the sound of Rachel dry-retching in the bathroom. Throwing off the covers, he dragged on his dressing gown and went to stand in the doorway.

She turned to look at him, eyes soft as a puppy's; pretty even now and looking as if butter wouldn't melt in her mouth. 'Oh, Jamie, I feel terrible.'

'It's your own fault.'

She groaned and rubbed her temples. 'Don't shout at me.'

'I wasn't shouting. Do you remember coming home last night?'

'No. Was I very noisy?'

'On the contrary, you were nearly unconscious and you'd thrown up over yourself.'

'Ugh. I hope you put my clothes to soak.'

Somehow, this was the final straw. 'No, I didn't. I'm damned if I'm going to clear up your messes.'

She didn't seem to hear. In a little girl voice, she pleaded, 'Best of darlings, would you *please* get me some coffee and four paracetamols? I've got *such* a headache.'

'Get them yourself. I'm going out.' He began to fling his clothes on, hearing her shuffle into the kitchen, groaning as she opened a cupboard.

When he started to unlock the front door, she called out in sharper voice, 'Jamie? Where are you going?'

'*Out!*' he yelled at the top of his voice, then slammed the door after himself.

He heard the door open again and she called, 'Don't go. Jamie!' But he didn't dare stay at home today to watch her nurse a hangover. In his current mood, it'd be all too easy to say something he might regret.

Might regret . . . or might not.

If he said what was on his mind at the moment, if it did come to that, he intended to say it after long and careful thought, not in the heat of anger.

And if a tear or two escaped as he strode along the street, because what he was thinking was agonising, there was no one looking at him on a blustery morning and the tears soon evaporated. People were too busy fighting against the wind and getting on with their grocery shopping to gape at passers-by.

He'd made a mess of his life. A bad one. No wonder his parents had never warmed to Rachel. They'd never said anything against her, that wasn't their way, but they had suggested he wait to get married and try living with her first. Only, her damned father had scotched that.

What would his family say if he—? He bit that thought off. He wasn't sure of anything at the moment.

He decided to go to one of the big London museums for the day, the V & A. Rachel didn't like museums, didn't have the slightest interest in history of any sort, even fashion history. He'd missed his cultural outings lately. He'd missed a lot of things, blinded by her beauty and the great sex they'd shared.

But the shadow looming over his life was so huge it prevented him from enjoying even his favourite museum. In the end he went to sit quietly by the Thames, watching some little children playing under their parents' fond gaze, trying not to think about his problems.

Failing, of course, because he could see only one course of action possible.

He went home as the day started to fade, not knowing how to face Rachel. But he found a note from her saying Tasha wasn't well and Daddy needed a partner for a function, so she'd gone out with him. She'd be back late, but not drunk, underlined heavily.

Did he care?

Not much.

Sunday was another working day. Molly didn't see Euan till he opened up the sales office, and as they weren't busy during the morning, he went back to his house to catch up on paperwork. He always seemed to have paperwork waiting.

'Don't forget, Molly! Give me a ring if you get busy.'

'Yes, I will.'

She felt at a loose end when he'd gone. She'd already tidied the office and sorted out the cupboards. She'd have to bring a book with her for the quiet times. In the end she faced the problem of drafting a reply to her son.

If he really had started acting responsibly, it'd be wonderful.

Dear Brian,

I was glad to hear from you and to learn that you're sorting out your life.

I'm well and you've no need to worry about me. I have a job, somewhere to live and I'm making new friends.

She was interrupted by some people coming to look round the houses and by the time they'd gone, she'd decided to give Brian her new mobile phone number. After all, no one could trace her from that, could they? And it'd be lovely to speak to her son again.

She checked that no one else had driven into the car park and went back to the computer.

I'll give you my phone number, but please don't use it during the daytime, unless you want to text me, as I'll be at work. And above all, don't give the number to your father. I don't want any further contact with him. Craig's behaved despicably.

Have you seen Rachel? How's she settling into married life? If you're in contact, give her my best wishes, but don't tell her the new phone number, either. She'd definitely pass it on to your father.

Love,
Mum

Only after she'd sent it did she realise that most of what she'd said had concerned Craig. She was still afraid of meeting him, still afraid of what he'd do.

How did you make yourself be brave when you'd been a pushover all your life? She worried about that.

That left her with nothing to do but think about Euan and worry about what she was going to wear tonight.

Had he meant it when he said he loved her? Did she dare love him?

No, she was going to be honest with herself, at least. She loved him already. It had seemed as natural as breathing to tumble in love with him.

But she wasn't sure she trusted that things would work out, that she wouldn't become dependent on him and lose the small start she'd made at independence.

Life wasn't easy at the best of times, but new love was even more complicated – at least, she found it so.

Did other divorced women worry about making the same mistake again?

Brian decided he could afford half an hour at an Internet café to investigate his collection of toys and see what they were worth.

Before he did that, he checked his emails and found one from his mother. It'd only just been sent and it sounded as if she was speaking to him.

He was so relieved to hear she was all right and had a job. What sort of job was it? He hoped it wasn't too menial, only she hadn't worked for so long, she had no experience, so it probably was. Still, you couldn't despise anything that brought in money, as he was proving. The café job was going to make all the difference to his finances.

He frowned. Why did his mother need to work? Surely she'd had a settlement from his dad? He'd heard his father ranting on about men being financially gutted by their ex-wives.

He still felt ashamed of how he'd mooched off his mother.

He was wasting his Internet time thinking. He needed to have a look for some of those boxed toys.

Five minutes later he sat back, shocked rigid at how much his toys might fetch – though of course you couldn't be certain of auction prices and you had to pay commission. He'd need to do more research, find an auction house that specialised in rare toy auctions.

What a bit of luck he'd kept those two boxes of toys!

He'd done it for sentimental reasons, but if it paid off his bank card debt, to hell with sentimentality! Even if he got top money for the toys, he'd still keep the job at the café. He actually enjoyed it there. Mel kept him hopping around, but she worked far harder than he did, and he admired her initiative. And the food was to die for, good solid food, not that airy-fairy stuff Tasha produced. It might look pretty, but it left you hungry an hour later.

Besides, working at the café was a good way of keeping in touch with Carrie, at least he hoped it was. She wasn't all over him like some girls, but she'd invited him out for coffee, hadn't she? And she'd been fun to work with when they were helping Mel.

He'd never met girls like those two, what with the private boys' school he'd been sent to and his father trying to steer him towards the 'right' sort of girl. Then there had been the debacle with Tasha's daughter, which still made him wince to think of it. Talk about a clone of her mother. *Not* his sort of girl, Geneva.

What was his sort of girl? He wasn't at all sure. But he wanted to spend time with Carrie, get to know her. He'd just take it easy and see if it led anywhere.

Or he would once he'd sold his toys and cleared his debts.

After his half hour at the computer was up, he went home, if you could call that hovel home. He decided to ring his mother. It was Sunday, after all. That'd be out of working hours and wouldn't cost him a lot.

He did want to speak to her.

* * *

Molly's mobile rang during another lull.

Euan called across, 'Go on. Answer it.'

'Not in working hours.'

'I hereby give permission – in triplicate, if necessary.'

Smiling, she caught the call on the last ring before it went to voicemail.

'Mum?'

'Brian? Oh, how lovely to hear from you!'

'I read your email, and I wanted to ring. I won't give this number to anyone, I promise. Thanks for trusting me. I don't deserve it.'

She didn't know what to say and there was silence from his end as well.

'I wanted to speak to you and now I can't think what to say.'

'I'm the same.'

'Tell me about your job.'

'I'm an amanuensis.'

'A what?'

'General factotum. Part PA, part sales. Whatever needs doing.' She saw Euan grinning at her from across the room and pulled a face at him.

'You didn't waste time getting a job, did you?'

'No.'

'Good for you. Oh, I thought you'd like to know. I read in the paper that Mr Benton had died.'

'I knew he was terminally ill. I hope he didn't suffer too much. Poor Jane. I must write to her.'

'I'm sure they'd want you to go to the funeral.'

'I can't risk it. I'm sure she'll understand. But I will ring her up.' She glanced outside as two cars drew up. 'Look, I have to go now. I'm at work and someone's turned up. I'll phone you one evening. Take care.'

'Yeah. You too.'

She sighed happily, then turned to face the door, ready to help someone else.

Chapter Twelve

Since she'd had a very late night, Rachel cried off from
having Sunday lunch with Jamie's parents, and she was
looking so heavy-eyed, he didn't try to persuade her to
go. She might not have got drunk, but she was obviously
hungover.

'You'll be happier on your own with them.' She took a
long drink of the coffee he'd brought her to bed.

'As you were happier on your own with your father.'

'Exactly.' She finished the coffee, then sighed and
wriggled down under the covers. 'No one knows how to
make a girl feel special like Daddy.'

She had no idea how rude this was to her husband,
Jamie thought. It was a pity she couldn't have married
her father! They were a matched pair. He got ready and
went out.

But it was difficult at his parents' because they guessed
at once that something was wrong.

'Want to talk about it, son?' his father asked quietly as his mother was serving up the roast dinner.

'Not yet, no. It's . . . difficult.'

'We're always here, you know. If you ever need help, come to us first.'

After that they talked about soccer and his mother's reading club, safe subjects.

When he left, he couldn't face going home, so went along to the pub. But his half pint went down slowly and he sat in a quiet corner, not making eye contact with anyone.

Could he actually do it? Was he making a hasty decision?

When Euan came to pick up Molly, she was still uncertain about what to wear to go out. She'd tried on the few smart clothes she'd brought with her and they didn't seem quite right. By now Craig would be criticising her harshly and she was dreading what Euan might say.

She gestured to herself. 'Is this the sort of thing you want me to wear?'

'I don't care what you wear as long as you're comfortable, though maybe you need a sparkly scarf to brighten up that top.'

She squinted at herself in the narrow mirror, then went to open the drawer. 'This one, do you think?'

'No, this one.' He flung it round her neck, using it to capture her and kiss her. 'It brings out the blue in the skirt, and it makes your eyes look bluer.'

A huge sigh of relief escaped her. 'That's sorted, then. Thank goodness.'

'Were you that worried? About clothes?'

She shrugged. 'Craig used to say I had no dress sense whatsoever. He got furious at me sometimes.'

'And since when has lack of dress sense been a crime?'

'He made it seem like one.'

'He really destroyed your confidence, didn't he?'

She nodded. She'd got so het up trying to choose what to wear that she was still on edge.

'Come and give me another kiss, then we'll get on our way.'

The kiss made her feel much better, so she put her arms round his neck and stayed there, cheek to cheek for a minute or two.

'I hate to break this up, but we have a booking and I'm really hungry.'

'Where are we going?'

'To a restaurant in what used to be a pub. I know the owner – Brett's wife worked for me a few years ago – and the food's great.'

The food was indeed wonderful and after the main course had been cleared away, she found herself enjoying a conversation with Brett about exactly how the dishes had been prepared. Then she told him about a cheesecake recipe she'd made up, using mascarpone instead of cream, for a friend who was lactose intolerant but could eat cheese.

'You sound as if you really know your stuff about cooking,' Euan said when Brett left them to enjoy the desserts.

'I love cooking. I used to cook for big dinner parties. It

was fun choosing a menu. You must let me cook a proper meal for you one day – but not in the caravan.'

'More hidden talents, my little treasure. I'd love you to cook for me.'

By the time they got back, they were both pleasantly tired.

'Do you want to come in?' she asked, but was caught out by a yawn.

'Not tonight. We're both weary. It's been an eventful week, hasn't it? Did you realise today was the anniversary of when we first met? A whole week we've known one another now.'

'Is that all? It feels as if I've known you for ever.'

'Me too. Now go to bed, Molly, my love, and remember you have the morning off tomorrow.'

She lay for a few moments, reliving the evening, then felt herself slipping happily towards sleep.

Molly, my love, he'd called her. *Molly, my love.*

She was beginning to believe he meant it.

After he'd put the phone down, Brian realised he still hadn't apologised to his mother, not properly, anyway. In fact, they hadn't talked about anything except trivia. But it'd been comforting just to hear her voice. She sounded happier, he couldn't figure out why he thought that, until he realised she hadn't been breathless and hesitant.

He did hope she really was happier.

He looked at the clock. What was he going to do? He didn't have the money to spend on booze or going out, and anyway, these activities had lost their attraction. He smiled. Maybe he was growing up. And maybe it wasn't as bad as he'd thought it would be.

If he sold his toys, if they really were worth so much, he might be able to afford a TV and a computer connection as well as paying off his debts. That'd make a big difference to his life. On that thought, he went to get out the boxes, spreading their contents all over the floor, for lack of a table, then making up a detailed list.

Next thing to do would be to research special toy auctions and see if there were any coming up in the near future. The sooner the better.

But he wouldn't try to sell everything at once. He wanted to check out the people doing the selling, try them out on two or three items. See how close his research had brought him to actual prices obtained.

His phone rang. He picked it up and checked who it was. His father. He didn't feel like speaking to him tonight, so let it go to voicemail.

It suddenly occurred to him that he should write a condolence note to Mrs Benton. A note would be cheaper than a card. And perhaps he should tell Rachel that Mr Benton had died.

He picked up his phone. 'Rach? I thought you should know that Mr Benton's died. You know, the old guy next door. You might want to send a note of condolence to Mrs Benton.'

'Why should I do that? I don't live there any more.'

'You lived next door to them for years, and she was kind to us when we were kids.'

'Yes, well, I've got troubles of my own and Mrs Benton won't care whether I write or not.' She started sobbing.

'What's wrong?'

'You wouldn't understand. You men are all alike.' She ended the call.

He put the phone away. Sounded as if she'd been quarrelling with Jamie. He didn't intend to get involved in that. Rach would go her own sweet way whatever he said.

He got out a piece of computer paper, folded it in half and wrote a brief note of condolence to Mrs Benton. He'd put it in the post tomorrow.

Then, because there was nothing else to do, he went to bed with a library book. First, he had to pull the air mattress across the room so that it was under the central light.

A good thing he still had a sense of humour. His friends would crack up laughing if they could see him now.

His smile was a little wobbly and soon faded. He concentrated on the book. He'd done enough thinking for today.

Rachel put the phone down and went to look out of the window. But there was no sign of Jamie. How long could a Sunday lunch take?

He must be upset at her going out and was staying away to punish her. Well, they'd agreed to keep up with their old friends, hadn't they? And she'd got back safely, so why this fuss?

She'd been careful not to drink too much when

she went out with her father. He didn't approve of drunkenness. But even a moderate amount seemed to have reawakened her hangover. It'd been the worst she'd ever had. She'd definitely be a bit more careful what she drank in future.

She'd spent rather a lot, too, having to dip into the housekeeping money. That'd be what had upset Jamie so much, but she'd show him she'd learnt her lesson, which would sort things out, surely.

She wished he'd come home. It was boring without him. She went to look in the fridge but didn't feel like fussing with food, so ate a banana, then fell asleep in front of the television.

It was nearly six o'clock before she heard footsteps on the stairs and a key in the front door. She turned eagerly to greet him. It'd be all right now. She'd take him to bed and show him how much she loved him.

Jamie didn't smile at her, didn't even come across to hug her, so she went across to hug him. He stiffened and moved her to arm's length, before walking past her into the bedroom.

'I'm sorry I got trashed the other night. I'll not drink as much next time I go out with my friends.'

He spun round, scowling. 'You still intend to go clubbing?'

'We said we'd each keep up with our friends. And you don't like dancing.'

'I also don't like my wife going out dancing with other men.'

'Oh, that. It means nothing. I was dancing with the girls half the time.'

'You probably don't remember, but one of your friends told me they'd had to stop you going off with some guy or other.'

She stared at him in shock. 'I didn't!'

'Only because they stopped you, apparently.'

'They were just joking. I wouldn't.'

'Somehow I don't think it was a joke. They were too drunk to do anything but tell the truth. *In vino veritas.*'

She watched resentfully as he hung up his outdoor things and shut the wardrobe door. Mr Perfect he was, always keeping things tidy.

When he went back into the living room, he picked up a book and began to read it.

How dare he ignore her? She twitched the book out of his hand. 'Don't read. Talk to me. I've been on my own all day, well, except for a phone call from Brian.'

He picked up his book from where she'd tossed it on the floor and straightened the pages, then put it carefully on the arm of his chair, keeping one hand on it. 'What did your brother want?'

'To tell me that Mr Benton had died, the old man next door to Mum's. Brian wanted me to write Mrs Benton a letter of condolence. As if.'

She'd dismissed that idea so casually, Jamie frowned at her. 'Can you not spare the time even to write a letter or send a card?'

'What's it to do with me? I don't live there any more.

Mum will write and—oh no, she's not living there now, either, so she might not know.' Her face brightened. 'But Brian said he'd write, so that's OK.'

It was the final straw, that casual dismissal of the death of an old man who'd been charming and whose wife of many years would no doubt be dreadfully upset. Jamie stood up, knowing he couldn't take any more. Just . . . couldn't.

It seemed wrong to say something like this sitting down.

He took a deep breath. This wasn't going to be easy. 'We made a mistake, Rachel.'

'What?'

'Getting married was a mistake. I don't want to spend my life with you. We don't have enough in common. I'm sorry, really sorry. I've been thinking about it for a while and I won't change my mind. I'll move out and leave this flat for you.'

She'd been staring at him in growing horror as his words sank in, but now she suddenly clutched his arm. 'You can't mean that. If it's about the clubbing, I won't go again. Jamie, tell me you don't mean that. Tell me you're just trying to frighten me into doing what you want. And I will. I promise I will.'

He had to unclench her fingers to get her hand off him, she was clutching him so tightly. 'I'm not trying to make you do anything, Rach. I'm trying to tell you that except for making love, you and I have nothing in common. Absolutely nothing. What's more, I don't like living with you. You're a slob. This place is filthy.'

He'd expected her to scream at him, but she didn't. She stood and stared in complete silence, her beautiful eyes huge; her whole face tragic.

The trouble was, he'd learnt that the expressions on her face meant very little. She got that tragic look if she spilt her favourite perfume or burnt a piece of toast and couldn't get it out of the toaster.

'I'll go and pack my things, get it over with.' He remembered suddenly the tales of women cutting up their husband's clothes because they were leaving, and changed his mind about taking only minimal stuff. He'd take everything in one fell swoop. His parents would let him stay with them temporarily, he was sure.

It took him nearly three hours to pack, and he had to fight her off to keep her from pulling his stuff out of the case again. It was a good thing he'd bought some new bin liners, because he filled them too.

She kept flinging herself between him and his packing, begging him to give her another chance.

He spoke to her gently each time. 'It won't work, Rach.'

'But we're *married*. And we've only been married for two months. You're not giving it a chance.'

'I think all the fuss about the wedding hid how incompatible we were before. We were so busy we never stopped to talk about anything else. Our marriage won't work. Not ever. We're too different, in every way that counts.'

'But we're so good in bed.'

'That's not what marriage is about, well, not the only thing.'

'What will people say?'

'I don't care what people say.'

She hurled his shaver across the room then turned to look for something else to throw.

'If you damage any more of my things, I'm calling the police.'

She lay down across the bedroom doorway.

He continued packing, then stepped across her, only she caught hold of his leg and tripped him up. He cracked his head on the corner of a table and for a minute could only lie there, stunned.

'I've killed him! Jamie, speak to me. Jamie! I'm sorry. Sorry, sorry, sorry.'

He got to his feet. 'I'm all right.' He caught sight of himself in the mirror. 'I'm going to have a black eye tomorrow, though.'

Someone knocked on the door. 'Mr Thomas! Are you all right?' He hesitated, then went to answer it and found the lady from the next flat looking up at him.

'You've hurt yourself.'

'Go away, you stupid bitch!' Rachel yelled. 'He's leaving me and I don't need you poking your nose into it.'

Their neighbour glanced from Rachel back to Jamie.

'I tripped,' he said.

'Or you were pushed,' she said. 'The walls are quite thin. I'm afraid I could hear a lot of what was going on.'

He shrugged, then turned as there was the sound of

something else smashing in the bedroom. He ran across to see Rachel standing triumphantly over the ruins of his computer.

He wanted to weep that it should descend to this, but he forced himself to think. 'Mrs Upperton, could you please come and witness this?'

'My pleasure.'

That reminded him that Rachel had upset their neighbour a few times now with loud music and been totally unrepentant. 'And if you could bear to stay while I take the rest of my things on to the landing?'

'Put them in my flat till you can call a cab.'

'Thank you.'

It was an hour before he was clear, and he took the ruins of his computer with him in case any data could be salvaged from the hard disk.

He didn't ring his parents, couldn't talk about this on the phone.

When he knocked on their door, his father answered, already in pyjamas and a dressing gown.

'I've left Rachel. Can I come here temporarily?'

'Of course, son. Need a hand with your stuff?'

'No. The driver and I can manage. Where shall I put them?'

'Your old bedroom is still empty. Why not go back there?'

He saw his mother standing in the doorway of the living room. 'I'm all right,' he assured her. 'I could do with something to eat, though, if you don't mind?'

She nodded and walked off to the kitchen.

When he'd got his things into his old room, Jamie went downstairs.

'You don't have to tell us the details, if you'd rather not,' his mother said. 'And you can stay as long as you like.'

Everything twisted round in his head then, and he found himself sobbing against her like a stupid child.

Chapter Thirteen

Craig went to work early on the Monday. Tasha was in a picky mood, and was letting him know it, so he decided it'd be a good day to go off to the gym. He grinned as he sat down at his desk afterwards. She certainly knew how to go straight for what she wanted. But she was good value as a wife, and he preferred her sharpness any day to Molly's slackness and poor appearance.

He had a good day and as usual time flew past. Most of the accounts he managed were flourishing and salesmen from his area were bringing in more orders than any other group in the company. They might grumble at the way he kept a close eye on them and directed what they did, but he always told them to look at the commissions they were earning and decide what they wanted out of life: money or a touchy-feely boss.

As he was crossing the hall to the executive coffee-making area, a woman came down the corridor from her husband's office. Sour-faced old bitch, he thought as he smiled brightly at her. 'Hi, Ginny. You're looking well today.'

She stopped and smiled back, pretending to be glad to see him, but he knew better.

'So are you, Craig. But then, you always do. Heard from Molly lately?'

'No. Should I have?'

'I thought you might have done now she's settled somewhere. We ran into her this weekend.'

He'd been going to move on, but swung round. 'Where?' Damn, he'd given himself away. She was smiling like a cat tormenting a mouse.

'Wouldn't you like to know?'

'Ginny, don't play games with me. The whole family is anxious about her because she's not the sort to cope well on her own. And she is still the mother of my children, even if we're no longer married.'

She pretended to consider, then shrugged. 'Well, for your children's sake, then. Molly's selling houses in Wiltshire – or more likely *not* selling them. One can't imagine her working successfully in sales, can one?'

'Wiltshire? Whereabouts exactly?'

When they'd finished their chat, Craig moved on, trying to work out what to do about his damned ex. He'd thought he was driving her gradually to the point of selling to him and now, it seemed, she'd not only rented the house to Stuart Benton, who wouldn't be easy to frighten off, but she was making a living – though he agreed with Ginny for once: a more unlikely saleswoman than Molly would be hard to imagine.

He didn't like to think of her living comfortably, not needing to sell the house. The stupid bitch didn't *deserve* a place like that, and if she wasn't going to live in Lavengro Road, why was she being so obstinate about selling it to him? He could raise his price a little, but he wasn't flush at the moment, because of the wedding, and he couldn't go much higher. Who'd have thought a one-day event would cost so much? But he only had one daughter, and even if she'd chosen a no-hoper, he'd wanted to see her off in style.

Well, Benton might have driven the lads away with his paint gun, but the game wasn't over yet. There were many ways to kill a cat. Benton's mother was living next door, and she would make a much more vulnerable target. It'd have to be planned carefully, though. As Tasha said, he didn't want to risk his job or his good name.

Whistling cheerfully, he began to plan a little outing for the following weekend. This was something he would enjoy doing.

Rachel didn't surface until eleven o'clock on the Monday morning. She thought for a minute or two it was Sunday, then suddenly everything came rushing back to her and she began to sob. Her head ached and her eyes were swollen. She couldn't possibly go to work.

It was nearly lunchtime when she plucked up the courage to ring her father. He might be angry, no, he *would* be angry, but he'd not let her down.

'Daddy, I—?' She started to cry again.

'Rachel? What's the matter, princess?'

'It's Jamie. He's left me.'

Dead silence at the other end, then, 'I'll just check my diary.'

She heard him muttering and prayed he'd have some time free.

'Sorry, princess, but I can't come over till after work. Killer day, here. I'll ring Tasha and see if she's free.'

'I don't want Tasha, I want you. I *need* you.'

'No can do, baby. Hang in there. I'll see you as soon after six as I can make it.'

She heard him put the phone down, and it was a while before she realised what the buzzing tone meant and put her own phone down.

She got up and stumbled into the bathroom, then went to make herself a cup of coffee. Almost as an afterthought, she made herself a piece of toast and spread it thickly with strawberry jam, suddenly ravenous. Three more slices and she felt a bit better.

Not knowing what to do, she wandered across to sit on the sofa. Noticing something on the floor, with just a corner showing, she picked it up. Some stupid fantasy novel. She hurled it across the room, but that wasn't enough, so she went to pick it up and began tearing out the pages.

'Try reading that!' she panted. 'You and your stupid books.'

She looked around for other stuff to take her feelings out on, but could find nothing of his left. Nothing, except for a few fragments from his computer cover.

She began to sob again as she swept them up.

It seemed a long day and in the end she fell asleep on the sofa.

Molly spent the morning catching up on her washing and cleaning the caravan, which didn't take long, so she sat and read a romance novel for a while, wishing she had the heroine's courage to go straight for what she wanted.

When she saw Euan open the sales office just after lunch, she strolled up, looking forward to work. It was so pleasant living here. Her life had really taken a turn for the better. Even the caravan now seemed like home.

He smiled at her and pulled her into his arms for a kiss, murmuring against her ear. 'Mmm. Nice.'

It was far more than nice. It made her whole body feel alive. She clung on to him, letting her breath out in a long, shuddering sigh, then nestling against him, loving the softness of his sweater against her cheeks, the extra kiss he dropped on her forehead.

'What did you do this morning, Molly, my love?'

'Mundane things. Cleaning, washing.' Who wanted to talk about that? If an imaginary heroine could take the initiative, so could she. 'Kiss me again, Euan.'

All thought was suspended till he moved away. She stretched her hand out, not wanting to stop touching him.

He took her hand but didn't move closer. 'We'd better not get too steamy. This place is rather public. Phew! It's been a long time since I felt like this.'

'It's been a long time for me, too,' she admitted. 'And yet, it seems so right.'

'Would you like to move into the house with me?'

Her breath caught in her throat but she couldn't quite take that leap. 'Isn't it a bit soon for that? We haven't even . . . you know, slept together.'

'I don't think it's too soon at all. I'm quite sure of my feelings. I knew within two days of meeting Karen that I loved her, and it's been the same with you. I'm so lucky to have met you. But if *you* need more time, I'll not push you. I'm sure you'll be well worth the wait.'

He raised her hand to his lips, kissing it to emphasise what he was saying, and she had trouble putting two words together, let alone think clearly. 'I'll . . . think about it. I . . . hadn't expected to meet someone – and especially not so quickly.'

'Quickly? You've been divorced for over a year, and must have been estranged for quite a while before that.'

'But I only started getting my act together a couple of months ago.' After the wedding, that dreadful wedding, which had been replaying in her nightmares ever since. 'Before that I let people – my family – walk all over me.'

'Shame on them!'

But she'd thought about it a lot since the wedding, knew she couldn't just blame others, had to take some of the blame herself. 'Shame on me too. I should have stood up for myself.'

'You're doing it now. I can't help hoping you won't make me wait too long to start sharing our lives, though.'

He sighed and indicated a pile of papers on the desk. 'These are messages from this morning when the phone was switched through to Avril. Aha!' He passed one to her. 'Looks like you've earned your first sales commission. The Sarcens have told Avril they definitely want to buy.'

Molly glanced down at it and happiness bubbled up inside her, not because of the extra money but because it showed she really could hold her own in the world. 'I never thought I'd make a sale, I just supposed I'd . . . you know, hold the fort when you were out.'

'You've got a good manner, and you don't push people too hard. It's how I work myself. Dealing with customers honestly.'

'I couldn't do it any other way.'

'I know. I must get you a company mobile so that you can start taking messages from your clients after hours – if you don't mind doing it, that is?'

'The Sarcens are coming in this afternoon to complete the paperwork. Could you go through it with me before then? Or better still, you could deal with the final stages?'

He gave her a wry smile. 'I'll go through it with you after I've finished checking these messages, but you're perfectly capable of finalising the sale and the Sarcens trust you.'

He turned back to the papers, so she dusted the displays and tidied them up, trying not to smile too broadly.

His phone rang and he picked it up. When he put it down, he stood up. 'I've got to go and see Dan. We need to sort out a few details before we start another row of houses.'

'When will the second row be ready?'

'In about a month, perhaps less. There's all the painting and finishing to do, but Dan has the teams lined up.'

When he came back, Euan went through the paperwork with her, and there seemed nothing difficult about it. Why had she been so afraid? It was no more complicated than the family accounts and household business she'd dealt with for years.

After that he went down to work in his own house and, since there was nothing else to do, Molly braced herself to phone her old neighbour on her mobile. 'I heard about Denis. I'm so sorry, Jane.'

'Thank you. We knew it was coming and at least this way he didn't suffer the final indignities.'

'It must be hard on you.'

'It was always going to be hard to be the survivor. We've been together such a lovely long time. Look . . . I don't know whether you can get back for the funeral.'

'I hope you'll forgive me if I don't. I'd rather not run the risk of bumping into Craig. I know it's cowardly, but I'm still learning to stand up for myself.' And was still frightened of meeting him.

'I'm not inviting *him* to the funeral, but I perfectly understand how you feel.' Jane sighed, and after a short silence said more briskly, 'So. Tell me about yourself. How are things going?'

When Molly put the phone down, she thought how brave Jane was being. She wished she were half as brave.

Someone cleared their throat and she nearly jumped out of her skin.

'Sorry, honey. Didn't mean to startle you.'

She turned to see an older woman with beautifully styled silver hair, wearing a skirt and top in a lovely dull rose colour that shrieked *expensive*. 'I'm so sorry. I didn't see you come in. I was just speaking to an old friend whose husband has died.'

The woman's face softened. 'No wonder you looked sad.'

'How may I help you?'

'I'd like to look round the houses. Do you have a brochure, floor plans? Are any of the houses ready to occupy? To tell you the truth, I'm in urgent need of a home in England because if I have to live with my daughter-in-law for more than a few more days, I'll strangle her. I'm Cindy Pavrovic, by the way. I'm American, but I reckon you'll have figured that out the minute I opened my mouth.'

Molly couldn't help laughing. 'Yes. I'm Molly Peel, one of the sales team, and I'd be happy to show you round.' Pulling out her home-made sign, she set it up on the desk and led the way down to the houses.

Cindy held up one hand just as Molly would have started talking about them. 'Let's just take a quick look at them first time through and then I won't waste your time if I'm not interested.'

'Sounds like a good plan to me.'

They went through the houses, with Cindy pausing now and then to study a room, or the outlook from a window. Then they stood outside at the back in the sunshine, looking down on the small lake just below the first row of dwellings. Molly waited for the other woman to speak.

'They're the best houses I've seen,' Cindy said thoughtfully, 'but houses in England are kind of small for what I want. I was thinking of something a little bigger and maybe more luxurious. At my age, I don't stint on my comforts.'

'Are you needing a holiday home?'

'I suppose you could call it that, though I'd hope to spend quite a bit of time here. I want somewhere close to my youngest son and grandchildren, who live in England. Now that my husband's dead, I'd like to see quite a bit more of them.'

Molly thought rapidly. 'Could you give me a moment? We do have another home, but I'm not sure if it's available for inspection today.'

'You go find out. I'll look over the biggest house again.'

Molly walked over to Euan's house and rang the doorbell. When she explained about Cindy, he ran one hand through his hair, frowned, then said, 'Show her round, but apologise for the state of the office and tell her I'll have to go on working for a few more minutes or I'll lose the thread.'

'All right.'

Cindy again wanted to look round in silence, so Molly explained that Euan was working, and as he didn't even look up when they stood in the doorway, she didn't introduce them.

Afterwards they came down to the great room and Cindy studied it carefully, then went round every room on the ground floor again, taking her time. 'This is the kind of place I want. Has someone already bought it? If not, I'd like to make an offer.'

Euan came down the stairs to join them as she said

this. 'Sorry I didn't speak to you before. I was at a crucial stage in a very important document. I'm the developer, Euan Santiago.'

They shook hands and Molly couldn't miss the open admiration on Cindy's face. She forgot how attractive Euan was when she was with him, because he was just . . . Euan. But the way other women looked at him kept reminding her that he was rich and very good-looking. She still couldn't understand why such a man would fix his sights on her.

Cindy came straight to the point. 'Is this house for sale, Euan?'

'I hadn't planned to sell it yet. I've been living in it for convenience and using it to show people what we can do that's a bit more upmarket.'

'Then let me put it to you straight: I'll pay any reasonable asking price if I can get into this house within a few days.'

He stared at her, then chewed the corner of his lip thoughtfully. 'OK. I think we might be able to do that, but the price will have to take into account the considerable inconvenience to me. Can you give me until tomorrow to sort out the details?'

She grimaced and shook her head. 'Could we say an hour? I'm desperate, Euan. If I don't find something here, I'll murder my daughter-in-law, so if this isn't available, I'll need to continue looking today. How about I go buy a coffee at that cute little hotel up the hill while you check out your options?'

She turned to Molly. 'Thank you for your help, honey, and

for not filling my ears with facts when I wanted to look and feel the atmosphere. You've got yourself a good saleswoman here, Mr Santiago.' She strolled up towards the hotel, turning a couple of times to look back at the development.

Molly watched her go in amazement. 'Whew! Talk about straight to the point. But I liked her. Are you really going to sell?'

'Yes. That's what we build them for, after all.'

'I'll move out of the caravan then, and let you move in. I'm sure I can find myself a flat nearby.'

'Hmm. Let me lock up this place, then we can go and have a coffee in the sales office while we discuss details. We'll hope no one else turns up for a while.'

When they got there, he went straight to the coffee machine and poured them each a mugful.

'I should be doing that.'

He grinned as he handed her one. 'You think this is below the boss's dignity?'

'My ex would never have done it for an employee.'

'We're already agreed that he's a prime numero uno rat. Next time you speak to him, watch his whiskers twitch. They're a dead giveaway.'

She choked with laughter on her first mouthful.

Euan went to sit at his desk, his smile fading. 'I hate to lose a sale like that, a cash customer. But I don't want to throw you out of the caravan.'

Silence, then she surprised herself. 'Why don't we share it, then?'

The words seemed to echo around her and he looked startled.

'After all, *you* asked me to live with you yesterday.'
She waited, wishing he would say something.

'Yes, but you didn't exactly leap at the idea.'

'I had to get used to it . . . and get used to . . . caring about you.'

His face lit up with happiness and he tugged her up to twirl her joyously around the sales office. 'And are you used to it now?'

'You're growing on me,' she teased.

He let go of her hand. 'I accept your offer, then. I'm looking forward to it, and not just because of sharing a bed. I want to share a life again.'

He spoke so openly and warmly, he disarmed her every time, and she felt as if the dark shadow Craig had cast over her life was getting fainter every day.

'Now, I have to work out how much to charge her. She's not getting it cheaply because it's going to cause me considerable inconvenience – not so much because of moving out, thanks to you, but because of losing a special show home. I wonder if she'll want to buy the furnishings as well? I hope so. Bring your chair over here and we'll work on pricing it together.'

Only after he'd gone striding up to the hotel to find Cindy did the doubts about her offer to live with him begin to creep back into Molly's mind. Well, not exactly doubts. She did love him, how could she not? He was so easy to be with and so altogether gorgeous. But was it the right sort of love? Would it last? Wouldn't a man like him want a prettier and younger wife one day?

Only . . . he spoke so warmly of his dead wife that he

must have had a successful marriage. Unlike her. Perhaps she wasn't the sort to keep a man happy. Perhaps he too would grow tired of her, as Craig had.

Oh, don't be silly! she told herself. Love doesn't come with guarantees. And Craig's no angel. You put everything you had into that marriage. And he took it.

Could she bear to risk doing that again?

Could she bear not to?

Euan brought Cindy back down to the office to sign some papers and promised to have her in the house by Friday. He turned to Molly as he said that. 'All right with you?'

Cindy looked from one to the other. 'Hey, you're an item! I can see it now.' She beamed at them. 'I think you'll be good for one another. I can usually tell.'

He was unfazed. 'I hope so.'

Molly could feel herself flushing.

Cindy nodded at her wisely. 'It's recent. You're not used to it yet. Don't hang about, honey, grab him while you can. He's a keeper! Now, about the furniture . . .' She switched seamlessly into business mode.

When they'd finished, she turned to Molly. 'I'd be grateful if you could show me around the neighbourhood, the shops – I'm not used to grocery shopping in England, but I like to cook. You two must come over for a meal once I'm settled.'

Euan didn't hesitate. 'We'd be delighted.'

'I think it'd be best if I introduced you to Avril,' Molly said. 'I'm a newcomer to the area too and I'm only just finding my way round. She's been here for ages.' She explained who Avril was.

'Let's go visit with her,' Cindy said at once.

Molly had met enough Americans to understand this meant chat to her. She looked at Euan. 'All right if I go now?'

He waved one hand.

'How long have you lived here?' Cindy asked as the two women walked up to the hotel.

'Just over a week.'

'Did you know Euan before?'

'No.'

'And you're already in love? That must be a strong attraction.'

Somehow Molly didn't mind the other woman's questions, because Cindy was so warm and friendly, you couldn't suspect her of ulterior motives. 'Yes, but I'm still a bit . . . surprised by it all.'

'My advice still holds. Grab him while you can.'

'I'm not used to diving into things head first.'

'You Brits are too uptight. Go get him, girl!'

Molly led the way past reception to the office suite. 'Here we are, Avril, this is Cindy, who's going to buy a house, and . . .'

She could see that the two older women had taken to one another, so left Cindy with Avril and returned to the sales office.

Euan flapped one hand at her by way of greeting, but he was immersed in something on the computer, so she sat at her desk and stared out at the beautiful rolling

Wiltshire scenery. She'd never lived so close to nature and watched in delight as a hare hopped across a patch of open land, and a parliament of rooks gathered to peck at the grass on the slope below the golf course. Such a delightful word for the flock of large black birds.

Euan pushed his chair back. 'Done! Are you still comfortable about me moving in? I can always get a room at the hotel, after all.'

'I meant it.'

'Good. I mean it, too.'

A car drew up and he swore under his breath. 'Maybe when we're living together we'll manage to finish a conversation. Can you handle these people? I have some appointments up at the hotel. I've been neglecting my other business interests. I definitely needed your help full-time.'

She turned to greet the newcomers, smiling as she realised she felt quite confident about dealing with them. She was definitely moving on. In so many ways.

Chapter Fourteen

It took Rachel a few moments to realise someone was ringing the doorbell. It couldn't be Jamie, who had a key, and she didn't want to see anyone else, so she ignored it.

It rang again and kept on ringing, so she got to her feet and went to check who it was through the peephole. What she saw made her fling the door open. 'Daddy! Oh, Daddy!'

He gave her a hug, then held her at arm's length, shaking his head at the sight of her face, before leading her back into the living area. 'Tell me exactly what happened.'

She faltered through the tale, trying to minimise the nightclub incident, but he homed in on it and forced the truth out of her.

'Not a good idea, princess. You're married now, not single. I'd not let my wife go out clubbing without me, especially if she was as pretty as you.'

'But Jamie doesn't like dancing. He just wants to sit and read or watch TV. He's working such long hours he's always tired at night.'

'Busy at work or needing the overtime?'

'Both. I sometimes think he cares more about his stupid clients than he does about me.' She looked at her father hopefully. 'Can *you* go and see him? Persuade him to come back. Tell him I'll do anything and—'

He held up one hand. 'Not a good bargaining position. And you were stupid to smash his computer. I never thought you stupid, princess. How many times have I told you it never pays to let go of your temper?'

'But you will go and see him?'

He looked at his watch. 'I'll go straight away.'

'Can I come and stay at your place for a bit, just till Jamie comes back? It's horrible here on my own.'

'Sorry, princess. Geneva's been a bit difficult lately and Tasha's found her a flat. Tash wants us to live on our own from now on. We never have, you know.'

'But I'm desperate, Daddy. I've never managed on my own before.'

He looked round. 'You have a decent enough place to live, Rach, though I don't know how you can live in such a pigsty. If you find it a bit difficult paying the rent, I'll help out. We don't have to make any final decisions about anything yet, do we? Let me go and see Jamie.'

She watched him drive away, then flung herself down in front of the TV, but started crying again. The box of tissues was empty, so she went to look for another one and found only two empty boxes. She'd bought some last week, surely? Or was it the week before? How did people keep track of all the stupid details of shopping? She went to get a toilet roll and used sheets of that to mop her eyes.

But the tears kept on coming.

Life sucked! Everything sucked. She couldn't wait for Jamie to come back. Having him to organise her life was worth never going clubbing again.

Craig pulled up outside Jamie's parents' house, relieved when he saw the car. He'd guessed right about where his son-in-law would go.

Mr Thomas senior opened the door. 'Ah.'

When Jamie's father didn't immediately invite him in, Craig said, 'I'd like to speak to your son, if that's all right?'

'I suppose you'd better come in. Go easy on him. He's still very upset.'

'So is Rachel. I'm sure we can sort this out.'

Mr Thomas turned round to call, 'Craig Taylor's here to see you, Jamie. I'll show him into the front room.'

Craig waited in the room, which was so old-fashioned in décor and so cluttered with ornaments, it made his lip curl. When the door opened, he turned round and was surprised at how much older Jamie looked, and haggard, as if he hadn't slept well. 'How are you?'

'All right. I suppose Rachel sent you.'

'Yes. Can we sit down?'

Jamie waited till he'd sat, then took a chair on the opposite side of the table. 'I shan't change my mind,

Craig. Rachel and I should never have married. We have nothing in common except sex.'

'That's a bit of a sweeping statement.'

'It's the simple truth. What's more, your daughter is the biggest slob I've ever met. Her mother must have run round all day picking up after her. I'm not prepared to wait hand and foot on Rachel, or anyone else, nor see my hard-earned money thrown away on cocktails and clubbing.'

That was the clue. 'It's the clubbing that sticks in your gullet, isn't it? Look, she's learnt her lesson there. Give her another chance. She won't do it again. And her mother may have spoilt her a little, but—'

'*Spoilt her a little?* That's the understatement of the year. Have you ever lived on your own with your daughter?'

'Well . . . no.'

'Try it. She expects dirty clothes to wash themselves, can't cook, doesn't bother to shop and thinks money falls from heaven to get takeaways or eat out every night.'

Craig tried to think how to give this a bit of a spin, but couldn't. 'It's not as bad as that, surely?' was the best he could manage.

'Yes, it is. Last week she bought a packet of new knickers rather than wash the dozens of dirty pairs that were lying piled up in the corner of the bedroom.'

'She can learn to do the housekeeping better. If you two are in love, you can work through this and—'

'In lust, more like. She threw my computer on the floor when I tried to pack, and hurled my shaver across the room. I've had to buy new ones.' He looked very steadily at Craig. 'I'm not going back to her, not ever, not for anything under the sun.'

'And if she's pregnant?'

'Good try. But she's not. She just had a period and we haven't made love since.' Jamie stood up. 'I think that's all we need to say, Craig. My lawyer will be in touch. I'll make sure he contacts you as well, so that you can help her deal with it all. No doubt Rachel will be living with you from now on. She's incapable of living on her own, that's for sure.'

Craig prided himself on knowing when he'd lost an account, and this bore all the classic signs. He went out to his car, thinking hard, and it was a few moments before he started it up.

No way would Tasha allow Rachel to live with them. And even if he did insist, there would be one row after the other, so it wouldn't be worth it.

Anyway, he'd seen the flat, seen the state his daughter was in, and Jamie was right: she was a slob. That was Molly's fault. Could his ex do nothing right?

But what was he going to do about Rachel? He was fond of her, proud of how she looked. He'd have to give it some thought.

She wept all over him, of course, when he told her, but he stuck to his point. The marriage was over. She had to move on. And she had to learn to look after herself, too.

Euan got back at seven-thirty. Molly felt her heart start beating faster when she saw his car pull up outside the caravan. She was apprehensive about spending the night with him, even though it was something she wanted very much. She went to unlock the door and wait for him.

He got out of the car and stretched.

'Did you drive to London?'

'Yes. It's easier to take a car when you're going here and there on the outskirts.' He stopped to smile at her. 'Do I have to say a magic password?'

She realised she was blocking the entrance and moved inside. 'I'm a bit nervous.'

'Ah, Molly, am I so fearsome?'

'No. But I don't want to disappoint you. I've only ever been with Craig, you see, and—'

'Molly, you're intelligent, fun, attractive, kind. Be proud of what you are.'

'I wasn't fishing for compliments.'

'I wasn't giving empty praise.' He looked round. 'It's cosy, isn't it? I've always felt good here.'

'I love it, too. Do you want something to eat?'

'Not till I've kissed you.'

He held out one hand and she took it, letting him pull her gently into his arms, raising her face for his kiss. This was more urgent than the others and she found herself responding, wanting more and forgetting to be shy or nervous, just losing herself in the loving.

Between caresses, they set up the double bed and when they lay down on it together, she felt so at home in his arms, she forgot to be nervous.

Afterwards she sighed with pleasure as they cuddled

closely. When he would have switched on the light, however, she protested. 'I've not got a young woman's body and I never was a sylph.'

'Who would ever want a scrawny woman when they can have you, Molly Peel? Soft and feminine, so easy to rouse.' But he didn't switch the light on, just pulled her close again.

They woke a couple of hours later, laughing at themselves for falling asleep, and he admitted he was hungry for food now.

She put on her nightdress, her best one, a silky affair, but had to put an apron over it.

'Now that is a very elegant look!' he teased as he put on pyjama bottoms. He couldn't find the top half, so settled for a scruffy old T-shirt.

Together they made omelette and salad, eating it with crusty bread, and then, since he was still hungry, slathering apricot jam on the remaining bread.

'We're like that scene in the old *Tom Jones* movie.' She licked her fingers slowly.

He chuckled and pulled her hand towards him, licking off a smear of jam and making her gasp.

'We're good in bed together,' he said as he pushed his plate away.

'Yes. It was great. I was so worried. I'm stupid, aren't I?'

'No. You're normal. Taking a relationship into intimacy is a very important step. I think we both passed with flying colours, don't you?' He yawned and then laughed. 'It may not be romantic but I'm exhausted,

Molly, and I'd like nothing better than to sleep.'

'I'm tired too.' She fell asleep in his arms, woke in the middle of the night with a start, realised who she was with and smiled in the darkness, snuggling down again.

It felt wonderful not to be alone, even more wonderful that it was Euan lying beside her.

Tuesday was overcast, with rain threatening. It seemed a very suitable day for the funeral of his father, Stuart thought.

The service was short, then he and Wendy stood by his mother's side at the crematorium as the curtains rolled silently round the coffin before his father slid away from them for ever.

His mother had her head bowed. She'd wept steadily throughout the service, unable to contain her grief. He watched her anxiously, wondering how she'd cope with the gathering of mourners afterwards.

But by the time they arrived at the pub, where he'd managed to book a private room, she was more composed. She laid one hand on his arm as she saw him looking at her anxiously. 'I'll be all right, darling. It's a relief to have that part over. Getting through it was hard. Why do we inflict this public ritual on ourselves?'

She greeted the mourners, accepted condolences gracefully and sipped a glass of wine. If she ate very little, he wasn't going to urge her to take more. He wasn't feeling particularly hungry himself.

Afterwards, the family went back to his house in a taxi and his mother said, 'Would you mind if I went straight home, darling? I'm exhausted.'

'Will you be all right? Do you want somebody to stay with you?'

'I'd rather be on my own. I've got the buzzer and security pendant if I need help. That's going to be such a comfort.'

'I'll walk you back, then.'

At the door he gave her a hug and she looked up at him anxiously. 'You need to weep as well, you know, Stuart.'

'Not my style, Ma.'

'It's human nature. But have it your own way. Grief will catch you out sooner or later. It always does, even after you think you've moved on.' She stretched up to kiss his cheek. 'Thank you for all your help, darling.'

As he went back home, he decided to email Molly this very evening about buying her house. It'd be something positive to do.

Brian got a phone call from his sobbing sister and was startled to hear that Jamie had left her. He couldn't believe the marriage had disintegrated so quickly.

'Look, I'll come round to see you after work tonight. No, I can't take the day off! You can tell me all about it – unless you've made it up by then.'

More sobbing, from which he gathered that even their father hadn't been able to persuade Jamie to come back to her.

'I have to go to work now but I'll be round at about six.'

She was still sobbing when he hung up.

He was dreading the visit all day. OK, she was his

sister and blood was thicker than water, but they'd never been close and he'd always resented the way their father had favoured her.

When Rachel opened the door of the flat, he was shocked at how dreadful she looked.

She turned and trailed inside, leaving him to close the door.

He was even more shocked when he saw the state of the place. He turned to Rachel, who was sitting on the sofa snivelling into her handkerchief. It never did any good to be kind to her when she got into a state like this, so he said sharply, 'Stop crying this minute!'

She hiccupped to a halt, staring at him resentfully.

'I'm not sitting down in this mess. Come on. We're going to clear the place up.'

'My life is ruined and you talk about tidying the flat!'

He yanked her to her feet. 'This place is a health hazard and I'm not going out for takeaway until it's safe to bring food back.'

He chivvied her into helping him tidy up and she trailed to and fro, following his orders, but not thinking of anything for herself. They had to take two big bags of rubbish out to the bins, and when he saw the pile of dirty washing, he gave her another blast and forced her to put the washing machine on, under his tuition.

'What's so hard about pressing a few buttons to get the wash cycle going?' he demanded. 'I don't even have a washing machine of my own. I have to use the one belonging to the block of flats. My place is a near slum, but my room is in a better state than yours.'

'Why are you living there, then?'

He lost patience totally. 'Because it's all I can afford, you fool!'

'If you're going to shout at me, you can go away again.'

'I'm your brother. I'm not going away. And I will shout at you if you act stupid. Grow up! You can't expect everyone else to look after you.'

Honesty made him add, 'Look, Rach, I was going down the same path myself, so I do understand how hard it is. But when Mum chucked me out, I had to face a few unpleasant truths. I'm working two jobs now to pay off my credit cards.'

'Two jobs?'

'Yes. I thought I'd told you: I'm working as a kitchen hand in the evening at the weekends. And *do not* give me that scornful look. It's fun, even if it is rough on the hands, and I get a pile of leftover food as well as my wages.' He didn't tell her about the toys. Well, there was nothing to tell yet. 'Now, get your jacket. We're going out for some food.'

'I can't go out looking like this!'

'I'll give you ten minutes to tidy yourself up. Don't tell me you can't hide most of that, because you're good with make-up.'

He was still having to order her around, though. How did you persuade someone to think and act for themselves? Maybe it was too late. Maybe she'd literally been spoilt rotten. He didn't like to think of that, though. She was his sister, after all.

Rachel insisted on turning her back to the other

diners, so they sat in a corner of an Indian restaurant. At first she toyed with her food then started to eat ravenously.

'You've not asked about Mum,' he said as they waited for their gulab jamun, his favourite dessert.

'After what she did at my wedding—'

'She had concussion.'

'Oh, don't you start.'

'She really did have concussion, Rach,' he said quietly. 'I'm not lying to you. And even if she hadn't had the accident, you and Dad treated her shamefully and I let you. I still feel guilty about that.' He saw that mulish look on her face. 'Rachel, if you don't believe me about Mum's accident, I'm leaving now and never coming back to see you.'

'But Dad said—'

'He'd say anything to paint things his way, you know he would. Where is he now? Is *he* looking after you, inviting you to stay with him? No, he isn't. I bet he's blaming not being able to have you on Tasha, too.'

She was silent, then, 'Mum really did have concussion?'

'Yes. I swear she did. Quite badly too, because they kept her in hospital overnight.'

'Oh.' More silence as she used her fork to rearrange the grains of rice left on her plate. 'Is she . . . all right now?'

'Yes. She's got a job and—' He remembered in time not to tell her the details.

'Mum's got a job? What as? A housekeeper?'

'Is that the only way you see her?'

'Well – yes. She's always stayed home, hasn't she? That's all she knows about.'

'Rotten sort of life she led, too, picking up after you and me, waiting on Dad hand and foot. Then he dumped her for a more up-to-date model.'

'You never used to take Mum's side.'

'I've had time to think. I can't afford a television yet and you can only read so much, then you start thinking.' And feeling ashamed of yourself.

When they came out of the café, he dragged Rachel into a late-night mini-mart and made her buy some fresh food, then walked her back to the flat.

'Don't go,' she said as she led the way inside. 'Stay here tonight. I don't like being alone. I've got some wine.'

'You've had enough wine. And I have to go to work tomorrow, which means getting a good night's sleep and ironing my shirt.' He moved to the door, then turned and said firmly, 'I should think pride alone would make you start to get your act together. Or do you consider yourself so useless at the age of twenty-three that you can't even manage a little washing and cooking? Do you really need looking after like a helpless baby?'

She scowled at him. 'I hate housework.'

'Don't we all?' A thought occurred to him. 'Have you been to work since Jamie left?'

'No. My life's fallen apart. I can't cope with working.'

'How are you going to live, then?'

'Daddy said he'd help.'

'He might for a week or two, then what?'

She shrugged.

He suddenly lost patience. 'You're a waste of space, Rach.'

She sagged against the door frame, clutching his arm. 'You will come back to see me, won't you?'

'I'll come to see you at the weekend early in the morning, before I go to the café. But I'm only staying to chat if this place is clean and tidy, and you're back at work.'

He heard her start sobbing again as he walked away, but hardened his heart. Life was a matter of sink or swim. And once you grew up, you had to learn to swim on your own.

He'd try to help Rach, but he wasn't going to do everything for her. He was having enough trouble managing his own affairs.

On Wednesday morning, Molly found an email from Stuart Benton waiting for her.

> *Hope things are going well. If you still want to sell your house, I'd love to come and discuss it with you.*
> *Stuart*

She read it through again. Sell the house! He must want to live near his mother now that Jane was on her own. She emailed back straight away to say she'd be happy to see him any time and gave him directions, but warned him that she was working most of the weekend.

When she went up to the sales office, Euan was waiting to go out to a series of meetings in London.

'You look pleased about something, Molly.'

'I think I've just found a buyer for my house.'

'That's good news.'

'Yes. But at the same time it's so final. I grew up in that house, and we moved back there after my parents died.'

'And when it goes, you'll be rootless.'

She nodded. Euan seemed to understand such things without her having to spell every detail out for him.

'You don't have to sell.'

'I do. The old Molly lived there. The new one isn't going back.'

'But it still hurts?'

When she nodded, he came across to give her a hug.

'Is it still all right for me to move the rest of my things in this evening? I'll not be back till nearly eight because I have to go up to London again.'

'Of course it is, you fool. I'll have something ready for you to eat.'

'Just something simple. I'll be having a big lunch, if I know my friend Alistair.'

'I could go across and move the food from the kitchen to the caravan, if you like.'

'Is there no end to the ways you support me? You don't have to.'

She looked at him very seriously. 'I think I was born to be a general factotum.'

He frowned. 'Not the best term to describe you

these days. I think "executive assistant" suits what you do better, because you go way beyond what an average employee would be able to handle.'

She tried it out. 'Executive assistant. Sounds good. You're on.'

'I have to get going now or I'll be late.'

She was left on her own, so phoned Avril to arrange cover for the lunch break, then sat thinking about her old house. She'd been ready to sell once and Craig had put paid to that. Would he do something to prevent Stuart buying? She'd better warn Stuart. But surely a man like him would be capable of handling Craig?

The next evening Brian rang up and after checking she was all right, said abruptly, 'I thought you ought to know, Mum. Jamie and Rachel have split up.'

'*What?*' Molly couldn't even think for a moment, it was such a shock.

'Yeah, surprised me, too, after all the fuss she made about the wedding. *He* left her, says she's a slob. And she is. I went round to see her and the place was toxic.'

'What does your father say about that?'

'Dad spoke to Rachel, then went round to see Jamie, but said there was no moving him. He rang to ask me to keep an eye on my sister, but he'd no need to. I'd already gone round to see her. She is in a big mess. If I ever think of getting married, I'll definitely live with the girl first to make sure we're compatible.'

She'd never heard him mention marriage before, except as a joke. 'Are you thinking of getting married?'

'No. But I've met a rather nice girl and she's agreed to come out with me, so I'm thinking of going steady. I won't be able to wine and dine her in style, though.'

'What does that matter?'

He laughed. 'It doesn't to her, and as for me, I'm quite a reformed character these days, Mum.'

'I know. I'm really proud of you.'

When she put the phone down, she was smiling.

Euan came back a little earlier than she'd expected and she had to tell him about her son's phone call.

'He's got two jobs now to pay off his debts. I can't imagine Brian working as a kitchen hand.'

'Good for him. What was the bad news?'

'You read me so easily. Rachel and Jamie have split up.'

'After only two months? That's quick.'

'Mmm. I'm not going to ring her, though. It's up to her to contact me. She didn't even give me a chance to explain at the wedding.' Her voice wobbled on the last phrase but she blinked away the tears.

His phone rang just then, his eldest son. Euan was on the line with him for fifteen minutes, smiling and nodding. She couldn't help overhearing and envied him that ease of communication.

When he put the phone down, he said thoughtfully, 'I need to tell the boys I'm with you. I think it'll be better to do that by email. I'm sure they'll be all right about it once they've met you. We've talked about the possibility of me finding someone else, and they're all right with the idea in theory, but they were fond of their mother, so it's best to tread gently.'

'I like the way you all loved her so much. I hope someone remembers me as kindly.'

He gave her hand a quick squeeze. 'They will.'

'I need to tell Brian about us as well. I was too shocked by the news about Rachel to do it today. And you're right, email will be better, so that I can think carefully about exactly what I want to say.'

'It's complicated, isn't it, going into a second relationship?'

'Is this a relationship?'

He didn't hesitate. 'It's the beginning of one and I hope it goes further.'

'Living with you isn't complicated, Euan. I'm surprised at how easy you are to be with, even in such cramped conditions.' She didn't say the obvious, that Craig had never been easy. She was trying not to mention him at all.

'If we can manage to rub along together in our present circumstances, I reckon we can manage anywhere.'

His eyes held a promise, but he didn't speak that promise aloud, and she didn't want him to – yet.

A little later, she sighed and said, 'I can't help worrying about Rachel. I don't know whether she'll be able to cope on her own. But if I pick up the pieces yet again, she'll never learn, will she? I used to threaten all sorts of things, but in the end I gave in and cleared her room up every now and then, because it was a health hazard. And she refused point-blank to learn to cook. You should have seen the messes she brought home from school. She spoilt them deliberately. Her father laughed but I hated the waste.'

After a minute or two she said, 'Let's talk about something cheerful now.'

'I second that. How about a glass of wine?'

'Excellent idea.'

Chapter Fifteen

On Thursday night, Jane woke suddenly. She lay for a moment or two, wondering what had disturbed her, then heard footsteps on the gravel outside and sat up abruptly, her heart pounding.

The security light hadn't come on, but whoever it was couldn't have got so close without waking her. She slept very lightly these days.

She was shocked when a voice yelled, 'Stupid old bitch!' and a rock was hurled through the window. Stuart had been nagging her to have double glazing fitted, saying it was safer as well as warmer, but she preferred the old glass, with its imperfections that turned some parts of her garden into wavery images. Besides, she liked the look of old-fashioned sash windows and she didn't want to live in a hothouse during winter.

Sitting upright in bed, with her heart pounding and fragments of glass everywhere, she reached automatically for the alarm buzzer and pressed it. There was the sound of another window smashing elsewhere in the house and she whimpered, afraid to stir from her bed. What if they got inside before Stuart arrived? What if they attacked her? Hooligans did attack old people for no reason.

More lights went on outside, the very bright spotlights next door, and she groaned in relief.

The voices yelled out, 'Go and live somewhere else or we'll make you sorry, you old hag!' Then she heard them running off down the street.

When there was the sound of a key turning in the front door, her heart seemed to skip in her chest. Stuart. It must be. But she couldn't move or speak, just couldn't move a muscle, because fear had gripped her so tightly.

Stuart saw two male figures running down the street, but his first concern was for his mother. He unlocked the front door and yelled, 'Mum? Are you all right?'

There was no answer. Terrified, he slammed the door shut so that it locked and ran up to the bedroom, not even putting the light on till he got to the top of the stairs. 'Mum? Ah, thank goodness! There you are.'

She didn't speak or move, and he'd never seen anyone look so terrified. But when he took her in his arms, she shuddered and collapsed against him.

He stroked her hair, upset at how fragile she felt. 'It's all right, Mum. I'm here. It's all right.'

But it wasn't all right. She huddled against him, shaking and clutching his hand, tears running down her cheeks, still not speaking.

Holding his mother close, he rang Wendy and asked her to come across. 'I saw them run away so it should be safe now. I'll watch out of the window as you come across. I can be with you in thirty seconds flat if you need me. No, Mum's not hurt physically, but she's in shock. We need to call the police and maybe the doctor, too.'

Wendy was there within a couple of minutes and took over with her usual brisk efficiency, leaving him free to go and investigate. He was furious with himself for not putting a better security system round his mother's house, but all the previous trouble had targeted the house he was living in and he couldn't understand why anyone would target his mother. He could only hope his own CCTV cameras had caught the intruders, though they'd probably been wearing hoods or masks.

The police arrived quickly and the officers were concerned that such an old lady had been attacked and terrified like that. They asked to see the CCTV footage and he promised to get the recording for them once it was safe to leave his mother.

By that time she was recovering a little, thank goodness. She refused to have the doctor called out, but her hands still shook as she raised the mug of hot, sweet tea Wendy had made to her lips.

Stuart's whole body shook too every time he looked at her, but with anger and outrage so strong he could barely keep his feelings under control.

What sort of person targeted an old lady who had so recently buried her husband? If this was Molly's damned husband, he was going to regret it. In fact, whoever it was, Stuart was going to find him and teach him a lesson he'd never forget.

But not till he'd calmed down a little, and not till he'd set up a better security system here. His mother didn't even have a lock on the inside of her bedroom door. Why had he not noticed that? He'd let her down. His own mother.

Then he thought of Molly. What would her ex do if he found out Molly was selling the house? Would he go after her, too?

Taylor needed bringing into line and Stuart already had an idea how to do that.

By Friday morning, the show house was clear of Euan's personal possessions, though he'd had to have a shed erected next to the caravan to store some of his things, because there was no room for them inside.

'Cindy's not short of money, if she can lay her hands on enough to buy this house outright within a couple of days,' he told Molly thoughtfully. 'You'd have thought she'd have gone for something more upmarket, a luxury flat in London maybe. She doesn't play golf, after all.'

'She said she liked the setting and the beautiful countryside nearby, and it's also close enough to her family, but not too close. I really like her and I'm glad she's moving in. She'll help set the tone for the group. I think she'll get on well with the Sarcens, too.'

'You like everyone.'

'Not everyone. I don't like Craig or his new wife. She's very hard; brittle is a perfect word to describe her. Her voice gets a viciously sharp edge to it sometimes, however polite the words.'

'And how does Craig react to that?'

'I gather from Rachel that he usually does as Tasha wants.' Molly smiled. 'In fact, I'm distanced enough now to believe he deserves her. It's a good thing our children are grown-up, though. I'd have fought tooth and nail to prevent a woman like her raising them. Even so, she still took them away from me.'

'Sounds like Brian's come back to you. Maybe Rachel will, too.'

She shook her head, sad now. 'I doubt it. Rachel is a daddy's girl through and through.'

When the doorbell rang, Rachel glanced out of the window, saw her father's car parked below and threw open the front door with a glad cry of, 'Daddy—oh, it's you, Tasha.' She took an instinctive step backwards.

Her stepmother walked in and did a quick tour, her expression growing more disgusted by the minute. 'I thought you told your father you'd clean this place up?'

Rachel looked round. It did look a bit untidy, but she'd cleared a whole lot of stuff up *and* done two loads of washing. Well, Brian had done one, but she'd done another all on her own.

'Did your mother teach you nothing about housekeeping?'

'I didn't need to learn. She could do everything better than I ever could.' She didn't admit to Tasha that her mother had tried and failed to get her to clear up after herself, or that she'd deliberately made a worse mess whenever her mother nagged about that.

'Everyone needs to learn to look after themselves. Unless you want to smell like a pig. Dirty places smell, Rachel, and make people who live in them smell, too.'

She looked at her stepmother in horror. *Smell!* She didn't smell. Did she? How did you know? Maybe you couldn't smell yourself. 'What's it got to do with you, anyway?'

'Mind your manners when you speak to me or I'll make sure your father never comes to see you again. And don't think I can't.'

Silence hung pregnant between them then Rachel began to cry.

'Stop that!'

She couldn't help crying even more loudly. This confrontation was just too much on top of everything else.

Tasha slapped her across the face and Rachel stopped crying to gape at her in shock.

'Someone has to take you in hand. I'm not having your father worried by this mess, just when he's got a big deal coming up. If you don't care about yourself, you should at least care about him after all he's done for you.'

'I do care about him.'

'Then why are you not at work?'

'I don't want to go back there. They'll all laugh at me.'

'They'll be sorry for you, you fool, especially if you're brave about it.'

Rachel looked at her doubtfully. 'Brave?'

'Yes. Don't cry or sob, and especially don't complain

or bad-mouth Jamie. Just blink away the tears and look tragic. I'm sure you can manage that. You're a good little actress. Your father can't always tell when you're lying, but I can.'

It sounded more like another insult than advice, but Rachel didn't know what to say, which often happened with her stepmother.

Tasha put her expensive leather handbag down. 'Right. We're going to have a lesson on house cleaning, and make sure you pay careful attention. I do not wish to see a pigsty like this again. I'll be back to check on you regularly, for your father's sake. At least my Geneva can keep herself *clean*, whatever her other faults.'

The scorn in her voice made Rachel twitch, but Tasha wasn't even looking at her, didn't care two hoots about her, only about her father.

If he didn't look after her, no one would, because no one else cared about her now. Her mother certainly didn't, and she might not have been able to help spoiling the wedding, but afterwards she'd gone away without saying where, in case anyone needed her, which showed how selfish she was.

Sulkily, Rachel did as she was told, hating the way the cleaning reddened her hands, because of course she didn't have any rubber gloves and Tasha did.

Why was her father letting this happen to her?

When Tasha got home, a man followed her up the path. He looked smart enough to allay any fears she might have about being mugged.

'Mrs Taylor?'

'Yes.'

'I'd like to see your husband. Would Craig be at home?'

'I certainly hope so. Please wait here. I'll see if he's in.' But when she walked into the house, the man gave her a nudge with his shoulder and as she stumbled through the doorway, he followed quickly, saying, 'Oh, sorry.'

She lunged for the panic button, but he was already between her and it.

'I'm not here to hurt you in any way, or to rob you. I merely want to make sure I see your husband face-to-face.'

She frowned at him, but he looked utterly respectable. 'Who are you? Why should he not want to see you?'

'I'm Stuart Benton.' He pulled out a business card and offered it to her.

She studied it. 'Security consultant. Is this a stunt to show us we need better security?'

'No. This call is on behalf of my mother.'

Craig called out, 'Tasha? Is that you?'

'Yes. You have a visitor. He's pushed his way in.'

There was the sound of footsteps running down the stairs, but at the sight of the other man Craig stopped a couple of steps from the bottom, looking poised to retreat. 'Benton, isn't it?'

'Yes. I'm here on behalf of my mother. Her house was targeted by vandals last night and this upset her considerably. Which has upset me.'

Tasha watched her husband put on his false look of concern.

'I'm sorry to hear that. What's it got to do with me, though?'

'As you and I both know, it has everything to do with you.' He turned to Tasha. 'My mother is over eighty, and she buried my father on Tuesday. She's normally a very plucky lady, but wasn't in the best of states to be facing intruders a couple of days after that, as you can imagine.'

He turned back to Craig. 'I would be very upset if anything else happened to my mother. Very. Make sure it doesn't.' He nodded to Tasha. 'See if you can talk a little sense into him.'

She watched Stuart leave, then looked at Craig. 'Tell me he's mistaken.'

He shrugged. 'I was just sending a little warning to him not to buy that house.'

She stood perfectly still, then said in icy tones. 'I can't believe you attacked a woman so soon after her husband's funeral.'

'How the hell was I to know the old chap had died? Anyway, no one touched her. I made a point of telling them not to. They just lobbed rocks through a couple of the windows.'

'Even that was a disgusting thing to do to an old lady.'

'Sometimes you have to make a point forcibly.'

'Not in that way. And not to ladies over eighty. I'm disgusted with you. I think I'll spend the weekend with my brother. You are *not* invited.'

She waited and when he didn't say anything, added, 'When I come back, I want to hear that you've severed your ties with those hoodlums and given up your plans to move back into Lavengro Road.'

He followed her upstairs into the bedroom. 'You're not going to your brother's, and I *will* get that house and we *will* live there. I'm owed it. Keep right out of this affair, Tasha. I'll sort it.'

For the first time ever, she found herself a little nervous of him. For the first time, she wondered if some of the other rumours she'd heard about him were true. No, surely not? He was a respected businessman, a man on the rise, not a thug. But she'd bear this in mind if she decided to take further action. With a shrug, she took her coat off and changed into more casual gear.

'What time is dinner?' he asked, as pleasantly as if he'd not just threatened her.

She didn't want to be alone with him till she'd calmed down and decided what to do. 'I'd like to go out to eat. Just somewhere casual. I'm not in the mood for cooking tonight after dealing with your stupid daughter.'

'Very well. Mario's suit you?'

She inclined her head and he went downstairs to wait for her.

At the restaurant, he said in his usual pleasant tone, 'I think we'll take a little trip into Wiltshire on Sunday. I want to visit Molly.'

'You're not going to . . . do anything else stupid.'

'Of course not. I'm going to make her another offer for the house, and in such a way she can't refuse it.'

When they got back, Tasha said she was tired, but he smiled as he continued to get ready for bed. He paid no attention to her protests and for the first time she didn't enjoy making love to him.

In fact, it was more like a rape as far as she was concerned.

That was a lot of firsts for one evening. But the last one upset her most of all.

The email Euan sent to his eldest son brought a rapid response. He called Molly over to his computer to read it on Friday evening.

'He hopes it works out for you,' she said. 'How nice your Jason sounds! How loving!'

'Have you sent an email to your son yet?'

'Yes. But I haven't had a reply.'

Even as she spoke, her email program pinged to let her know a message had arrived and she found it was from Brian.

> *Great to hear that you're making friends, and have found a new guy. Hope it goes well for you.*
>
> *Rachel still not coping well. She rang to say Tasha went round and gave her a forced lesson in cleaning and now her hands are all red. Made me laugh to think of it.*
>
> *Going to work now.*
>
> *Brian*

She felt relief shudder through her. She didn't know what she'd been expecting, but this cheerful acceptance of her relationship made her feel good.

She called Euan over. 'Come and look at this.'

'That's great. I'd like to meet your son. I think you've definitely got him back again, Molly.'

She nodded, tears threatening. 'I'll invite him to visit sometime, but he works weekends so I'm not sure when he'll be able to manage it.'

She felt more cheerful after that email and hummed to herself as she got ready for bed. Things were really looking up, and if she could sell the house as well, she'd feel really good about her future. She might even buy another house one day, or she might not need to do that on her own. She'd have to see whether the relationship with Euan was going anywhere.

Please let it continue, she prayed as she turned into Euan's waiting arms. *I do love him.*

Chapter Sixteen

Saturday was busy at the sales office, probably helped by it being gloriously sunny, just the sort of day to bring out sightseers instead of serious buyers, Euan said, with a wry grimace. Molly was glad he was there all day, unlike weekdays when he sometimes had other business appointments.

Apart from any other considerations, they were able to chat quietly during the short periods without customers, getting to know one another better, sharing hopes and fears about their children, also one or two tales of their own childhoods.

She felt utterly comfortable with him and still marvelled at that.

They were both tired after that long day, so strolled up to the hotel for a quick meal in the bar. Euan knew several people there, but avoided joining them.

He took her hand on the way back. 'Nice to be a two again.'

'Very nice.'

'And nice to be going home together.' He swung her round for a quick kiss and suddenly she felt young and carefree, happier than she'd been for years.

Could it last? It really might.

Stuart vanished into his tech room, as he called it, coming out looking concerned.

'Something wrong?' Wendy asked as he came to join her for lunch.

'Yes. Taylor is planning to visit his wife tomorrow.'

'He didn't find the listening device you planted when you went to visit them, then?'

'No. He'd not be looking for it. I've been eavesdropping on his phone calls from home ever since.'

'Poor Molly. She'll be so upset to see him. I remember before they split up how she used to change when he was with her, how hesitant she became. It used to upset your mother so much. I wonder what he wants with Molly.'

'The house, of course. It's the only thing he wants from her now.'

'I suppose so. Are you going to email her to let her know.'

He had a think, then shook his head. 'She might try to stop him going. I reckon we need to catch him harassing her and finish this once and for all.'

'Stuart—'

He grinned. 'Don't worry. I'll make sure he doesn't hurt her, let alone get the house. I really like this place, not because it's on Lavengro Road, but because it's a lovely house. I know we've moved all over the world and never put down roots before, but I can put them down here, I know I can. Not to mention being there for my mother.'

'Is it any use my asking you to stay on the right side of the law when you deal with Taylor?'

His grin broadened. 'Don't I always?'

'No. Oh, and you haven't forgotten that I'm going out today to lunch with Wives Reunited.'

'I'm sure you'll have a great time with your friends. You usually do. I'm not sure I'll be in when you return.'

He wandered off again, thinking hard. How did you know what was the best thing to do? It wasn't about his job now, it was about his family's happiness. Far more important, that.

Sunday not only brought showers, but there were thunderstorms forecast for later. At Molly's suggestion, they'd bought a dozen golf umbrellas to lend to people going round the houses and these were well received.

Towards the end of the morning she was on her own when she heard a car drive up. One couple had just left and another was going round the houses for a second time, accompanied by Euan because they wanted to discuss the design details more seriously. Another sale, she hoped.

When a car drew up she was tidying the umbrellas and didn't bother to look out of the door. Footsteps came towards the office and she turned to greet the newcomers. Her smile froze on her face when she saw who they were, and her heart began to thump.

Craig came into the office and looked round scornfully.

'Trust you to work for a second-rate organisation.'

Molly tried desperately to think of something to say, but her lips felt numb and her brain too. All she wanted to do was run out and get as far away from him as she could. She took an involuntary step towards the door.

He gave her a predatory smile and took two quick sideways steps to block her exit.

Tasha, who had followed him in, said nothing.

'Not going to offer us brochures, Molly? This is no way to treat a customer.'

'What do you want, Craig?'

'For you to show us round the show houses, of course.'

She could hear how her voice fluted with nervousness and despised herself for it, but couldn't seem to pull herself together. 'We . . . um, ask our visitors to go round on their own the . . . the first time and then—' She hauled in a deep breath and forced out more words, 'We suggest they come and ask for further help if they're seriously interested. I . . . um . . . Here are the . . . the brochures you need.'

She fumbled for the brochures and only managed to scatter them across the floor. 'Oh . . . I'm s-sorry.'

'Take one of her brochures and look round the houses, Tash.'

'Go easy on her, Craig.' But when he didn't reply, Tasha frowned at him, then picked up a brochure and walked quickly out, thin high heels perfectly balanced, tapping out a sharp rhythm on the wooden floor.

She didn't look pleased at what he was doing, Molly thought. He hadn't even noticed that. He didn't notice the subtleties of how people were reacting to him, only whether he'd got what *he* wanted.

Craig gestured to the desk. 'Sit down. We have things to discuss.'

Habit had Molly sitting down where he indicated before she realised what she was doing. She tried to gather the shreds of her composure together, but couldn't; felt sick with nerves.

Before he could say anything, another car drew up and she heard doors opening and voices coming from the car park.

Craig moved away from the desk. 'Get rid of them.'

He pretended to look at the house plans on the wall.

She got up and moved towards the door, but the two women from the car were already walking down towards the houses.

He took her arm in a hard grip and swung her back to the desk. She sat down because she was no match for him physically. He'd never manhandled her before. Why was he hurting her now? She was sure her arm was bruised where he'd gripped her, sure he'd done it on purpose, too.

He came to sit on the edge of the desk, looming over her. 'We need to discuss the house, how much I'm going to pay you for it. I will raise my offer, but it won't be a market offer, because you don't deserve it. I put a lot of effort into that house too, and I have as much right as you to it.'

'I'm not selling it to you.'

'Oh, but you are.'

'I'm n—'

He smacked his clenched fist down on the desk. 'Shut up and damned well listen!'

She drew in a shuddering breath.

'You have a daughter on the verge of disintegrating. Jamie has left her and good riddance to him. But Rachel needs help, a lot of help. I'm willing to provide it, but only on condition you sell me the house.'

Her voice came out a little more strongly this time. 'That's no inducement.'

'It will be. I can push Rachel right over the edge if you don't cooperate.'

She gaped at him in horror. She'd never have believed he'd go to such lengths. 'I thought you loved Rachel. She's your *daughter*, for heaven's sake.'

He laughed gently. 'I loved getting between her and you. That amused me. I also love the fact that she's so pretty. That does me credit. I think I know how to make use of it when I help her pull herself together. But whether I take the trouble to do that or not depends on you.'

'No, it doesn't, because I won't.'

'Can you really stand by and watch Rachel crumble, maybe go on drugs? Lose her home?'

'You wouldn't let that happen.'

'Wouldn't I? Are you prepared to stake her happiness on that assumption?'

She could only stare at him, horrified by this threat.

'Anyway, it's a win-win situation. Come on, Molly. Get real. You *want* to sell that house as much as I want to buy it.'

She felt even more nauseous because she was suddenly quite sure he meant what he said. He really was prepared to use Rachel in any way that suited his purpose – or destroy their daughter.

Could she let him do that?

As Stuart drew up behind a couple of middle-aged women, he noted Craig's car parked next to the sales office. He looked round carefully before he got out and saw Tasha come out of one of the show houses, look up at the sales office with a worried air, shake her head slightly then go into another one of the houses.

From that, he assumed Craig was in the sales office with Molly and that Tasha was worried about what he was doing.

Just as he was about to get out of the car, a man came out of the show houses with a smiling couple and stood talking to them, then they went into the first house.

If Stuart's guess was right, this would be as good a time as any to eavesdrop on what was going on inside the sales office. His rubber soles making no sound on the tarmac, he moved quietly to position himself below an open window. He hoped he couldn't be seen from the houses, but would have to risk that.

He listened for a few minutes, feeling the anger that had been there ever since the attack on his mother's house flare up again as he heard what Craig was threatening Molly with. When he risked a glance through the window, he could see that she was afraid, and that she believed the fellow.

He felt sorry for her. Poor Molly had been browbeaten for years.

People didn't always think straight when they were afraid of someone. He'd seen it in ex-prisoners, blackmail victims, new recruits who'd been put under a particularly nasty sergeant.

He checked his equipment, moving to a slightly better position.

Well, she wouldn't be on her own this time.

Another car drove up and he bent to tie an imaginary shoelace. Then he saw the man who'd been talking to the couple come striding up the hill, so went back to his car as if looking for something. He'd wait for a moment or two, then see what was going on before he acted.

There was plenty of time for what he intended to do today.

Molly looked up, but it was another couple. She thrust brochures at them, suggesting they look round the houses and get back to her if they needed more information. It was one of the worst explanations she'd ever made. She stuttered and jerked the words out as if she didn't really know what she was doing. The woman looked at her scornfully, and no wonder.

'What idiot employed you as a saleswoman?' Craig said once they'd left.

Euan had waited to let the couple out, then stopped as he saw how afraid Molly looked. He heard enough to guess who the man was and walked into the office.

'This idiot,' he said firmly. 'Only she's actually a very good saleswoman.'

Craig made a faint but distinctly scornful noise.

Thunder rumbled suddenly in the distance and Molly shivered. She felt ashamed to think Euan had heard her stumbling through what was usually a well-rehearsed spiel. And she knew she wasn't coping well with the situation, was showing her fear of her ex.

Craig turned round, all charm again. 'I'm sorry. I shouldn't have said that, only I know how my ex-wife crumbles under pressure and I was worried about her. She's not going to be happy in a sales position. You're not doing her any favours by employing her here.'

Euan ignored him, looking at her and she felt tears of embarrassment well in her eyes. She gave him one look, then stared down.

Craig leant against the wall with supposed casualness and waited. But he was blocking Euan's way across to the desk. 'Look, I wonder if you'd mind leaving me and Molly to continue a rather private conversation about our daughter? We have a bit of trouble in the family.'

Euan took him by surprise, shoving him out of the way, and went to stand beside Molly, one arm round her shoulders. 'Rat was the correct word to describe him,' he said quietly.

He could feel her shaking against him, so turned to stare back at her ex. 'I'm not leaving you to bully her. In fact, I don't even like you being on my premises. You're upsetting one of my employees and I'm not having that.'

'I'm not leaving till I've finished my conversation with Molly.'

Euan looked at her. 'Shall I throw him out?'

She closed her eyes and shook her head. 'I think I'd better . . . speak to him. About our daughter.'

For a moment triumph blazed on Craig's face, to be replaced by an ugly smile.

Outside, Stuart switched off his recording equipment. It was time to intervene. He ran lightly up the steps into the office. 'Don't deal with him, Molly, or you'll never be rid of him.' He turned to Euan. 'I'm Molly's tenant, Stuart Benton.'

Euan held out his hand and the two men shook.

Two strong men, Molly thought, but not bullies like her ex. She saw Craig looking at her behind their backs and making a beckoning movement with his right hand.

She jerked to her feet and took a step forward, then stopped abruptly.

Stuart made a small shushing sound as Euan opened his mouth.

Molly looked at her ex-husband and thought about the terrible threat he'd just made. If he was capable of that, there was no way she could ever trust him to keep his word. If he cared so little about Rachel, it would do their daughter no good to be rescued by him.

'I can't sell you the house, Craig, because' – she had to stop and take a deep breath – 'I've already sold it to Stuart.'

Stuart nodded confirmation, though they hadn't actually got as far as a sale.

There was silence, then Craig said, 'There hasn't been time for you to exchange contracts yet, so we can still negotiate, still come to some agreement – for Rachel's sake.'

'No. We can't. For Rachel's sake. And for my own.' Her voice grew stronger. 'I won't negotiate with you, Craig, about anything. Ever again.'

His expression turned ugly. 'You're going to regret this.'

Euan moved to her side. 'She won't, you know. I'll make sure of that.'

'Who are you? Some struggling developer with a few houses for sale? I don't think you've got much power to do anything.'

Euan smiled at him. 'I'm the main shareholder of Crest Hayle Holdings, actually. I started up the company, but though I've sold part of it now, I think I still have a little clout in business circles.'

Craig stopped in his tracks. 'The shopping centre developer? I don't believe you. Someone with that much behind him wouldn't be fiddling around with a tinpot development like this one.'

Euan smiled even more broadly. 'Every man's entitled to a hobby.'

Craig stared at him as if he'd suddenly grown horns.

'Anyway, what I do or don't do isn't your concern. But believe me, I do own most of Crest Hayle and, more importantly, I can keep Molly safe.'

Stuart stepped forward. 'And if you have any further doubt, you might try listening to this.' He pressed the play button on his recorder and first Tasha's then Craig's voice filled the room.

'I can't believe you attacked a woman so soon after her husband's funeral.'

'How the hell was I to know the old chap had died?
Anyway, no one touched her. I made a point of
telling them not to. They just lobbed rocks through
a couple of the windows.'
'Even that was a disgusting thing to do to an old lady.'
'Sometimes you have to make a point forcibly.'

Then Stuart pressed another button and today's
conversation between Craig and Molly was replayed.

'Do you really want this to be made public?' he asked
with a smile.

'That's blackmail,' Craig snapped.

'I haven't asked you for anything. How is it blackmail?'

Craig lunged for the tiny tape recorder.

Stuart easily shoved him back. 'Careful, Mr Taylor. We
don't want you getting hurt. And for your information,
I have copies of the first recording in a safe place, and it
can easily be sent to your employer if you don't behave
from now on.'

As they all stood there, waiting for Craig to speak
or move, footsteps tapped up the wooden steps into
the office.

Tasha stood there, her face expressionless.

Craig smiled at her. 'Would you wait for me in the car,
darling? I won't be long.'

'I don't think so.'

He looked at her in puzzlement.

'I've been listening to you for a while, from the back
of this place. Threats against Molly, against your own
daughter – *your own daughter*, for heaven's sake. And

two days ago you virtually raped me. I've been raped once when I was younger; I vowed then never to accept it again without speaking out.

'I'm taking the car and I'm going to my brother's. He will ensure that I'm safe when I go to remove your things from our flat. Be sure to bring a van with you when you return tomorrow, because if you don't take your things away I'll send them all to the tip. Your beautiful suits, your expensive ties, all the trappings that dazzle the unwary – till people get to know you and see what's behind the facade. You even dazzled me, and I thought I was good at recognising that sort of trickery.'

He lunged towards her and Stuart stepped forward, twisting his arm behind his back so quickly it had happened before Craig knew it.

'Thank you, Mr Benton.' Tasha turned to look at Molly. 'I apologise for the way we've treated you. He can be very convincing. I really thought you were a malicious fool.'

'I was definitely a fool, but never malicious,' Molly said. 'I should have left him years ago.'

'Well, you stood up to him today. Better late than never.' She studied Euan. 'And it seems to me, Molly, that you've found someone better in every way.'

She smiled bitterly. 'I thought I'd met a man with solid ambitions, and he turns out to be a minor thug.'

'Tash, I can explain!' Craig stretched out his free arm towards her.

'No, you can't. Because I heard the truth today, and even you haven't enough weasel words to twist the facts round and put our marriage back together.'

She turned and walked out of the office.

Craig tried to follow her, but Stuart made sure he didn't get to the door in time.

As the car pulled away, Euan said, 'I'll arrange for a car to take you to London, Mr Taylor, because I don't want you staying here a moment longer than necessary. But if you ever set foot on my property again, I'll have you forcibly removed. Please wait in the coffee shop at the hotel. Perhaps you'd escort him up there, Mr Benton, then come back and join us?'

'My pleasure.' Stuart gestured towards the door and followed Craig out, winking at Molly.

Euan watched them go, then turned to Molly, who was looking as if she'd just run a marathon.

'I'm ashamed that it took such an extreme situation to make me stand up to him,' she muttered.

'Don't expect miracles of yourself. You're taking one step at a time. Many women need years of counselling before they can stand up to a husband who's abused them verbally for so long. I had a cousin in a similar situation.'

He pulled her to him and hugged her. For a moment she hugged him back, then moved out of his embrace with an apologetic smile.

'I'm still afraid for Rachel. The trouble is, I don't think she'll listen to me if I tell her what her father said.'

'Why don't you ring your son? Ask him to explain the situation to her. I'm sure Stuart would give him a copy of the tape to play to her.'

She glanced at her watch. 'I'll do that. I hope I can catch Brian in a break.'

Euan moved towards the door. 'I'll keep the sightseers at bay.'

'No. It makes more sense for me to go down to the caravan to phone in private. And Euan . . . thank you.'

'I love you, Molly.'

'I don't know how you can.'

She was gone before he could refute this.

He made a quick phone call to the hotel reception, then turned to deal with the customers who'd just returned from looking at the houses.

Molly's hand was shaking as she pressed the button to ring Brian. 'Hello? Oh, thank goodness I've caught you.'

'Mum? Are you all right?'

'I am now.' She explained what had happened.

When he'd finished swearing, she got to the point of the call. 'Can you go and see Rachel, tell her what happened?'

'Yes. But Mum . . . I don't think she'll believe me. She still thinks he's Mr Miracle.'

'I'll get the recording to you.'

'She won't listen to it.'

Molly sagged against the caravan window. 'We can't force her to do anything, I know, but we have to try to make her see sense.'

'*I* believe you about him, Mum.'

'I'm glad.'

'I have to go now; I'm due at work. I'll have to ring and explain that I'll be late.'

When she switched off the phone, Molly sat there for a few moments, feeling as if she'd been run over by a tractor. But out of the corner of her eye she saw yet another car draw up. Euan would be struggling to deal with all these people.

She gave a wry smile as she tidied her hair and put on some more lipstick. The show must go on. And it'd probably be as well to keep herself occupied.

Brian rang his sister's doorbell.

She opened it, keeping the security chain across it. 'What do you want?'

'Can I come in?'

'No. Daddy just rang. He said you'd all ganged up on him, were trying to make me believe lies with a doctored tape.'

He blinked in shock. That was fast work. 'If you'll just let me in, I'll explain.'

'You're not coming in. Daddy needs someone to stand by him. He hasn't even got anywhere to sleep tonight, thanks to Mum and that flaky fellow she's shacked up with. Well, he's still got me and he's sleeping here, so I have to clear up.'

She slammed the door in his face.

He stood there for a moment, then shrugged and went back to work. He wasn't surprised at her reaction.

When the last customer of the afternoon had gone, Euan turned the sign to 'CLOSED' and shut the office door firmly. 'Thanks for coming back to work today. It can't have been easy.'

'It was easier than sitting on my own, thinking and worrying.'

'I like Stuart.'

'So do I. His mother's lovely, too. I'm glad he's going to buy my house.'

'You could probably have got more money for it.'

'Who cares? I like to think of him near Jane if she needs help. I like to think the house will be loved, as I used to love it.'

After a moment's silence, he said quietly, 'Let's go down to the caravan.'

She felt a sense of loss as she walked inside, because of course she couldn't stay there now. She'd shown herself up as a coward, for all Euan's kind words. He wouldn't be able to respect her now. She didn't respect herself.

'I think I can guess what you're thinking,' he said gently.

'Can you?'

'Oh, yes. I told you my cousin was in your situation, so I do understand. But I meant what I said. You standing up to him today took a huge amount of courage, and you did it without any counselling or help.'

'Even so, I'm no fit partner for a man like you.'

'Shouldn't I be the one to judge that?'

'You're a kind man. And you'll go on being kind to me for a while, then . . . you'll leave me.'

'I won't, darling. I love you, the Molly you are now, not the cowed woman put down by her whole family. The Molly I love is moving on. And will move still further.'

But still she shook her head.

'What can I say to persuade you?'

'I didn't know you were the man behind Crest Hayle Holdings. I thought you were struggling to find the money to finish this development.'

He smiled and took her hand. 'I am. It's a challenge I set myself, to see if I could still do it, make something from almost nothing.'

'Why should you want to do that?'

'Avril told me I was getting soft and spoilt. She was right. I've worked hard on this.' He gestured around them. 'I'm juggling pennies, where I usually juggle millions. And do you know what – it's fun. I've not felt so alive for a long time, not since Karen died and I buried myself in financial work. And it's brought me you, which is the best thing of all about the venture.'

'But I'm so ordinary.'

'No, you're not. You've got many useful skills, you're kind, you're fun and pretty. I don't want a clothes hanger of a woman who spends half her life looking after her body. I want a woman who'll work beside me, hop on a plane at the drop of a hat and nip to Paris for dinner, or tell me off if I've left the place untidy, not to mention whipping up gourmet meals on a few minutes' notice.'

She took a hesitant step towards him. Dare she believe him? Dare she take the risk? 'I do love you, Euan.'

'That makes me very happy. And do you believe I love you?'

She looked at him and nodded.

'Does that mean you'll take a risk on me, share my life?'

'Yes. If you'll do the same with me.'

Then she was in his arms, crying and laughing, kissing and loving. She knew it was a risk, but how could she not try for the moon?

Chapter Seventeen

Her old home seemed so different already. Molly had to stop in the hall to take a few deep breaths and get her bearings. They'd exchanged contracts today and this was now Stuart's house. She was here to check whether she wanted any of the furniture that was left, but she already knew she didn't.

Beside her, Euan whispered, 'All right?'

She turned to smile at him. 'Very right.' In the month they'd been together, still in the tiny caravan, she'd smiled a lot.

Stuart threw open the door of the sitting room and a whole crowd of people yelled, 'Surprise!'

Jane was closest and she moved forward first to hug Molly. 'Welcome back, my dear.'

'It's so good to see you.'

Behind her was Brian, with a pleasant-looking young woman by his side.

'This is Carrie, Mum.'

'I'm pleased to meet you.' And Molly was. You could tell at a glance that this was a nice person, devoid of malice or slyness. You just could. She was learning to trust her own judgement about people.

With squeals, her friends threw themselves on her, and her cousin Helen grinned at her from behind them, waiting for a hug.

'This is Euan,' she told them proudly.

'Nice one,' Nikki said. 'You've hit gold this time.'

Molly let out a gurgle of laughter as Euan blushed. She'd learnt by now that he was embarrassed by his own good looks. You could say it was his Achilles heel.

'Hands off, girls!' she said. 'I saw him first.'

Rachel wasn't there, of course. But then, Molly hadn't expected her to be. She had to hope that some day her daughter would find out for herself how untrustworthy her father was.

'I didn't know it was going to be a party,' she said, 'or I'd have dressed up.'

'No, heaven help us. Don't let her dress up, Euan. It doesn't suit her,' Di said. 'Keep her simple.'

Everyone laughed and Molly with them. She'd got confident enough to be amused at her own lack of dress sense, because Euan had taught her how unimportant that was compared to what sort of person you were.

At one stage, Brian cornered her in the bay window. 'I just wanted to tell you how much two of my old toys fetched at auction.'

She gaped at the sum he named. 'For two little toy trucks?'

'In their original boxes, almost pristine. I never knew I'd be thankful that I tired of things quickly and you put them away out of harm's reach. I've paid off my debts, Mum, and I'm not getting into any more.'

'Good. And I like your new friend.'

'So do I.' His eyes raked the crowd and he saw Carrie in one corner talking animatedly to Jane. 'She's taught me a lot about life. I don't think there's anyone she can't talk to and enjoy the company of.' He hesitated. 'No more trouble with Dad?'

'No. Stuart's keeping an eye on him, so is Euan.'

'And Tasha's really divorcing him?'

'Oh, yes. She's an ambitious woman, but she's not into skulduggery, and I gather he did something that really upset her.'

He burst out laughing. 'Skulduggery! I'd forgotten that word even existed.'

When everyone had gone, except for the Bentons, Molly and Euan, they sat over a final glass of wine.

'I'm so glad you've got the house,' she said to Wendy.

'So am I. And I'm never moving house again. It was hard uprooting ourselves every couple of years.'

'Change is always hard,' Molly said before she could stop herself.

Wendy patted her hand. 'But we change when we have to. I hope you and Euan will be happy together. I really like him.'

Molly smiled, hoping Euan couldn't hear this or he'd be blushing again. 'I'm beginning to believe we can.'

'Don't doubt it. He obviously loves you deeply.

Everyone commented on the way he looks at you.'

When the chauffeur-driven car came to pick them up, Molly subsided on the back seat and reached for Euan's hand. 'It's tiring being happy, isn't it?'

'Are you happy?'

'Oh, yes. Very. I do love you, Euan, and thank you for helping Stuart to arrange this party. It's the right way to end my association with that house.'

'I'll arrange a lot more happy occasions, I hope, because I love you more each day.'

He said the most romantic things – but best of all, she believed he meant them. She snuggled against him, feeling happiness settle round them like a warm cloak.

Life wouldn't always be perfect, she knew that, but she was quite certain this man wouldn't let her down or bully her.

He was definitely a keeper.

ANNA JACOBS is the author of over eighty novels and is addicted to storytelling. She grew up in Lancashire, emigrated to Australia in the 1970s and writes stories set in both countries. She loves to return to England regularly to visit her family and soak up the history. She has two grown-up daughters and a grandson, and lives with her husband in a spacious home near the Swan Valley, the earliest wine-growing area in Western Australia. Her house is crammed with thousands of books.

annajacobs.com